PHY
SICAL
EVI
DENCE

PHY SICAL EVI DENCE

GARY METRO

PHYSICAL EVIDENCE

iUniverse books may be ordered through booksellers or by contacting:

iUniverse
1663 Liberty Drive
Bloomington, IN 47403
www.iuniverse.com
844-349-9409

ISBN: 978-1-6632-5743-7 (sc)
ISBN: 978-1-6632-5741-3 (hc)
ISBN: 978-1-6632-5742-0 (e)

Library of Congress Control Number: 2023920573

Print information available on the last page.

iUniverse rev. date: 02/02/2024

This book is dedicated to my wife, Debbie, an excellent writer and copy editor. Her love for me and support of my writing meant everything.

CONTENTS

ACKNOWLEDGEMENTS FROM THE AUTHOR

This book would not have been possible without the final read-through and content edit of my manuscript by the late John Skipper, a many-times published author and a journalistic icon in Mason City, Iowa. I also must credit the late Wilson Ruff of Sheboygan, Wisconsin, a retired newspaper editor who coached, critiqued, and encouraged me. Kudos also for the oversight of an earlier literary effort by novelist and musician Dennis Hetzel, who put me on a better path to completing a novel. I also want to acknowledge the support of my writing by my friend and colleague Mark Hertzberg, a superb photographer who lives in Racine, Wisconsin. Most especially, this book reflects the content and copy editing of my wife and literary coach, Debbie. She read every word of my every effort and provided continuous encouragement and support.

It wouldn't have been possible for me to earn a living as a writer without the encouragement and support of the faculty at Valparaiso University, especially from Dr. Carl Galow, and the freedom to write provided by Bob Roth and his leadership team at the Chicago Reader. Finally, I also want to credit the coaching from City Editor Chris Boultinghouse at the Racine Journal Times and earlier efforts by Art Techlow, the managing editor of the Oshkosh Northwestern and Joe Sayrs, the paper's city editor.

CHAPTER 1
EARLY JUNE

Our county's highway commissioner probably has an unflattering nickname for me. I have no tolerance for litterbugs or for highway workers who dawdle in removing the mangled carcasses of deer, raccoons, skunks, and the occasional cat and dog. I'm up at dawn for my workday commute to the city and see a lot of fresh roadkill. It bothers me to think of children on school buses looking at the bloody remains of wild animals and household pets that wandered into the paths of nighttime joyriders and speeding truckers. So, I'm often on the phone with Pat McCurdy, a cigar-chomping highway boss with a short fuse.

I'll be first to admit I wasn't very diplomatic in reporting my latest roadside findings—blue plastic bags thrown into ditches and nearly obscured by weeds growing unchecked since spring.

"What's taking your guys so long to pick up the trash bags in the ditches?" I growled into my cell phone.

"You *again*? What izzit this time?"

"Some dipshit's dumping trash by the side of *your* roads. Looks like he's using those blue recycling bags from the city."

"My guys ain't seen nuttin like dat. I'da heard about it."

I then gave him the locations of the five bags I'd seen. The bags were spaced about a quarter mile apart on the same county road. It looked deliberate and planned, I said.

McCurdy said nothing in response.

"Did you get that, McCurdy? Do you know where to look?"

"I ain't stupid. Goodbye!"

•⁂ •

Curtis Hobart hated every minute he spent inside the Howard County Jail. He'd served nearly half of a one-year sentence for driving under the influence, shivering through the winter months and now baking in early-summer heat. But his behavior was exemplary thanks to his jailhouse-enforced sobriety, in part, and his strong desire to remain a member of the trustee program. It meant outdoor work during the warm-weather months, which, though tiresome and sweaty, was infinitely preferable to reading from the library's meager offerings or watching TV programs dictated by the tough Black prisoners who ruled the dayroom.

Curtis looked forward to working on highway crews. His uncle, Pat McCurdy, gave Curtis jobs that were shunned by the full-time staff, who were well-paid union workers. He also provided Curtis with cigarettes and allowed him to smoke while working, in violation of trustee and jail rules.

Curtis smoked hungrily as McCurdy drove a five-ton dump truck along the route he'd been told about earlier that morning.

"Supposed to be blue trash bags in the ditches. Probably nothing. Guy who called is never happy, always complains."

"That a blue bag over there?" Curtis said through a thick cloud of smoke.

"Go take a look. Take your time. We got all day."

Curtis finished his smoke, crushed the butt in the roadside gravel, and pulled on the heavy work gloves issued to highway crews. He tucked his cuffs inside his work boots, snugged a bright yellow hard hat on his head, and stepped into the overgrown bramble. A corner of a blue bag protruded from the weeds.

"Bring the whole thing up here," McCurdy bellowed. "I wanna closer look."

"It's kinda awkward, Uncle Pat. Give me a second, OK?"

Curtis tugged the bag through the weeds. It was heavyweight plastic, and the opening had been sealed with zip ties. He could see dark stains on the underside of the bag.

"Might be motor oil in here, along with something else," he said. "Can't see through the bag."

"I'll get it," McCurdy said as he pulled a buck knife from the sheath on his belt.

He split the bag quickly, without thinking. What he and Curtis saw inside the plastic would remain in their thoughts forever.

Throughout the day, I brooded about McCurdy hanging up on me. By the time I was driving home from work, I was really pissed off. I barely heard the radio, which, unfortunately, didn't offer any baseball broadcasts on this day. I listened to games of the Milwaukee Brewers, Chicago White Sox, and Chicago Cubs—all were on strong-signal stations in the state-line region of Wisconsin and Illinois. I guess you'd say I was a fair-weather fan. Whoever had the best team was my favorite that season.

For some reason, I switched from NPR to an all-news station. A commercial for the local *Action News* telecast teased the day's big headlines.

"And, finally, highway workers in far southeastern Wisconsin's Howard County make a gruesome discovery. Sarah Livingston has a live report at six."

I rushed into the house just before six; kissed my wife, Becky; and headed into the TV room. In just a few moments, the booming theme music of *Action News* filled the room, followed by a tight-focus shot of Pat McCurdy and his ever-present cigar.

"I cut a blue bag open with my knife and seen a bloody leg. A human leg. Thing was covered with bugs. Almost puked when I seen it."

"Five bags were found today," Sarah Livingston said to the live camera. "Legs were found in two bags; the arms were in two others. The heaviest bag contained a headless torso. Sheriff's deputies believe the remains are those of a young man, but the investigation is only beginning."

It must have been the look on my face when I returned to the kitchen. I hadn't said a word. I guess I was stunned to learn the roadside trash I'd reported as a nuisance was physical evidence of a crime.

"What is it?" Becky said. "What happened?"

"Looks like a murder, not far from here."

"Oh my God! Who?"

"The cops don't know. They've got missing person reports, but it won't be easy figuring out who got killed."

"Why?"

"All they've got are body parts."

I poured myself a glass of red wine and another for Becky. We sat down at the kitchen table, and I told her what I'd seen along the roadside and how I'd reported it. Then I repeated the contents of the TV news broadcast.

"I hope the cops don't think you had something to do with it."

"Me too. But I'll bet they'll want to talk to me."

"Why? You didn't do anything."

"They don't know that. And neither does Pat McCurdy. All they know is that a big complainer called the highway chief to report blue trash bags in roadside ditches. And they found human body parts in the bags."

I took another swallow of wine, then heard the sound of a vehicle crunching up our gravel driveway.

"Hear that?" I asked.

"I don't hear anything. You're paranoid."

A few seconds later, there was a heavy knock at the front door. I could hear the static crackle of a police radio as I walked to the door. I pulled it open, and a brown-shirted deputy sheriff in mirrored sunglasses greeted me with a few terse words.

"You Edward Norwood?"

"Yeah. People usually call me Ed or Eddie."

"You the same Edward Norwood who called Pat McCurdy this morning just after six?"

"That's me, Officer."

"Come with me, please. We'd like to talk to you about what you saw. You can ride with me in the squad car."

The brown cruiser was idling in the driveway. A seven-pointed star and "Howard County Sheriff's Department" were painted in gold and black on the front doors.

"Am I under arrest?"

"No, sir, you are not. But we're working a homicide investigation. You are the person who brought this matter to light. We need to know exactly what you saw and when you saw it."

I turned to Becky. "Better not hold dinner for me."

A look of terror was on her face. I thought she might weep. The deputy must have noticed too.

"I'll make sure he gets a sandwich, ma'am. Try not to worry, OK?"

Her face brightened slightly, and she managed a smile. She waved as the cruiser backed out of our driveway and onto the county road. The evening sun lit her brunette curls, which spilled across her shoulders. She looked just like the willowy college student I'd wed twenty years earlier.

It's funny how that detail stands out, even today. There were whole chunks of the same day and the preceding week that I couldn't fully explain at the sheriff's department.

Memory is a funny thing.

CHAPTER 2
THE HOMICIDE INVESTIGATOR

It had been an unexpectedly long and gruesome day for Ida Mae Rollins. That was the nature of a detective's job. Feast or famine. She'd hoped to dig deep into a cold case homicide, but the discovery of newly scattered body parts changed her plans.

Ida spent most of the day picking through the bloody contents of blue trash bags, taking photographs, and measuring various distances, including the spaces between bags and the gaps between the bags and the roadway. The putrid scent of death and decay lingered in her nostrils.

A team of deputies followed Ida's instructions as they walked through the nearby brush and along the shoulders of the road, looking for evidence. They also went to nearby houses and asked those who were home whether they'd seen or heard anything unusual along the road. Ida suspected the area search would be useless, but it was a mandatory task in any death investigation. Nothing was found. Nobody heard or saw anything.

Ida stayed in the field until the medical examiner's team took custody of the dismembered remains. The victim was a young man who had not been sexually mutilated. The unscathed genitals struck Ida as an oddity in a killing otherwise so brutal. It also was strange that the head, hands, and feet were missing. The killer knew something about cutting meat—and eliminating identity evidence.

"Whatcha make of this mess?" Deputy Scott Brooks asked.

"He's dead—that's for sure. But it doesn't look like the work of a spurned and enraged lover. My criminal textbooks won't help."

"I don't understand, Detective."

"Lovers' quarrels sometimes turn especially ugly. Multiple stab wounds and mutilated genitals are not as unusual as you might think. This doesn't look like that."

"Whatcha gonna do next?"

"We need to talk to the guy who reported trash along the road."

"Want me to pick him up?"

"Yes. Guy's name is Edward Norwood. He lives on this road, not too far away."

Ida sat at her desk and began writing the first of many reports on the homicide. She munched potato chips and swigged diet cola as she began typing details into her laptop. Only the shuffle of heavy footsteps interrupted her work.

"Got a minute, Detective?" Sheriff Peter Clark asked.

"For you, sir? Anytime," Ida said.

"Take a good look at this guy Norwood. He gave us the exact location of each bag. Also, he specified there were five bags."

"Maybe he meant five bags that he saw."

"Or did he *know* there were only five bags?"

"I'll give him the full treatment, sir."

"Good girl, Ida. I'd stay, but my fundraiser is tonight. I'm the guest of honor."

"Good luck, sir," Ida said with a sigh of relief.

Ida tolerated the sheriff, who knew little about homicide. She especially bristled whenever he said, "Good girl, Ida." It sounded like he was talking to a dog.

Peter Clark was an old-school cop who'd been appointed sheriff after the death of his boss. He got the job mainly because he'd been second-in-command and consistently campaigned for law-and-order candidates. Most shared a political vision of a state covered with prisons, all linked by interstate and four-lane highways. As sheriff, Peter Clark spent most of his time working for reelection every two years. He was a bungler as a detective. He might successfully arrest a bloody killer who walked into the sheriff's department, surrendered a murder knife, and confessed on video. But maybe not.

"Thank God he's gone," Ida said to herself. "He's as useful as tits on a bull."

Ida heard Deputy Brooks report his arrival on the department's radio.

"You must be Mr. Norwood," Ida said with a smile and a handshake. "I'm Detective Ida Mae Rollins. Please call me Ida."

"OK. I like to be called Ed."

"Are you hungry? Deputy Brooks is getting me a cheeseburger and fries. I hate to eat alone."

"I've only got five bucks on me. Is that enough?"

"Keep your dough, Ed. This is on the county's dime. You're a taxpayer, ain't ya?"

As they ate, Ed and Ida talked about their lives and families. Ida habitually used small talk to open interviews, easing conversation and defusing tension. Ed did most of the talking, but Ida described how she'd been raised on a farm in southern Illinois, just outside the small town of Cobden. Her family grew peaches and apples, kept hogs and chickens too.

"My mama and daddy worked from before sunrise until late at night," Ida said. "Daddy ran the farm and worked in a bread bakery near Anna. Mama managed the home and raised me and my four sisters. I had a baby brother too, but he died."

"I'm sorry. What happened?"

"Mama found him dead in his crib. Sudden infant death syndrome."

Ed explained that he'd graduated from the University of Wisconsin–Oshkosh. That's where he met his wife, Becky. They married in her senior year and lived in an apartment on Jackson Street while Ed worked at a paper mill in Neenah. They'd moved to southeastern Wisconsin because Becky got a teaching job near Whitewater. Ed told Ida he'd been a business major and knew how to write a business plan and get financing for a promising venture. He'd wanted his own business.

"My dad loaned me five thousand dollars for a down payment, and I got a business loan to buy a diner on the lakefront, just south of the

Milwaukee city limits. After some remodeling and cleaning, I opened the place in 1996. Maybe you've heard of it? Eddie's?"

"Nope," Ida said. "I don't get out much, Ed."

Ed went on to say that he and Becky didn't have children and that she wished he spent less time on the job. They'd bought a country home midway between Becky's school and Ed's diner. It was practical and priced below market value, but the driving time added to Ed's hours away from home.

"We're just a breakfast-and-lunch place, but if you're running any kind of food service, you've got to be there before opening and long after closing."

"Why's that?" Ida asked.

"Your help can ruin you. I watch everything seven days a week. I keep the books, pay bills, and do all the ordering after we close at three in the afternoon."

"Can't you hire a manager?"

"Tried it once. Left the guy in charge on weekends. Turned out he was collecting full payment from customers, but he'd ring up lower receipts and keep the excess cash."

"Go on for long?"

"Caught him after two weeks. I was as much as fifty dollars short every day he was in charge."

"What did you do? Call the cops?"

"I just fired him. It happens all the time in food service. Cops in the city don't have time to pursue small-time crooks."

"Sounds like a tough business."

"I've got a great cook and good servers, but you can't leave the place for more than a few minutes. They get too generous with portions and sometimes fall for sob stories from people who don't want to pay."

⁕ ⁎ ⁕

Becky Norwood took her meat loaf out of the oven, stopped boiling water for rice, and put the frozen vegetable medley back in the freezer. This was no night for carrots and broccoli with pearl onions. But once her hands weren't busy, her thoughts ran wild. She didn't see much of Ed, and it was especially nerve-racking to be home alone on this night. One of the homes on the sparsely populated road might be sheltering a killer.

Becky poured another glass of wine and phoned Caroline Connelly, who lived within a quarter mile. There was a light on in Caroline's kitchen, and Becky needed to talk. The women had learned to rely on each other, though it had taken several months before they'd first met at a yard sale.

"Hey, Caroline," Becky began. "It's me."

"Hey! Did you hear about the murder? It really gives me the creeps."

"That's why I called. Ed was the guy who spotted trash bags in the ditch. He thought it was litter, so he called the highway department."

"Oh my God!"

"He's down at the sheriff's department now. I hope they don't think he had anything to do with it."

"When would he have the time for it?" Caroline said. "He's away almost as much as George. I never knew a union carpenter would be on the road so much. But George says he's got to travel to keep working steady."

"I thought Ed would have more free time than he does. He owns the business, after all. I'd especially like to see him more in the summer. I don't have to teach until right after Labor Day. It gets lonely out here."

"I know what you mean. Hey, do you mind if I come over and keep you company? I'll bring a bottle of wine."

"That would be great. I'll cut some cheese, slice a few apples, and wash some nice fresh grapes. It'll be like a slumber party, I guess."

"See you in five minutes," Caroline said.

Both women were dozing at opposite ends of the couch when the sound of an approaching car could be heard in the driveway. Then a car door slammed shut and Becky heard footsteps slowly tromping up the front steps. She recognized Ed's worn-out walk and dashed to the door.

"Ed! Thank God you're home! It's almost midnight. What happened?"

"Detective Ida Mae Rollins had a lot of questions but no answers."

"What do you mean?" Becky asked.

"She asked how I knew where the bags were. I told her I'd seen the stuff driving to work. I often report litterbugs, I said."

"That'll check out. What did she say?"

"We started talking mostly about our lives. She's a good conversationalist. But when she started asking about the blue bags, all she did was frown and look at the next question on her list. Then she asked how I'd known there were only five bags."

"What did you say?"

"I told her I'd seen five bags and reported each. I didn't know if there were others that I couldn't see."

"What did she say?"

"Nothing. Just kept making notes and asking more questions. She wanted to know where I'd been and what I'd done for the last ten days. I told her I worked every day, that I left home every morning at six and got home every night about six."

"Or seven or eight," Becky said.

"Then she asked me what I did at night. I told her we ate dinner, watched TV, and I was asleep by eleven."

"More like nine thirty or ten."

"I doubt it matters much. She kept asking me the same questions. I hope I told her the same thing each time. I was getting really tired and confused."

"Did you eat?"

"Yeah. Ida and I had cheeseburgers and fries. She offered me a diet cola, and I asked for a beer."

"That must've made her laugh."

"Didn't even smile. Listen—I've got to get some sleep. If I go to sleep right away, I might get close to five hours."

"So," Caroline asked, "are they done with you?"

"I sure hope so, but I doubt it. Ida has my cell, business, and home numbers. She said we'd be in touch."

"Does that mean you're in trouble?"

"She said I'd probably be needed as a witness if they make an arrest."

⁕ ⁕ ⁕

Becky welcomed the sound of a ringing telephone at ten o'clock the next morning. She'd already washed the small pile of breakfast dishes, watched a news broadcast, and put out bowls of water and kibble for the cats Ed kept in the barn. He'd learned they killed more mice, moles, gophers, and other pests if they were well fed. Becky was amazed continually by her husband's eclectic recollection of arcane facts.

"Hello. This is Becky Norwood," she said into the phone.

"Good morning, Mrs. Norwood. This is Ida Mae Rollins from the Howard County Sheriff's Department."

"The detective my husband talked to?"

"Yes, ma'am. Do you have a few minutes? You live near where we found body parts that your husband reported."

"He didn't know they were body parts when he called the highway department."

"That's what he told us."

"You don't believe him?"

"We're just collecting information, ma'am. We don't know what a lot of it means—not yet."

"Ed didn't have anything to do with this."

"No one said he did. We didn't even ask him if he did. What makes *you* ask about it?"

"I just don't want you to get the wrong idea about Ed. I know he's away a lot, but he's a good man. He doesn't hunt and can't bear the sight of someone baiting a hook. I grew up fishing, but he doesn't like it a bit."

"How often is your husband away?"

"Every day, working at the diner. It's called Eddie's."

"He told me that. When does he leave and come home?"

"The diner opens at seven in the morning, so he's on the road by six. It takes time to make the coffee and get food ready to cook."

"Sounds like hard work. When does he get home?"

"He's usually home before eight, sometimes as early as six."

As Becky spoke, she noticed her reflection in the upper oven's glass door. The morning sun didn't favor her. It spotlighted the gray in her hair and made the tiny lines near her mouth and eyes look more like crevices. A kitchen phone was mighty handy, but no woman wants a sudden reminder of her age from the nearby stove.

"Oh my," she said, unintentionally worrying aloud about her face. It was a knee-jerk type of reaction.

"What's that, Mrs. Norwood? Is everything OK out there?"

"I just saw a coyote trot across our yard into the cornfield," Becky said.

"Keep your pets indoors, ma'am. Coyotes are heartless killers."

"We have barn cats. It's lonely out here, sometimes a little scary. Especially now."

"Why's that?"

"We might have a killer living nearby."

"It's more likely the work of someone living elsewhere."

"Maybe you're right. But I'm still keeping the doors locked all the time."

"You can never be *too safe*, ma'am."

Then there was a long, awkward pause. Becky heard the crackle of the detective's police radio and Ida saying something in a muffled voice—as though she was covering the mouthpiece with her hand.

"Are you still there, Detective?"

"Yes, I am. Sorry about that. I needed to talk quickly with the sheriff."

"Why? Is something big happening?"

"Not especially. Sheriff Clark pays special attention to major crimes."

"Sounds like a demanding job."

"At times, it sure is. Well, that's about all I need for now, Mrs. Norwood."

"Are you sure? We've got nothing to hide."

"Thanks for your time, ma'am. Perhaps we'll talk again. Is this the best number to reach you? I'd also like your cell and school numbers."

"I won't be in school until after Labor Day."

"I understand. I'm just being thorough, ma'am."

Becky gave Ida the numbers and wished her well.

"Same to you, ma'am. Hope you have a blessed day."

It seemed an odd way to ring off, Becky thought. She couldn't remember the last time she'd been wished "a blessed day." It sounded so old-fashioned, like the way people talked in the old black-and-white movies on TV. It made her wonder about Detective Ida's upbringing. Had she been poor? A churchgoer?

Ida also thought about what she'd been told by Becky. She wondered about the hours Ed kept. Was it significant that Becky said he was away from home more than he admitted?

If the diner closed at three and Ed often was as late as eight getting home, that left up to four hours unaccounted for some days. It wasn't likely that the ordering, bill paying, and cleanup lasted more than an hour or two most days.

Where did Edward Norwood spend those hours? Ida didn't know a great deal about the dismemberment killing and certainly hadn't identified a suspect. But she knew that until the question of Ed's whereabouts was satisfactorily answered, he'd remain a person of interest.

CHAPTER 3
THE PHONE CALL

I wasn't surprised when Becky called me at ten thirty. She knew the breakfast rush had ended and it was before the hurry-up for lunch. We often talked at this time, sometimes for as long as thirty minutes. I'd hoped the calls eased her loneliness, especially during the long summer months. She didn't have the all-consuming school-year work of a teacher to keep her company.

"Ya know," I said, "I was thinking about what we could do to make our place more secure. Especially now."

"Ed! Did that detective say we're in danger?"

"No, not at all. I was just thinking it might be smart to get a dog. Some big guard-dog breed with a loud bark."

"I hate dogs," Becky said. "They tear a house apart. And they stink."

"A dog would be good company for you."

"When I get lonely, I can always call Caroline."

"What are you doing today? Everything OK out there?" I finally asked.

"I was on the phone just now with your friend Ida."

"Detective Ida? What the hell did she want?"

"Don't get excited. I live here too. She wanted to ask me a few questions."

"What about?"

"Mostly about you, the hours you keep. Nothing big."

My heart hiccuped as a bead of sweat rolled from my gray and thinning hair. I wiped the sweat off my brow with the back of my right hand. My left hand seemed to involuntarily tighten its grip on the diner's main phone.

"I've got to call you back on my cell," I said. "I'll call from my office. Give me a minute or two."

The "office" was a beat-up desk and a rusty filing cabinet in the basement storeroom. It was a private space, however. I couldn't be heard upstairs.

"Does Ida think I'm a suspect?" I asked, speaking too loud and too fast.

"Don't get all worked up. She's only doing her job. It's just a routine thing."

"But why does she keep asking about my hours? I told her all about that."

"It's just a double check, I'd say."

"What did you tell her, Becky? What did you say about my hours?"

"I said you work seven days a week from six in the morning to as late as eight at night."

"Why the hell did you say that? I work from six to six. That's what I told Ida."

"I said you *sometimes* get home at six."

"Almost always, you mean."

"Maybe it seems that way to you, but I'm looking at the kitchen clock until you walk in the door. I worry about you driving tired in all the city traffic."

"I'll try to be more prompt tonight," I said angrily. "I've got to get ready for the lunch crowd."

"OK, then. See you later, honey."

"Bye-bye," I said.

I thought about our conversation while prepping for lunch—making hamburger patties, slicing tomatoes, and getting bags of frozen potatoes ready for the fryer. It was strange, hanging up without saying "I love you" to each other.

It was a habit of ours, something I'd started because of the way my grandparents parted. Grandpa Norwood was late meeting his buddies for the annual drive to their deer camp. He accused Grandma of stalling as she made sandwiches and poured coffee into his big red-and-black thermos.

"Goddamn it! You made me late again," he said as he banged the kitchen door shut.

They were the last words he ever spoke to her. Grandpa suffered a heart attack and died in the field early on opening-day morning. He'd shot a deer and was moving the carcass when he was stricken.

I thought about calling Becky back immediately, but the crush of lunchtime customers made it impossible. It was a missed connection.

It wasn't the only thing I missed that morning. I later learned from a subsequent interview with Ida that a new customer at the diner, "Arnold from Milwaukee," wasn't named Arnold and didn't come from Milwaukee.

It was a plainclothes detective from the Howard County Sheriff's Department, an older man who'd said he was hard of hearing. He'd been asked by Ida to see what happened in the diner around ten thirty, the time she expected to finish her conversation with Becky Norwood.

When Ida later told me I'd been watched, it felt as if a hot band of iron were tightening where my white diner cap rested above my ears. She'd been told that I had been a gregarious and hearty host as breakfast ended but my demeanor changed after a phone call with my wife.

Ida had been told I suddenly looked very nervous, said something about calling Becky back on my cell, and vanished downstairs.

Could that detective somehow have heard me talking on the cell? Was he wearing a listening device that looked like a hearing aid? Or had a high-tech cop parked outside snagged my cell signal and eavesdropped electronically?

I couldn't stop thinking about it.

CHAPTER 4
THREE MISSING MEN

Becky kissed Ed when he walked into their home at 5:55 p.m. But it was a coolish peck on the lips, a message to Ed that he might have been convicted in absentia for failing to say "I love you" in their telephone call.

"What did you do today?" Ed asked, initially oblivious to the freshly baked apple pie on the kitchen table and spotlessly clean kitchen, dining room, and TV room. He also failed to instantly detect the scent of a sirloin tip roast in the oven or notice the chopped salad or the potatoes waiting for express baking in the microwave.

"Not much. Drank wine, ate chocolates, and watched soap operas on the television," Becky said with a grin.

"What? Hey, wait a minute. That's sarcasm, right? Because it sure looks like I'm getting a great meal tonight."

"Very good, Captain Obvious. See anything else that wasn't here this morning?"

"No, I guess I don't ..."

"Have you looked in your recliner?"

Ed darted to the TV room and returned with a calico kitten cradled in his arms. It pawed softly at his bristly chin and appeared to welcome Ed's muscular hand stroking its little head, neck, and back. The feline purred loudly.

"Who's this? Where did he come from?"

"She's a female. She's from the new litter in the barn. She's been responding to my voice. Today she played with some yarn I dangled. I picked her up, and she started purring. She was still purring after I carried her inside."

"What are you going to do with her?"

"I'm taking her tomorrow to see a vet in downtown Howard. She'll get all the vaccinations a kitten needs and get checked for worms. She'll need to be fixed too, but that has to wait until she's a little older."

"You've thought about this a lot. Anything else?"

"I think her name should be Muffin."

"Muffin? As in a baked good?"

"She's as cute as a little muffin," Becky said, taking the kitten from Ed's arms and holding it aloft, as if for inspection.

"She's awful cute—I've got to admit."

"I'm going to keep her in the house for company. You said I could use some company, remember?"

"I was thinking of a dog. A cat won't provide any protection for us."

"Sit down, Ed. Let me get you a beer. I've been thinking more about a dog. Maybe you're right about the protection we'd get."

Ed had put Detective Ida out of his mind, at least momentarily. He sipped his beer and listened to Becky's thoughts.

"Caroline and George have cats and dogs living in their house. I think the dogs are a German shepherd mix."

"They've never caused any trouble when we visit," Ed said. "Usually they're all asleep."

"But remember what happened when they heard noises in the driveway? Those dogs growled and barked so furiously I got scared."

"Me too, but it didn't bother their cats. They kept sleeping."

"Maybe it would work for us too. I'd make sure the dog was properly trained. You know, gentle with family and protective against outsiders. That's a Shepherd trait, according to what I read online."

"I think George once talked about their dogs being protective by nature."

"You can ask about it a week from Saturday," Becky said. "You remember we're having dinner with them, don't you? He's going to barbecue country ribs."

"You must have talked to Caroline too."

"Just for a minute. It was a busy day."

"I'll say. Don't forget about talking to Detective Ida."

"How could I?"

"But you also were cooking, cleaning, bringing a cat into the house, and researching guard dogs."

"Anything was better than thinking about that detective and the awful murder."

Ida's day was long but not especially helpful in the homicide investigation. She'd received phone calls from worried mothers in Milwaukee, Racine, and Kenosha. All had sons in their early twenties who hadn't been seen or heard from in more than a week. It was out of character for each, especially the Milwaukee man.

"He might have found some new friends at the concert in Milwaukee," Ida told the Kenosha woman. Her son was last seen heading out with friends for a rock concert on the lakefront. "Some kids hook up with the band and their crew; others decide to follow the band's tour dates. He'll probably call when he runs out of money."

She'd also learned the missing Racine man had been seeing a lot of an older woman, a blond flight attendant in her thirties based at O'Hare International Airport in Chicago.

"He's talked about going to Europe on one of her flights," she told Ida, "but he didn't call or leave a note."

"Is this a woman you approve of?"

"Hardly. She's been divorced twice. My son is a college student. That woman could ruin his life."

"I'll bet he gets in touch with you pretty soon," Ida said. "Give me a call when he does, OK?"

Ida didn't have a quick answer for Martha Thomas, the mother of a missing twenty-one-year-old Milwaukee man. He'd lived at home with his mother while enrolled at the University of Wisconsin–Milwaukee.

John Michael Thomas, a politically minded young Democrat, had told his mother he'd be campaigning for a state senator who was testing the waters for a gubernatorial challenge. He failed to meet a campaign driver who'd expected young Mr. Thomas to be at a rural intersection at an agreed-on time.

"Do you know exactly where he was that night?" Ida asked Martha.

"Not really. He said it was out in the country. I'm sure it was outside of Milwaukee."

"Could it have been in Howard County?"

"I hope not. But maybe it was."

"What was the name of the campaign driver? When did he contact you?"

"The driver called the next day, asking for my son. They wanted him to work on the campaign again. The driver assumed my son accompanied another worker."

"The driver must have given you his name, didn't he?"

"He said he was William Johnson, a volunteer for Kent Cofield. He's that state senator who wants to be governor. I've seen him on the TV news."

"Do you know any other campaign people your son worked with?"

"No, I don't. John Michael is a grown man. He works twenty hours a week on the campus, in maintenance and groundskeeping. He's very responsible, so I paid less and less attention to his daily activities."

"Has he ever failed to come home before?"

"Never. He always called me if he was staying with friends. I'm a widow, and he doesn't want me worrying about him."

"I see," Ida said. "If you hear from him, or come across the names of anyone who worked with him on the campaign, please call me."

"I will."

"I can be reached twenty-four seven through the Howard County Sheriff's Department. Tell the dispatcher it's about the recent homicide."

"Thank you, Detective. I hope to call you soon with good news."

"I hope you do too."

As Ida got ready for bed, she thought more about the missing man. After wiping away the little makeup she used, she brushed her teeth thoroughly and carefully. The repetitive, mindless activity let her thoughts wander over the calls she'd taken that day from worried mothers.

There was no reason yet to pursue DNA matching between the victim's remains and any of John Michael Thomas's personal items—perhaps a hairbrush that only he used, or underwear that hadn't yet been washed.

Pubic hairs might be found in his bed, or nail clippings in the bathroom wastebasket. It wouldn't be difficult to find something positively linked to Martha's son and only him, but such expensive testing could not be authorized without sufficient cause.

All Ida had was a hunch. But it was a deep sense of dread, the same feeling she'd had when her dad was in the hospital back at home and her bedside phone rang in the middle of the night.

She knew before answering that her father was dead.

CHAPTER 5
AWAY FROM IT ALL

Ida liked the independence of living alone. She'd tried marriage, but it didn't work out. Maybe it was a mistake to marry a classmate after graduation from the Illinois State Police Academy. Since that day, she had spent ten years in law enforcement and had rarely seen happy marriages between cops.

There was friction almost immediately with Bill Rollins, who'd advanced since their divorce into a shift commander position at a suburban police force near Chicago. As a newlywed, he'd expected Ida to wait on him, clean the house, and eventually bear his children. Ida thought it unfair. She worked just as hard as Bill in her postgraduate job as a patrol officer for a small department near Harvard, Illinois—west of Chicago, but too distant and rural to be considered a suburb.

Bill made fun of her job almost immediately. He thought it was hilarious that her department considered a trek to downtown Harvard "going to town."

"It sure ain't going to a city," Bill said. "No city would have a statue of a cow in the middle of downtown."

Ida laughed at the joke, but it grew old for a girl who'd been raised in the country. Bill wasn't at all interested in the town's dairy history or its annual Harvard Milk Days celebration.

"Bust any jaywalkers today? Nab any library book thieves?" was his customary greeting when Ida's shift ended. He never even bothered to listen to her reply.

Ida might have been able to tolerate Bill's dumb jokes, but she chafed when he minimized her accomplishments. All of them. The day she was promoted to investigator, he went out drinking with his cop buddies instead of taking her to dinner or celebrating at home.

It led to a long and furious argument. It ended when Bill threw her to the floor and slapped her when she tried to stand. Ida called in sick the next day, packed her belongings, and moved into an apartment above the feedstore in downtown Harvard. She'd served Bill with divorce papers within a week.

Life without Bill was sometimes lonely, but not as torturous as living with him had become. Ida wondered if she'd been so smitten by the ex-jock's rugged good looks that she was blind to his apparently deep-seated hatred of women. By the time she'd joined the Howard County Sheriff's Department, she'd stopped thinking about Bill. She got the company she needed in frequent phone calls to her mother, Lula Belle Budslick, who still lived near Cobden.

Ida's murder investigation was going nowhere, despite almost two weeks of nonstop police work. She took advantage of the lull to visit her mother. It was a long drive to the family farm, but Ida had the time to spare. No duties were being neglected. The comforts of home provided time for thinking. It was a comfortable and peaceful place, perfect for collecting one's thoughts.

Ida spent her Saturday night reading as her mother knitted and watched TV from the rocking recliner Ida had given her the previous Christmas. There was plenty of time for talk too. Ida found herself speaking as if she'd never left the farm.

"That murder you're workin' on; I was just wonderin'."

"What's that, Mama?"

"Don't you have any ideas about who was killed?"

"I've gotta hunch. That's all."

"Tell me about it, honey."

"Yeah, I never see Barney or Spike in the cornfield between our houses. I wouldn't mind, though."

"Watch the meat for a minute, Ed. It looks like them dogs are tearing up some small animal."

Ed watched as George trotted into the field. He was in his late forties, but George still ran like an athlete. He suddenly stopped and grabbed both dogs by their collars, then led them back into the yard.

"Get in the barn, boys," George told the dogs. "Your food bowls and water are in your pen. That's it—be good dogs."

"Something wrong, George?"

"Real wrong. Them dogs were gnawing and pawing at something. I'd never seen 'em act that way before."

"A rabbit? Raccoon?"

"I wish it was. I didn't look too closely, but it looks like a human head."

Ida wasn't interested in the movie her mother wanted to watch on TV. She munched on the pepperoni pizza that had been delivered piping hot by a nearby convenience store that made pies and delivered until midnight. Take-out food had been a rarity when Ida was a child, and food delivered to the door had been decades away in tiny Cobden. Since then, there had been many other changes too.

Lula had served her family food at the kitchen table unless it was midsummer and too hot indoors. Then she used the picnic table under the maple tree in the backyard. They ate the chicken and hogs raised by Ida's father, Earl Wayne Budslick, and of course there were always fresh and canned peaches from the family's orchard. Fish was served often too, usually catfish and crappies her father caught in nearby streams.

Ida thought about those times, which never were easy but now took on a warm sepia tone in her mind's eye. She wondered what Earl Wayne would think of eating pizza from paper plates in front of the TV.

He wouldn't like it a bit, I'll bet, until he took a bite, she thought. *Then he'd join right in. Like it was his idea in the first place.*

Ida took another slice of pizza from the disposable delivery box. It probably would have been used as fireplace tinder when she was a child. Most of the wintertime heat came from the stone fireplace in the living room, augmented by the kitchen stove and small coal-burning space heaters that sometimes were needed in winter.

The home now had central air and heat, her father's final improvements. Earl Wayne hadn't done the work himself, but it took years of raising peaches and baking bread in a full-time job to raise the money. It nearly emptied his savings account, but he didn't want to be indebted in any way.

"We pay for what we need, when we need it," he'd say. "If we can't pay for it, we don't need it."

Ida wondered what her father would think of cable television, a big flat-screen TV, and stereo sound. She imagined him sinking into a recliner, loosening his bib overalls, and kicking off his boots.

"He'd like it fine as long as he could watch John Wayne or Randolph Scott," Ida said.

"What's that, honey?" her mother asked. "Didja say somethin'?"

"I was just thinkin' about Daddy. Guess I didn't realize I said something out loud."

"I talk to him all the time. It helps me get through each day. Sometimes it seems—wait, what's that noise? Is it comin' from the TV?"

"No, Mama. That's my cell phone. I've got a special ringtone for calls from work."

"Ringtone? I remember when phones only rang like a bell."

Lula had a bad feeling when her daughter answered the call and quickly walked into the kitchen. She couldn't hear what was being said, other than a final, somewhat loud "Yes, sir. I understand. Right away, sir."

Ida was shaking her head and wringing her hands when she returned from the kitchen.

"Ooooh, Mama, sometimes I hate police work."

"You're going to work, aren't ya?"

"That's right. It was Sheriff Clark on the phone. I'm heading back to Wisconsin."

CHAPTER 6
THE WORST CALL

Before heading home for the weekend, Ida had spoken to Sheriff Clark. He'd stressed her need for time off.

"This murder is going to be top priority for months," he'd said. "I don't know when you'll see your mother again. Go home now or wish you had."

She soon wished she hadn't. All it took was the Saturday-night phone call.

Ida listened in horrified silence as Peter Clark explained he would lead the death investigation until Ida returned. His words likely were intended as supportive, but Ida heard only an unexpressed threat to her by-the-book investigation.

She imagined her old-school boss and a big team of overtime-hungry deputies and scent dogs shredding the farm field where the decapitated head had just been found. The delicate search for evidence she'd intended to lead would be pointless if the good old boys and their hounds started trampling, uprooting, and snuffling at daybreak as planned.

"Please, sir—I need to be at the scene," Ida had said. "I'll be there before six. Don't take anything out of that field."

"Even the head?"

"Especially the head. Make sure those dogs don't get back in the field."

"OK, Ida."

Ida hit the road after ten o'clock that night. It was more than four hundred miles to Howard County, but Ida knew she'd be at the crime scene faster than the average motorist. The V-8 in her late-model Ford Mustang had enough giddyap to average eighty miles per hour on the route linking Interstate 57 to I-294 around Chicago, then to I-94 into Wisconsin. She'd have enough time for breakfast and coffee and still be in the field by six in the morning.

That kind of speeding might earn Joe or Jane Six-Pack a trip to jail, but not a law enforcement officer. Ida smiled at the Illinois State Police officer who pulled her over near Mattoon. Then she uttered the magic words: "I'm on the job, Officer. May I show you my badge?"

Although Ida was clocked at eighty-seven miles per hour, she got the go-ahead to proceed if she kept her speed to no more than eighty. Ida complied and learned a few hours later she'd made the right decision going to the crime scene—which was a textbook case of poor police procedure. Half a dozen squad cars were parked on the roadway and in the gravel tractor paths linking the pavement and the borders of the field. All had their red-and-blue lights rolling, and radio transmissions were blaring from the squads' loudspeakers. All that was missing was a lit billboard proclaiming "Major Crime Scene."

Ida took a deep breath, steadying herself. Then she stepped from the Mustang, grabbed her mug of coffee, and squinted at the yellow crime scene tape that had been lashed to four metal stakes, forming a rectangle. Deputies stood at three corners, the sheriff at the corner nearest the road and Ida.

"Mornin', Ida," he said. "Everything look OK to you?"

"Not so much, sir. Can you get everyone to kill their lights and loudspeakers?"

"Sure thing. But why?"

"You probably kept the neighbors awake all night. We don't want TV choppers coming in here. They'll draw a crowd. Let's keep this low-key. It's Sunday morning, a quiet time. Maybe that'll help us."

As Peter Clark issued his calm-down orders, Ida walked to the edge of the yellow tape. The head was easily seen. The face had been horribly disfigured, maybe by the dogs but perhaps by the killer. It appeared to be the head of a young man with collar-length brown hair. Ida looked at the remains, then at a photo of John Michael Thomas she'd been given by his mother. A solid identification wasn't possible, but Ida could see the hair looked like it did in the photo. It might be Martha Thomas's boy.

"That poor freakin' kid," Ida mumbled to the nearest deputy.

"You know who this is?"

"Maybe. Just maybe."

The sheriff approached as Ida looked at the head and the surrounding ground.

"What do you need, Ida?" he asked.

"We need evidence technicians, the medical examiner, and photographs of everything out in this field. Hey, how was this found?"

"Let's talk in my squad."

Ida kept quiet until she and the sheriff were seated.

"That house over there," she said, pointing a finger, "that's the residence of Edward and Becky Norwood. Who lives in the nearest house?"

"George Connelly and his wife, Caroline. George called us after his dogs found the head. His voice was shaking. He sounded very upset. It was before I called you, an hour or two. George and Caroline were barbecuing with the Norwoods. The guys saw George's dogs ripping and tearing at something in the field."

"The head, right?"

"They thought the dogs were killing a small animal. George pulled them away and found the head. Didja notice how neat the cut was made on the neck?"

Ida nodded.

"It's strange that all this stuff is found near Ed Norwood, ain't it?"

"Could be coincidental."

"He knew the exact number of bags we'd find. He reported the specific locations."

"That could be coincidental too. The highway boss says Ed reports litter all the time. And he reported *seeing* five bags. If he'd seen six or seven, he'd have reported it, Ed said."

"What's the guy's wife like?"

"She's a schoolteacher. We talked on the phone. She was defensive, but that's normal."

"Maybe not. Her husband works in *food service*. A guy who runs a diner must know a lot about cutting meat. He's probably got bone saws, butcher knives, and cleavers."

"I don't think Ed Norwood is a killer, Sheriff."

"Why not?"

"It doesn't feel right. He wasn't trying to hide anything when we talked. And he wasn't trying to figure out just what I knew."

"Just the same, don't rule him out."

"I won't, sir."

"I talked a little bit with George Connelly. He's a union carpenter who works out of town during the week. He's a barbecue nut, knows a lot about cuts of meat."

"What'd he say about the head, sir?"

"He said it looked like Barney and Spike dug it up. Those are his dogs. There's a hollowed-out place in the dirt where they'd been digging. It's inside the taped-off area."

"You don't think he's got something to do with this, do you, sir?"

"Seems unlikely. But you should talk to him. See if his story is the same as he told me. It's hard to remember lies."

It was a long, hot, and tiring day in the field. But everything that would be needed as evidence, and many other things that potentially could be evidence, had been properly collected, cataloged, and transported to safe storage in the morgue and the department's climate-controlled evidence room. Ida badly needed sleep, but there was another task to be completed.

It was the worst task: calling the possible next of kin.

Martha Thomas had attended Sunday-morning services at Peace Lutheran Church, where she was a lifetime member. She'd married Arnold "Arnie" Thomas in the church and had her only child, John Michael Thomas, baptized there. Her husband's funeral had been in the church two years ago. The congregation's widows and widowers were her closest friends.

"How're you getting on, Martha?" the Reverend Jerome Driscoll asked when the service ended.

"Thanks for asking for prayers for my son. I'm so alone without him. He's been such a help since I lost Arnie."

"God's plan isn't so easily understood."

"If only Arnie hadn't ridden his bike to work that day. It was my fault. I needed the car for some reason, but now I can't even remember why."

"Don't blame yourself."

"I know I shouldn't. Arnie really loved riding his bike to work."

"It's great exercise. Arnie was in top shape thanks to biking and running."

"John Michael said his dad could outrun all his friends—athletic kids, most of them. But he was only human. I still can't understand how a trucker could run him down from behind."

"He said the sun was blinding that morning, especially as he crested the hill where Arnie was riding."

"I've tried to understand what happened, but I just can't. And now I'm crazy worrying about my boy."

"I'll be praying for you, Martha. So will your friends. Take comfort in the power of prayer."

Martha spent the rest of the day at home. She made herself a small lunch with a frozen chicken potpie and a tossed salad, then worked in the garden Arnie had carefully fenced against rabbits and the ever-increasing number of urban raccoons. The weeding never stopped, and the dry weather required more watering than she would have preferred. Water was plentiful in Milwaukee, but it wasn't free.

After a cooling shower, Martha made herself a pot of tea, then watched the TV news and worked a crossword puzzle from the Sunday newspaper. Martha's worries about John Michael grew unbearable unless she kept her hands and head occupied.

When the phone rang shortly after seven, she hoped it would be Helen Vorhees, a church widow ten years her senior. They talked to each other nightly.

"Thomas residence, Martha speaking."

Ida was not surprised when Martha answered on the third ring. Martha had told the detective she'd been staying near her home phone as much as possible. She had a cell phone but didn't like using it.

"Hello, Mrs. Thomas. This is Ida Mae Rollins from the Howard County Sheriff's Department."

"Oh my God. Something's happened, hasn't it?"

"We found something, Mrs. Thomas. It could help us identify the remains."

"What did you find?"

"I'm not able to talk about it on the phone. May I visit you in your home, ma'am? Is tonight OK?"

"Yes, of course. I'll have a fresh pot of tea waiting."

"Thank you, Mrs. Thomas. I'll be there in thirty minutes."

Martha called Helen Vorhees and told her she was expecting a detective to visit.

Helen and Reverend Driscoll got to Martha's front door just as a squad car rounded the corner and pulled to the curb.

"We're here for you, Martha," Helen said.

"Thank you. Please come inside. There's a pot of tea and cups in the kitchen. I'll meet the detective here and bring her to the living room."

"Her?" Driscoll asked.

"Her name is Ida Mae Rollins," Martha replied. "Here she comes now. Welcome, Detective."

Ida offered a handshake to the minister and Helen, then followed Martha into the living room. It was a formal setting, spotlessly clean and free of distractions other than the ticking of a cuckoo clock, framed original art—watercolors of pastoral settings—and healthy-looking houseplants.

"This could be very upsetting, Mrs. Thomas," Ida began. "Please sit down."

"I've had the worst feeling since you called. What did you find?"

"There is no easy way to tell you this. We got a call from a man who lives on the road where we found body parts. He saw his dogs messing with something in the field near his house."

"Just tell me, Detective. I was a hospital nurse for nearly forty years."

"The dogs recovered a human head. It's probably from a young man with collar-length brown hair. The hair looks about the same as your boy's in the photo you gave me. That's all we know at this point."

·⁖·

It was midnight before Ida went home for the night. Coffee and adrenaline had kept her going through the long, hot day of police work, which was physically demanding. But it wasn't as tiring as the time she spent with Martha Thomas. That visit was emotionally draining.

Martha had fainted and toppled from her chair when Ida explained the details about the severed head that had been found. She knelt at Martha's side, felt a strong but rapid pulse on Martha's neck, and politely kept Helen and the minister from doing too much.

"Mrs. Thomas? Can you hear me?" Ida asked in a soft voice. She gently patted Martha's hand and asked Helen for a glass of water—no ice, not too cold.

"Is she going to be OK?" Reverend Driscoll asked.

Ida moistened her fingertips, then dabbed the water on Martha's lips. In seconds, Martha opened her eyes.

"What happened?" she asked.

"You fainted, Mrs. Thomas. How do you feel?"

"All I can think about is what you told me. Was it John Michael?"

"We don't know. I'll have to ask you for your son's dental records."

Martha said their family dentist had the records.

"I'll contact him tomorrow," Ida said. "Will you call him in the morning? It will make my job a little easier if he's heard from you first."

"I'll call the office at eight. I'll say it's a dental emergency. It is, isn't it?"

"Yes, ma'am, for you it certainly is an emergency."

As she turned off the lights in her apartment, Ida thought about the time she'd spent with Martha. Before getting into bed, she switched on the window air conditioner in her bedroom. The sound of the unit masked noise from the street, mostly late-night traffic after the bars closed. Downtown Howard was noisy compared to Harvard.

Ida had been shaken when Martha fainted but had quickly determined it was not life threatening. Martha apparently had a strong will to live, perhaps an even stronger wish for justice. Ida was relieved when Helen Vorhees offered to spend the night, but she also had a sense that Martha would have been fine by herself.

She's a survivor, Ida thought as she pulled the sheet and lightweight quilt to her chin. Then she switched off the bedside light and fell into a deep sleep.

CHAPTER 7

VICTIM OF CIRCUMSTANCE

I didn't kill anybody, but the unsolved murder near my home troubled me endlessly. I battled grogginess in daylight but couldn't sleep at night.

"For God's sake, Ed, get up and read. I can't sleep with you thrashing around," Becky said as the digital alarm pulsed to 2:25 a.m.

"I get up in a couple hours. How can I work all day without sleep?"

"You're not sleeping now. Make yourself some tea and read in your recliner. You'll nod off. I'll wake you when the alarm sounds."

"I hate fuckin' tea."

"Make some cocoa, then. You're driving me nuts."

When Becky woke me at five, I'd been asleep in my chair with Muffin on my lap for little more than an hour. It was more sleep than I'd logged several nights since learning an undercover officer had visited my diner. He'd seen my reaction to a phone call from Becky after she'd talked to Detective Ida Mae Rollins. That really spun the hamster wheels inside my brain. They turned relentlessly. Were my phones tapped? Were the cars behind me driven by cops? Were my emails being read? Was I under surveillance around the clock? Had anyone seen the visitors who entered the diner through the back door? Were license plate numbers being checked and logged?

Knowing I wasn't a killer helped, but it wasn't a miracle cure for paranoia. For one thing, I doubt there's anyone alive who doesn't have a secret that cannot be revealed. Or several secrets.

When Detective Ida interviewed me again, this time at the diner, it was obvious she was trying to connect all the dots in my life. That was after George's dogs uncovered a severed human head in the field next to his home. It felt as though she was looking straight into my soul when she asked me again what I did after the diner closed at three in the afternoon. Don't let anyone tell you that brown eyes convey warmth. Ida's suggested the dark orange fires of hell.

It felt as if I were gagging on a golf ball when Ida told me a detective had seen me act very nervous when Becky called. I finally managed to swallow, but I sweat my way through her other questions.

"Does it take several hours to order supplies, get food ready for the next day, and keep the books? Every day?" she asked.

Seconds passed as Ida looked in my eyes and waited for an answer. She said nothing. It seemed she never blinked, took a breath, or swallowed. It was obviously more than unnerving.

"There's more to running a diner than cooking and using a cash register," I finally said.

"Your wife says you don't get home till eight. You told me it was six. Who's tellin' the truth?"

"She wishes I didn't work so hard. She gets lonesome, especially in the summer."

"You're both telling the truth?"

"I guess so. That's the way it *seems* to her, I mean."

It wasn't a long conversation, but it put my teeth on edge. Ida portrayed herself as a simple southern girl who'd grown up on a farm. But she'd have never earned a detective's badge without curiosity, confidence, and intelligence.

Ida was investigating a dismemberment murder, and I lived near the crime scene. I'd known exactly where the bagged body parts were. I knew how many bags were found. It also was obvious that a diner operator would have access to sharp knives, cleavers, and other tools used by butchers. And she knew from talking to my wife there were days when I couldn't fully account for as many as five hours.

This was a real problem. I had a secret. And it wasn't the kind of thing I could share with Ida. I'd be slapped with handcuffs and taken to jail if I tried explaining that I was a bookie.

Legalized wagering on sports was a few years away. But I'd been taking sports bets in the diner. It was the kind of betting that eventually became perfectly legal once the government got its cut, like in Vegas. It was all a matter of greasing the right palms—those of Uncle Sam.

It was pretty small-time stuff, guys betting a few hundred on baseball, basketball, and *especially* football. You wouldn't believe how much money changes hands over the Sunday-afternoon games of the Green Bay Packers and Chicago Bears. And you wouldn't believe how quickly a winner wanted his money.

A buddy in Kenosha, a guy named Angelo Calacia, helped me get started. He ran a sports book through his barbershop. My book was kind of a franchise for him, since I'd give him 30 percent of my monthly net. He had other guys doing the same around Wisconsin and northern Illinois. I don't know any of their names. It wasn't in my best interest, should I ever get busted. That's what Angelo said.

"You don't know nothin', you don't say nothin'" was the way he explained it.

The book was a more lucrative business than the diner, which did OK but never brought in enough money for a big home on ten acres in the country. The sports book was a great cash-and-carry business. Fans would bring me their cash, and I'd carry most of it away. Too many people bet with their hearts instead of their heads.

Most gamblers gave me the money in advance, so I usually didn't have to collect debts. I paid the winners promptly too. I didn't want any arguments over money and kept very detailed books—nicknames only— in case an unhappy gambler asked a lot of questions. I always had answers. I kept the books and cash in a safe hidden in the diner's basement. A crook would never find it. Cops would.

This never seemed like a criminal enterprise to me, but I sure didn't want Ida to report her findings to the feds. Sports gamblers sometimes got busted in Wisconsin, usually in connection with a network of small-time bookies. Like me.

I was courting disaster, and not just from a possible publicized bust followed by criminal charges. Even if my reputation eventually was restored, the court-ordered fines and income tax penalties would ruin me.

These were among my thoughts late at night. Even after I drank a few beers or glasses of wine, visions of newspaper headlines ran through my head, always in a black-and-white film noir setting.

"Diner owner grilled on gambling rap" was one.

"Eggs over easy or Packers plus six?" was another.

"Cookie or bookie, feds will decide" was my favorite.

Think it's funny? I'd see the humor, too, if it was another guy in the soup. It *would* be comically ironic if a gambling arrest cleared me in a murder probe. It'd make a great plot twist in a dark comedy.

But I sure wasn't laughing.

CHAPTER 8
YOU NEVER KNOW

A disappointed Martha Thomas called Ida early Monday morning. She reported that her dentist was vacationing in Alaska and his office was closed.

"His bookkeeper and dental hygienist are on vacation too," Martha said. "I can't ask about John Michael's dental records until next week."

"That's unfortunate."

"It's terrible. I don't think I can stand waiting. Isn't there another way to identify remains?"

"DNA testing, but it might take months to get results. I'll need to visit your home and collect evidence from his bedding, clothes, and grooming supplies."

"Can you start today? I'll be home."

"I'll need to bring an evidence technician from the state crime lab. They're usually pretty booked up. Dental records are our best bet for quick results."

"Can't I just look at the remains? That's how they do it on TV."

"I'm not sure you'll be able to stand the sight of what we've found, Mrs. Thomas."

"I'm a mother. Don't I have a right to view the remains?"

"I can arrange a viewing, maybe as soon as tomorrow. I still don't think it's a good idea."

"Helen and Reverend Driscoll will take care of me. I told you I was a nurse, didn't I? I've seen a lot. I identified my husband's body after he was run over by a truck."

"I'll set up a viewing and call you back. But we'll still need dental records and DNA testing. I'll let you know when the evidence technician is available."

"Thank you, Detective. You've been very kind."

"Just doing my job, ma'am. And I'd sure appreciate being called Ida."

"I'll do that, Ida. Please call me Martha, OK?"

"Thank you kindly, Martha."

Howard County had an elected coroner who oversaw all death investigations. Clyde Sternberg was an undertaker who consoled the bereaved and counted on their support at election time. In his duties as coroner, Sternberg relied solely on the investigative abilities of the county's medical examiner, Dr. John Azarian, a nationally known pathologist.

But Sternberg wasn't entirely an empty suit politician. He kept nonsense away from Azarian, who deeply appreciated the coroner.

Ida called Sternberg to arrange a viewing.

"How can I help you, Detective? Hope it doesn't concern the body parts we've got in the morgue."

"Afraid it does, Clyde. I've got a widowed mother from Milwaukee who thinks we've got what's left of her son. She wants a look."

"You want me to work with Dr. John?"

"Yep. We've got to present the remains in the most humane way possible."

"Without damaging any physical evidence, right?"

"Have I said this before?"

"Maybe a dozen times. When does she want to take a look?"

"Could you get it set up for tomorrow afternoon?"

"I'll have it ready by two. It won't take more than an hour, will it?"

"It shouldn't. The mother, Martha Thomas, is a retired nurse. She's a survivor, but this won't be easy. I doubt she'll look at the remains for even ten minutes."

"That's good. Dr. John likes to close his shop at four. He's at work every morning at four, unless he's called during the night. Then he just keeps working."

"You'll be there, won't you, Clyde? Do whatever you can to make the face look better. You know what to do."

"I'll give it my best, but Dr. John won't let me do too much."

"I understand. See you tomorrow."

The morgue was in the basement of the Howard County Medical Center. Sternberg and Dr. Azarian ensured the brightly lit room was spotlessly clean and free of any odors aside from cleansers and disinfectant. There was a noticeable sheen to the stainless steel doors of the body drawers, and all the tools of the medical examiner's trade were stored out of sight.

What remained on display was an examination table in the center of the room, beneath a bank of high-intensity lamps. A human-looking form was on the table, entirely covered by surgical sheeting.

Martha Thomas arrived ten minutes early, escorted by Reverend Driscoll and Helen Vorhees.

"Are we too early, Ida?"

"No, ma'am—er, I mean Martha. We're ready. Have you prepared yourself?"

"I've prayed for strength. I'll do my best."

Sternberg gently pulled the sheeting away, but he left it covering where the feet and hands had been severed. Ida noticed that the head looked better than it had in the field. It was positioned atop the torso and legs on a human silhouette sketched on disposable medical paper.

"Thank you, Coroner Sternberg and Dr. Azarian," Ida said. She'd often seen ghastlier displays and made a mental note to send a thank-you note to Clyde.

Martha kept her composure. Helen Vorhees and Reverend Driscoll put their arms around her as she walked about the examination table.

"My son's about this size and build," Martha finally said.

"What about the face?" Ida asked.

"I can't tell for sure. The hair doesn't look quite right, though."

"Did your son have any scars, tattoos, or birthmarks?"

"He had a small star tattooed on the back of his left hand. Can I see that hand?"

"I'm sorry," Ida said. "The hands are missing."

"I didn't know that. The news said a torso, arms, and legs were found."

"We deliberately kept some things out of our news release on the homicide. If we questioned a suspect and he mentioned missing hands and feet, well, that's something only he would know, other than us."

"What kind of person could do such a thing?"

"Someone who wants to eliminate fingerprints and as many distinguishing characteristics as possible."

"You're smart, Ida."

"You learn a lot about all kinds of things in this line of work, Martha."

"I'll bet you do. A lot of things you'd rather not know."

"Sometimes it's hard to sleep. Does John Michael have any scars or significant birthmarks?"

"He didn't have birthmarks of any kind. Arnie and I couldn't believe how perfect our baby boy was," Martha said through tears.

"This might not be your son," Ida said.

"I hope not."

"What about scars?"

"None that I know of."

"I don't want to rush you," Ida said, "but do you need more time here? Take as long as you need."

"I guess I'm ready to go home."

"OK, then. I'll be in touch. Take care, Martha."

Ida conferred with Sternberg and Dr. Azarian as Martha, the minister, and Helen left the morgue and walked to the nearby elevator. The morgue door closed behind them and automatically locked with a metallic clunk.

"Good security system," Martha said. "I guess they need to protect evidence."

"That sounds so cold and clinical," Helen said. "Those drawers hold human beings."

"That wasn't John Michael's face," Martha said. "I can't be certain, but I have a strong feeling about it."

"Maybe he's OK," Reverend Driscoll said. "Young men sometimes disappear. Maybe he'll call or come home soon."

"I have a strong feeling about that too. Something's happened to my boy. Something terrible."

They were silent as they stepped into the elevator and ascended to the first floor. The tears Martha had fought in the morgue finally forced her to grab a handkerchief from her purse and dab her cheeks and eyes.

"You want to sit down, Martha?" Helen asked as she took her by the elbow and guided her to a padded chair.

"Thanks. I just need to catch my breath. I'll be all right."

"Take your time. And don't worry about being alone tonight. I can stay with you another night, if you'd like."

"Thanks," Martha said. "I don't think you'll need to, but I sure appreciate your kindness. You're a wonderful friend."

"The whole church is looking out for you," Reverend Driscoll said. "And praying too."

"Thank you, Pastor."

"I'll bring the car up to the main entrance, Martha. Helen will stay with you and walk you out."

"I'm sure glad you drove me here, Reverend. My legs feel weak, and my hands are trembling. I've been in morgues before, but usually as a nurse. This was just as terrible as seeing Arnie."

Ida was surprised by Martha's toughness but thankful for it. She wasn't thankful for the other surprise that was waiting for her in the detective bureau. Sheriff Clark was standing in the meeting room, fielding questions from a bevy of TV, radio, and newspaper reporters.

"We don't have the hands or feet," Clark said. "We think it's possible the killer was trying to hide scars or tattoos or birthmarks."

In the twenty minutes Ida witnessed, the sheriff ticked off a laundry list of physical evidence known only by the police, medical examiner, and coroner. The killer would be the only other person in the world with the same knowledge and might have unwittingly revealed some of it when questioned by police. That would be powerful evidence for a trial, but it would be rendered valueless after the six o'clock news and morning papers.

"I didn't know you were going to hold a press conference, Sheriff," Ida said after the media herd departed.

"It was kind of a spur-of-the-moment thing. I was talking to Calvin Krebs of the *Howard Register-Press* and giving him more information than you put in the press release."

"So what? Krebs is a goofball, and nobody reads that paper."

"Every elected official in the county reads it. All the business leaders too."

"So what did you tell Krebs?"

"The same stuff I gave out at the press conference. This ain't my first rodeo, Ida."

"I know that, sir. I just wish you'd kept the missing hands and feet our little secret."

"Everything will work out fine, Ida—you'll see."

What Ida saw in the morning wasn't fine. The front page of the local paper was devoted entirely to the dismemberment killing under the huge headline "Thrill Killer Still Loose." It included a high school yearbook photo of John Michael Thomas with the boldfaced caption "Possible victim?" There also was a photo of Edward Norwood lifted from an ad for his diner and another bold-faced caption: "Person of interest?"

It was a sensational scoop for Krebs, who would be interviewed during the day by both CNN and Fox News, as well as the big newspapers in Milwaukee and Chicago.

"It was the kind of digging any good reporter could have done," Krebs said to the TV reporters.

What actually had happened was Krebs had recorded everything Sheriff Clark uttered. He'd also surreptitiously read the investigative reports left on top of the sheriff's desk as Clark notified all of the department's media contacts of a scheduled press conference. Krebs carefully wrote down the names, ages, and addresses of the possible victim and person of interest. He later made a single attempt by phone to contact John Michael Thomas's mother, who was having dinner in the home of Helen Vorhees and ignored the vague message Krebs left on her voice mail. She thought he was selling subscriptions. Krebs also attempted to contact Ed Norwood at the diner, which at the time of his call had been closed for hours.

"Attempts to contact Martha Thomas and Edward Norwood were not immediately successful" was the final line in Krebs's lengthy story.

Martha quickly answered her phone early Wednesday morning. She thought it would be a call from Ida, but it was a man she didn't know.

"I'd like to speak to Martha Thomas, please," he said.

"Speaking. Who's calling, please?"

"You don't know me, Mrs. Thomas. I apologize for calling so early. My name is Ed Norwood. Have you read the newspaper this morning?"

"I read the *Milwaukee Journal Sentinel* with my coffee every morning. Why?"

"I'm sorry. I mean the *Howard Register-Press*. I get the paper at home."

"I don't get that paper. I live in Milwaukee, not Howard County."

"Today's Howard paper has a front-page story identifying your son, John Michael Thomas, as a possible murder victim. That's your son, isn't it?"

Martha's heart fluttered. Perspiration dotted her upper lip. She felt faint and quickly sat on a stool near the kitchen phone.

"Mrs. Thomas, are you there?" Ed finally asked.

"Yes, you gave me quite a shock. What else does that story say?"

Ed read the entire story over the phone, even as the diner filled with customers. He'd asked his staff to cover for him.

"How can they identify my son without my permission? Do I need a lawyer?"

"Think about how *I* feel. I didn't know your son, and I wouldn't hurt anyone. Calling me a 'person of interest' is like calling me a murder suspect. I'm calling a lawyer."

"I don't know what to do, Mr. Norwood. The detective investigating the murder was very kind. She isn't mentioned in the article, is she?"

"You mean Ida Mae Rollins?"

"Yes, that's the detective I've been talking to."

"The only cop named in the newspaper is the sheriff, Peter Clark."

"How could he say all those things? I've never talked to him."

"He's only quoted a few times. Almost everything else is explained as something 'deputies said' or 'according to sheriff's department reports.'"

"What's the reporter's name? Does it give a phone number? I'm going to call that man today."

"You might want to talk to a lawyer first. That's what I'm going to do."

Before ending the call, Martha paused, grabbed a pen and paper from the counter, and jotted down Ed's name and contact numbers, as well as the reporter's phone number. Then she wondered whether Calvin Krebs was his real name.

•⸱• •

Krebs was enjoying his sudden celebrity. He had been giving interviews throughout the day and, finally, at four in the afternoon, was sipping cola and feasting on a cheeseburger smothered with onions. He'd been regaling fellow reporters with the inside story of how he'd identified the possible victim and suspect.

"Sheriff Clark left the investigative reports on top of his desk, in plain view. I was alone in the office for five minutes, maybe more. I just had to lean across the desk to read the names and addresses."

"How did you know the stuff was legit?" the newest hire asked.

"I asked Clark point-blank if John Michael Thomas was a possible victim, if Norwood was a person of interest."

"What'd he say?"

"He answered in the affirmative," Krebs said in cop-speak while reaching for a jangling telephone on his desk. "Newsroom, Krebs."

"Mr. Krebs, my name is Martha Thomas. Perhaps you've heard of me."

"Yes, Mrs. Thomas, I'm glad you called. I tried to contact you yesterday."

"What gives you the right to print my name and address in the paper? Who told you it was OK to report my son may have been murdered?"

"Everything I reported came from the sheriff's department. It's a public record. The other papers and TV are reporting the same stuff today."

"You'll be hearing from my lawyer, young man."

"He'll have to take a number. I cover police news, and people are always threatening to take me to court."

"You must be a bitter, hateful person to do that kind of work."

"It's a living."

"I've thought about what you did all day. Mr. Norwood read me your story first thing this morning."

"I couldn't reach him last night, and he hung up on me today."

"He's already got a lawyer."

"So sue me," Krebs growled as Martha hung up the phone.

Ida made it a point to stay away from the sheriff, but he walked into the detective bureau at the end of the day and sat in the chair next to her desk. Sheriff Clark crossed his meaty arms and stretched his long legs to the nearest wastebasket—which he used as an impromptu ottoman for his hand-tooled cowboy boots.

"How's it going, girl?" he said with a smile.

"I've been better. I doubt Martha Thomas will let me in her home when I bring a crime lab evidence technician to look for her son's DNA samples."

"We can get a search warrant if we need to."

"That shouldn't be necessary. And now you've given Ed Norwood a reason to keep his mouth shut."

"He's said plenty already."

"This is a small department, sir. We're supposed to have two detectives, but I've been alone for three months. My work is tough enough without you putting up roadblocks all over the place."

"Now, Ida, let's keep this professional, OK? I'm getting close to making a hire. I'm hoping the county board will come up with the money. It's not a sure thing."

"Just what I thought. But it's not my biggest concern. What am I supposed to do about this mess of a murder investigation?"

"I've been around a long time, Ida. We used to release a whole lot more information years ago. People would see it in the papers or on TV. They'd remember seeing something that looked out of place. We'd get some good leads."

"The eyes and ears of the public, right?"

"Something like that. I know you don't get along with Krebs, but at least his story included the CrimeWatch anonymous tip line."

"I spent half the day listening to new information on that line, all of it useless. One guy even read me stuff right from Krebs's story."

"Be patient, girl. I've put you up for a bonus with the county board. They'll rubber-stamp it. And I've got a feeling we're close to a big break."

"I hope you're right about something good happening soon. Daddy always said it was darkest just before dawn."

CHAPTER 9
FACING TOUGH ODDS

I was near the end of my rope. Life's normalcy ended after I innocently reported ugly roadside litter. It was deeply upsetting to find evidence of a dismemberment killing near my home. But my nerves really unraveled after a detective questioned me about it and the newspapers and TV stations labeled me as a person of interest in an unsolved homicide.

I talked with a lawyer after closing Eddie's late Thursday afternoon. It meant driving into downtown Milwaukee at rush hour and facing a jumble of snail's pace traffic. But I wasn't going to hire a small-town yokel to sue a newspaper. Turned out I wasn't going to sue anyone, at least not after talking to attorney Peter Fitzpatrick.

"So what do you think of my chances with the *Howard Register-Press?*" I asked after spilling my guts.

"Not much, unless you've got a bottomless pit of money," he said. "A newspaper can afford to delay things until you're broke. They *buy* justice. The justice *they* want."

"But they labeled me a murder suspect. I never even got a chance to talk with their so-called reporter, that asshole Calvin Krebs."

"Actually, they called you a person of interest and attributed it to the sheriff's department reports. You'd have to prove otherwise or demonstrate Krebs maliciously fabricated your role in discovering body parts. That alone made you a person of interest in the broadest sense of the term."

"All I did was report roadside littering. Now they've got a lady detective asking me questions and at least one undercover guy watching me at the diner."

"That's upsetting. But you've done nothing wrong. How often are undercover guys visiting the diner?"

"Once that I know of. Could be others, I guess."

"I don't blame you for being upset. And you absolutely could find a lawyer willing to sue. But you'd be paying the lawyer's fees and all expenses. No lawyer would go against a newspaper on a contingency basis."

"Contingency?"

"Plaintiff attorneys agree to bill some clients after winning. They get a significant percentage of the final award, a third or more."

"Couldn't I find a lawyer who'd bill me on a contingency?"

"No one who's reputable. Top lawyers do it for cases that look like winners. Yours doesn't. Newspapers have deep pockets *and* the First Amendment."

"I've got some money. How much would it cost?"

"More than you'll earn in your life. You run a diner. That paper is owned by National Media. They own more than fifty papers. They've got lawyers on the payroll who'd drag this thing out until you were broke. I don't think you should sue."

"But what about the principle? I've been wronged. Any jury would agree."

"Principle is a rich man's game, Mr. Norwood. This mess will blow over, and you'll still have a savings account, your home, and your wife."

I was plenty pissed off after leaving Fitzpatrick's office. But as the night wore on and Becky and I talked it over, I realized he probably was right. I couldn't remember anyone successfully suing a Wisconsin newspaper during my lifetime. What made me think my claim was special?

There was an unexpected, good result from the sudden publicity, I must admit. Eddie's was attracting new customers. The Friday-morning breakfast crowd stood in a sizable line outside the diner's front door. The quiet ones just wanted to have a look at the possible killer. The chatty ones asked me the same kinds of questions I'd heard from Ida.

"How didja know the exact locations and number of bags?" a delivery driver asked between heaping forkfuls of scrambled eggs and hash browns.

"I hate litterbugs. I saw thrown-away blue plastic bags on the way to work and reported the locations to the highway department. You'd have done the same thing. Anyone would."

"Maybe. Gimme another shot of coffee, wouldja?"

Friday was the best day I'd ever had at Eddie's. I almost expected to be kidded at our bank about the size of the day's cash receipts. If the diner had always done so well, I'd never have started taking sports bets.

My cell phone rang as I started to lock up for the night.

"That you?" a gravelly voice asked.

"Yeah, man."

"I been reading about ya in the papers. You're too hot for me. You're outta business, as of now. Ya got any money, ya better give it all back."

"But, but—"

"This ain't a discussion. You're done. End of story."

I fumbled for something to say as the call ended. It was Angelo Calacia, of course, and he was doing more than offering friendly advice. He pulled a lot of strings from his lakefront home in Kenosha. He'd eliminate me as a problem unless I did just what he said. I'd heard about dead guys being found in submerged cars off the Lake Michigan shoreline. I wasn't much of a swimmer to begin with, not that stroke mastery would do me any good inside a car's locked trunk.

I spent more time than I should have away from the diner on Saturday and Sunday, returning the money I'd taken for baseball bets on the Brewers, Cubs, and Sox. There were some hard feelings from guys who expected a payday on a good bet, but they calmed down when I explained the heat was on. Anybody being looked at in a murder better stay below the radar, I said. I didn't want a federal gambling rap, I said, and didn't want my friends snagged either.

So that was my weekend, aside from drinking too much beer and whiskey shots and lying about it to Becky. I'd quickly learned how to sneakily drink myself into a level of numbness that approached sleep. It left me foggy in the morning, but it made the hamster wheels stop spinning at night.

I'd never expected to talk with Martha Thomas again. But she called me at the diner Monday, right before I locked the front door at three in the afternoon.

"Mr. Norwood, how are you doing? This is Martha Thomas."

"I'm doing a little better than when I called you. The newspapers and TV people stopped calling me after I kept cursing them and hanging up."

She wanted to know whether I'd talked to a lawyer, so I gave her the short version of my meeting with Peter Fitzpatrick.

"That doesn't mean *you* wouldn't have a case, though," I said.

What she said next was a complete surprise. Turned out that a woman reporter from a big Chicago paper—some lady with a hyphenated last name—had come to her home the day after Krebs trashed us in his paper.

"We had coffee together, and I talked about my son. She stayed for three hours and looked through my photo albums with me. She seemed to understand I'm lonely without Arnie and John Michael."

"She was just looking for a story, Mrs. Thomas."

"That's probably true. But it was a beautiful story in the Sunday paper. Other papers printed it too. Detective Ida even said it might help the investigation. People try to help others who are suffering. Maybe one of them knows something or saw something."

"I hope you're right. Why did you call me?"

"I guess it seemed like a kindness. You're suffering too, aren't you?"

"You got that right. Thank you."

"We all hunger for the milk of human kindness. That's what my mother taught me when I was a little girl."

"Have you heard anything more about your son?"

"I should know *something* tomorrow or Wednesday. Ida was planning to get John Michael's dental records this morning. My dentist was on vacation last week in Alaska, but he was supposed to have the stuff ready for Ida before noon."

"I hope your boy walks in the door tonight or tomorrow."

"I do too. But something tells me that's not going to happen."

CHAPTER 10
ANOTHER SETBACK

Ida hated to admit it, but her investigation was stalled. She'd just learned that John Michael Thomas's dental records were lost when the family's dentist moved into a new office. Ida was no closer to identifying a murder victim than she'd been when the arms, legs, and torso were found in ditches along a road in Howard County.

Martha Thomas would have to deal with weeks, perhaps months, of uncertainty about her son's disappearance. Unless he returned home or telephoned, the results of DNA testing were needed. And there was no certainty those results would identify John Michael as the victim of a dismemberment killer. Or when the results would be known.

Ida kept the news from Martha until she visited her Milwaukee home with Stewart Rosen, an evidence technician with the state crime lab.

"I want to be alone with Martha when I break the news about the dental records," Ida told Stew as they got out of her sheriff's department squad car.

"Works for me," Stew said. "I'd just be in the way."

Martha opened the door before Ida had a chance to ring the bell. Looking anxious and pale, she sighed loudly as she fidgeted with a kerchief in her right hand.

"What did you find out?" she asked.

"We'll talk about the dental records while Stew collects DNA samples. It's standard procedure in homicides."

"How can I help?"

"Just lead us to John Michael's room," Ida said. "Stew will take it from there. Evidence collection is what he does. We also need your son's laptop and phone bills. Does John Michael have an address book or diary? Any mail that he kept?"

"It'll be returned, won't it? Why do you need it?"

"It's necessary, Martha. Maybe a friend of his knows something. His possessions will be returned, but it will take some time. I'm sorry."

"We don't have to watch the DNA search, do we?"

"It's probably best to leave Stew alone, actually."

Martha led Ida into the kitchen and dinette. She poured two coffees and sat down. Ida walked about, sipping java, then stopped at a stairway to the basement family room. Ida took a peek. Dark wood paneling covered the stairway walls, which served as a photo gallery of the Thomas family. There were color portraits of Martha, Arnie, and John Michael, with many more photos of John Michael's life from cradle to college. Ida felt a tiny pang in her heart as she looked at the pictures—a tinge of what she felt when visiting her family home. She felt great responsibility to treat Martha honestly and kindly.

"Did the dental records help?" Martha asked.

"The records were lost when your dentist moved."

Martha set her white porcelain cup on its matching saucer, dabbed her lips with a napkin, and looked out the bay window into a fenced backyard. Ida noticed the delicate blue flowers edging their cups and plates. She thought the set probably had been shared by Martha and Arnie at the very table where she sat.

Ida also noticed bluebirds and robins were using a stone bath at the edge of the garden. Finches and other small birds pecked at seeds in a feeder. It was a lovely green escape from the nearby city streets.

"I like watching birds," Martha finally said. "Life goes on for them. It does for us, too, somehow."

"People search for answers when a loved one disappears," Ida replied. "It's got to be agonizing, but at least there still is hope. Maybe you can take some small comfort in that."

"Thanks, Ida. Until we learn otherwise, John Michael is still alive."

To Martha's inner ear, the hopeful words she'd just uttered had a hollow timbre. It felt almost as if she'd whistled in a graveyard.

If Ida felt the same way, she didn't let on. But her silence said a great deal as she finished her coffee and rose to her feet.

"I'll see how Stew's doing. He might need to look around other rooms. You keep a mighty neat house, Martha."

"I haven't done a thing in John Michael's room. He always kept it clean. It's the same today as the last day I saw him, but dustier. I should have cleaned it up for you."

"It's a good thing you didn't. Stew's job would be harder if you had."

Ida and Stew left Martha's home in her squad car and drove straight to the state crime lab's Milwaukee office. Stew was confident about recovering solid DNA samples, mentioning a hairbrush that John Michael hadn't picked entirely clean.

"I hope the DNA shows the remains aren't John Michael's," Ida said. "I'd still be at square one, but that's not so important to anyone other than a cop."

"You've got a good heart, Ida. My job is science, but you work mostly with people."

"Sometimes it's troubling."

Ida spent her evening reviewing every report about the unsolved killing. Perhaps she'd missed something critical. Maybe the deputies who'd helped her canvass the homesteads near the crime scene noticed something she hadn't. Wanting to help, the people living along the rural road welcomed the deputies and Ida into their homes. But they hadn't seen or heard anything unusual other than the sudden heavy presence of law enforcement near their homes.

"George and I feel just terrible about this," Caroline Connelly had told one of the deputies. "Our dogs found that head in the field right next to our home."

Ida had talked with George for more than an hour about the grim discovery. He didn't know anything about the murder other than what his dogs uncovered and what he'd heard from his neighbors and the news. Caroline knew even less.

"I'm worried about a killer still being around," she'd told a deputy. "I'd feel a lot better if Maddy were here."

Ida gulped hard and dropped her plastic ballpoint pen onto the report she'd been reading. The pen then clattered off the desktop and onto the tile floor. It wasn't much, but Ida had found something new: Who was Maddy?

Ida telephoned Caroline Connelly early Thursday morning.

"Would it be OK if I stopped by your place today? It's nothing urgent. I'm just trying to tie up some loose ends."

"George will be home tomorrow night. Could you stop by tomorrow around seven?"

"I need to see you today. I'm trying to learn as much about your neighborhood as possible. I can talk to George later, if it's necessary. It's OK with me if you want to invite Becky Norwood."

They set the visit for two in the afternoon. Caroline then called Becky, who agreed to meet with Ida.

"She scares Eddie," Becky said, "but Ida seems OK to me."

"She's easy to talk to. Kind of cute, too, with that spiky blond hair and southern drawl. I don't want her spending time alone with my George."

"She's a cop! How can you say such a thing?"

"She was a woman before she was a cop. You can never be too careful."

Ida had worn her uniform to work, mostly to please her tradition-loving sheriff. She preferred the three-button polo shirt with the department's gold star on her left breast. Worn with police-duty khaki chinos and rugged trail shoes, the alternative uniform was more comfortable and better suited to fieldwork.

For the visit to the Connelly home, however, Ida decided it would be best to dress entirely in plainclothes. She went home for lunch and changed into a periwinkle blue blouse, tailored denim capri pants, and running shoes. It was a look she hoped would make Caroline and Becky feel at ease.

I look like Sally Suburban, Ida thought. *All I need now is a horse and a few kids.*

Ida drove onto the Connelly property at 1:50 p.m.

"You're early, aren't you, Detective?" Caroline asked.

"It's the way I was raised. Daddy said early was on time and on time was late."

"What if you're late?"

"You better be early the next time," Ida laughed.

Caroline led Ida to a sunporch at the rear of the home. It offered a view of a well-manicured lawn, a small vegetable garden, and a large red barn leading to farmland. Ida took a chair with a view of the yard as Becky Norwood opened the front door.

"Anyone home?" she said.

"Ain't nobody here but us chickens," Ida replied.

Caroline laughed, perhaps too loudly, and Becky giggled as she came into the sun-drenched room. The chuckling sounded a little forced to Ida.

"I don't know what made me say that," Ida said. "I was talking about Daddy a minute ago. Maybe he's channeling me?"

Caroline poured three glasses of iced tea and sat down on a chair closest to the kitchen. "I'll get us cookies when you girls are ready. Fresh-baked chocolate chip?"

"I'm ready, girl," Ida said. "Never met a cookie I didn't like."

"Caroline's the best," Becky said. "Even Ed says he likes her cookies better than mine."

"Is Ed OK? I think he got a little spooked when we talked. I was just being thorough."

"He'll be alright—I hope. The newspaper stories made him a nervous wreck, but he seems to get better each day."

After Caroline returned with the cookies, the talk gave way to snacking. Ida was very curious about Maddy but decided to move slowly. She ate a cookie and sipped tea. Ida wanted everyone at ease, as if the three women were neighbors and friends.

"Thanks for the hospitality," Ida finally said. "I agree with Becky about the cookies, but the tea is good too. Kinda like my mama's but not as sweet."

"I'm sorry, Detective, but I've just gotta know. Are you from the South originally?"

"Please, ladies—I'm Ida. And yes and no to your question, Caroline."

"How's that?" Becky asked.

"I'm from deep southern Illinois, about two hours south of Saint Louis.

We fought on the Union side in the Civil War, but I'm more of a magnolia blossom than a northern pine."

"Does it get hot down there? I was in Saint Louis one summer for a visit, and the bank thermometers read a hundred and one degrees at eleven a.m."

"We'd go to Saint Louis to cool off," Ida laughed. "The air around our little town gets so thick you can grab chunks of it and roll it into balls. You've got snowball fights here. We had humidity fights at home."

Becky and Caroline laughed again, this time more naturally.

Ida subtly shifted gears.

"This is quite a place you've got here," she said. "I didn't really notice how beautiful your barn is. My daddy would have loved a big barn like that. Ours was big enough for a peach grower, but he made room for a few dairy cows. We had a chicken coop and pig shed too."

"It's a nice day, Ida. Let's go outside. I'll show you the barn."

It took a bit of walking to reach the barn. Caroline slid the barn door open, and light flooded the spacious interior. A small tractor, ATV, and mowing equipment were stored neatly in one corner. A horse stall was in the nearest corner, next to an open window. A single chestnut-brown horse with a black mane nibbled at hay, swished flies with its black tail, and occasionally turned its head to look at the women.

"Fine-looking mare," Ida said.

"He's a gelding, I'm afraid," Caroline said.

"I knew he wasn't a stallion," Ida laughed. "You do a lot of riding?"

"I don't ride, but someone has to feed and water the poor thing. I let him out in the pasture later in the day, when it's cooler."

"So, George is the rider?"

"He doesn't ride either. The horse belongs to Madeline, our daughter. Everyone calls her Maddy."

"Poor thing is lonely, I bet. What's his name?"

"Maddy calls him Lucky, but I don't know why. He's anything but lucky—neutered, alone, and neglected, other than the little time I spend with him. But Maddy won't even think about finding him a better home."

"Doesn't she see much of him?"

"Maddy is a free spirit, you might say. She's a licensed cosmetologist and nail artist. She follows warm sunshine when it's cold and then moves to the mountains when it's too hot."

"That sounds expensive. Does she hire movers?"

"Nooo. Maddy travels light. She hauls everything she needs in an SUV. I don't know when I'll see her again," Caroline said with a laugh.

"How does she find a job?"

"Maddy always finds work. Hair and nail people change jobs a lot, I guess."

"You must miss her."

"She was here not long ago. Stuck around a few months, then headed west."

"She must be pretty rugged," Ida said. "Sounds like my kinda girl."

"She's a bodybuilder and runs marathons too. That's her bench and weights on the other side of Lucky's stall."

"I like that stuff too. Mind if I have a look?"

"Go right ahead. Becky and I are gonna grab those cookies and bring a pitcher of tea out here."

Ida saw what she expected with the exercise gear—free weights and a multistation bench that offered a full-body workout. She also noticed an assortment of heavy Velcro straps in varying lengths hanging from hooks on the wall, as well as a wheeled metal cart that held wrist, ankle, and hand weights. There also was an open-topped wooden box on the cart that contained white plastic zip ties in a variety of widths and lengths.

Ida then noticed a large drain in the center of the barn's concrete floor. She walked to the drain and knelt for a closer look. It probably was used for draining wash water from Lucky's stall. Ida had expected it to be bone dry in the hot summer, especially since the horse's quarters obviously needed a good cleaning, but the drain was a little damp. It gave her a funny feeling.

Ida quickly looked through the barn door. There were no signs of Caroline or Becky. She grabbed a multiuse knife from her shoulder bag, then used the screwdriver blade to pry the drain cover off the pipe. She scraped the underside of the cover and the rim of the pipe with the sharp blade. She then wiped the blade inside a clean sandwich bag she'd carried in her shoulder bag—which also held her badge, police radio, service pistol, and other police gear. There still was no sign of Caroline or Becky.

Ida made a deeper knife swab inside the pipe, then wiped the residue into another resealable bag.

Ida replaced the drain cover and walked to the barn door. She tucked the knife into her bag after seeing Becky and Caroline stepping through the home's back door. Ida wouldn't be alone for more than another minute or two.

She knew what she'd scraped up would have no value as evidence, should it test suspicious– positive for traces of human tissue, blood or bodily fluids. The Connellys weren't suspected of any criminal activity. And Ida didn't have a search warrant or permission to remove anything from the property.

It wasn't a textbook police tactic. Such actions were officially discouraged. But her ex, the loathsome Bill Rollins, had plenty of street smarts that he'd shared before their breakup. Some of it was useful.

"My uncle Phil was a Chicago cop," Bill had said. "He always carried a strong lock-blade knife and a throw-down gun. I do too, and so should you."

"What for?" Ida had asked.

"You can use the knife to scrape up stuff near a crime scene or crash site. If you kill someone, ya can plant a knife on 'em or fix 'em up with the throw-down gun. You shot in self-defense. Case closed."

Ida refused to carry a throw-down gun. Her conscience ached at the thought. But a good knife made sense as a tool, if not as a ruse reason for a fatal shooting.

She'd instinctively reached for the knife while kneeling at the drain. Ida trusted her heart as much as her head.

Ida took a step toward Lucky's stall, and the big horse approached the gate. Ida stroked his muzzle and broad neck as she heard a screen door slam from the house. Soon she heard the voices of Caroline and Becky.

Caroline was carrying a pitcher of tea and glasses. Becky carried the plate of cookies.

"Stay away from those cookies, Lucky!" Ida said as she grabbed one for herself.

Becky gave Lucky half a cookie as Caroline poured tea for Ida.

"I'd love to have a place like this someday," Ida said. "I don't have enough time for all the work, but I love horses."

"Lucky's a good boy," Caroline said. "But he needs more attention than I can give him."

"Does this area of the barn get much use?" Ida asked.

"This used to be a working farm. George stores his tools here, sometimes a load of lumber. It's way more room than we need."

"Do you use the loft?" Ida asked as she nodded toward a heavy wooden staircase.

"Maddy lives up there when she's home."

"In the loft? That must be awful hot in the summer, freezing in the winter."

"Not our loft. We've got a fully furnished apartment up there. It has a full kitchen and bathroom. There's a high-efficiency furnace and central air too."

"Sounds like a lot of expense for not much company," Ida said.

Ida's cell phone rang as they wandered about the barn.

"It's the sheriff," she said. "I've gotta go."

"I'll walk you to your car," Becky said. "I need to get home and think about fixing something for dinner."

"Do you need anything more from me, Ida?" Caroline asked.

"Nope. I don't think so. Thanks for the cookies and tea."

Ida shook Caroline's hand and walked off with Becky.

"I feel sorry for Caroline," Becky said as they neared the squad car.

"Why? This looks like a good life."

"That Maddy has been in a lot of trouble. She was expelled from high school. She ran away from home several times. Then she tried to kill herself when she was pregnant."

"Oh my God. What happened then?"

"Caroline gave her the money for an abortion. Even George doesn't know that. They give her money every time she comes home. She always has a stack of unpaid bills, bounced checks, and big plans—if only she could have five thousand dollars."

"Caroline's lucky to have your friendship, Becky. You seem like a good soul."

"I wish I could get Caroline to see what Maddy's doing to them. She's a grown woman, nearly thirty. But she expects Mom and Dad to fix all her problems."

"She'll bankrupt the family eventually," Ida said. "It happened to my uncle Bob and aunt Gladys. Their youngest son, Caleb, cleaned out their bank account and took off. He was twenty-seven and knew he was doing wrong. Bob and Gladys had to sell the farm and auction all their possessions."

"I'm sorry, Ida. I never thought of police officers having troubled families."

"My daddy told his brother that Caleb was a bad seed. They ended up in a fistfight and broke some furniture."

"Think I could do anything that would help Caroline and George?" Becky asked.

"I doubt it. Maddy probably needed a damn good spanking when she was little. My mama wouldn't have put up with tantrums and threats to run away or kill herself."

"Mine wouldn't either."

"My daddy loved me. But when I was naughty, he'd slap my butt with his big leather belt. And then my mama would tell me how much I'd disappointed and hurt her. She'd make me look her in the eye. She talked real slow and gentle."

"It worked with you, right?"

"I guess so. But my mama's tears hurt me a lot worse than my daddy's belt ever did."

CHAPTER 11
VIEW FROM THE TOP

Peter Clark had been slow to accept the digital age as a reality, but to subordinates, the sheriff of Howard County eventually established himself as an emailing demon.

It was a rare day when Ida didn't waste her time with at least a half dozen of her boss's emails, all marked urgent and requiring a speedy reply.

The one she read while eating lunch was typical.

"See me soonest," Clark wrote. "Have some ideas."

It would have been easier for the sheriff to chat with Ida by walking twenty steps from his office to the detective bureau. But it would have denied the portly lawman the joy of issuing an order.

"You need me, Sheriff?" Ida asked.

"Shut the door, Ida. We need a heart-to-heart."

"Am I in trouble, sir?"

Clark didn't answer her question. Instead, he asked one of his own.

"How long are you waiting on that DNA testing?"

"Almost two weeks, sir. I called the crime lab yesterday. Stew said they're really backed up. He said work's getting tackled in the order it was received."

"Does that mean if there's another Jeffrey Dahmer, the Milwaukee PD will have to wait their turn?"

"I doubt it, sir. Milwaukee has more clout than Howard County."

"That's a problem. It's especially a problem for you. Where are you at in finding our slasher?"

"Almost nowhere, but you know that. It's tough to find suspects when you don't know who was killed."

"I'm listenin'."

"When someone's murdered, we look close at their lives, relationships, and relatives. You know all that. So maybe John Michael Thomas is our victim, but I can't prove it. Not yet."

"So it's a hunch, huh? Is that feminine intuition or something?" Clark said and smirked.

Ida felt like pushing everything on top of the sheriff's desk into his beefy lap, except for his tankard of hot coffee. She'd pour that on his balding head. But she kept her cool.

"John Michael Thomas went missing during the same time frame as the killing. He had collar-length brown hair; so did the head recovered in the field. John Michael was the same height and build as the reassembled body parts. But his mother couldn't be certain because of the mangled face. She said the hair didn't look quite right either."

"I've heard this before, Ida. What I'm concerned about is the trail growing cold as you wait for DNA results."

"I've checked John Michael's Facebook page and emails. There wasn't anything that stood out. He was an Eagle Scout and on the dean's list every semester at UW–Milwaukee. His mother said he wanted to run for office someday."

"Big deal. Look what it got me."

"It goes to his character, sir. When John Michael got his first computer, he had to make a promise to his mom and dad. He promised he'd never write anything he wouldn't want to see in the newspaper. His social media tracks are clean."

"What about his phone?"

"He's got an iPhone, which is password protected. But the cell disappeared with John Michael and hasn't been used since, according to the phone company. His past calls were to home, school, work, or to friends known by his mother."

"What about his laptop?" the sheriff asked.

"Stew says it was used almost exclusively for schoolwork, other than Facebook and emails."

"Does he have more than one laptop? Other identities?"

"I don't know. I'll check. What more would you do, sir?"

"I'd bring that guy from the diner, Ed Northgate, in for more questioning."

"Do you mean Ed Norwood, sir?"

"Whatever. Get him relaxed and talk about his business and family. Then ask softball questions about the body parts. Look at your reports as he answers, like you're seeing if he's telling the same story."

"Maybe you're right, sir," Ida said, hoping to end the useless and insulting conversation. She wasn't a rookie. She knew how to run a homicide interview.

"That's it, girl. Watch his reactions. Then, at some point, ask if he killed and cut up a young man. See if he's willing to take a lie detector test."

"You can't be serious, sir. Ed and his wife have tried to help us."

"I'm not only serious—it's an order."

"Yes, sir," Ida said as she stood up and walked to the sheriff's office door.

"Hey, one other thing," Clark said. "Wasn't Northwood—er, Norwood—being watched after work?"

"That's correct. He spent his time after closing the diner going to a number of locations around Milwaukee."

"He's having an affair, maybe?"

"It didn't look that way. He stopped often in barbershops but never got a shave or haircut. He also stopped in a plumbing supply business, hardware stores, pool halls, bowling alleys, and a pawnshop. The stops took no more than ten minutes."

"Drugs? Is he a drunk?"

"Usually all he did was shake hands with another guy, sometimes hand him some money. He doesn't look or act like a druggie to me. The eyeball we put on Norwood says he couldn't find any drug connections to the places he visited either. And he wasn't drinking. He was seen talking and shaking hands with other guys, sometimes handing over cash."

"Who was the eyeball?"

"Your nephew, Deputy Todd Schultz."

"My sister's kid? That doofus wouldn't know his ass from a hole in the ground."

"His undercover look was good. Maybe a little heavy with hats and sunglasses, but not bad. He drove beaters from the impound lot. Changed vehicles daily, his clothes too."

"We're still tailing Northgate, aren't we?"

"Yes, we're still looking at *Norwood*, sir, but I think it's time to pull the plug."

"Why is that?"

"He stopped running around a week or so after we started tailing him. Musta got spooked. Now he goes straight home after leaving the diner."

"He must have realized he was being followed."

"Maybe. I'll have him tailed a couple days a week, different days each week. If he starts making pit stops again, I'll find out."

Clark leaned back in his wooden desk chair and squinted at Ida.

"My nephew did good work on this?"

"Looks that way, sir. He says he wants to be a detective."

"What about the money he was handing out? Did Todd have ideas about that?

"Todd says Norwood's either a loan shark or gambler."

"Let me see his reports. Some of the locations might ring a bell."

"Right away, sir. Are we through?"

"For now, Ida."

In the morning, Ida found Sheriff Clark sitting in her office, looking through the day's headlines on his smartphone. The file containing Deputy Todd Schultz's report rested on his right leg, which he'd crossed over his left knee. The file looked as if it had been thrown down a flight of dusty stairs and then quickly patched together higgledy-piggledy.

"Had yourself a good look, didn't you, sir?"

"I dropped it on my garage floor this morning. You're gonna have to get it back in the right order, I'm afraid."

"No problem, Sheriff. The pages are numbered and dated."

"I recognized a couple addresses. Your guy's a gambler or hangs out with gamblers. When I was a detective for the Milwaukee PD, I used one of the barbers he visited and a plumbing supply guy as snitches."

"They'd tell you stuff?"

"*Some* bad guys can't keep their mouths shut. When my guys heard about a big score, maybe a burglar trying to fence stolen TVs or jewelry, they'd tell me about it. It kept me off *their* backs is what they figured."

"So what kind of gambling did you ignore?"

"Sports betting. It's bigger than you think, and it never ends."

"What do I do next?"

"Have a conversation with the feds. If they start asking Norwood about gambling, other stuff might spill out."

"Or he'll lawyer up and never say another word to us."

"That's pretty much where we're at now, ain't it, Ida?"

CHAPTER 12
END OF SUMMER

I looked up from the computer in Becky's upstairs office as the morning sun slanted through maple leaves shading our roof. The angle of the light somehow reminded me of the gruesome discovery a few months ago. The light was a golden spray of sunshine, but today it also hinted at cooler days ahead and the maple's approaching autumn cloak of salmon, gold, and red.

I realized my life was more under control as autumn was approaching. I'd at last gotten over deepening paranoia about my chances of getting arrested for gambling and then somehow being squeezed for incriminating information on the nearby evidence of a murder. It didn't seem to matter that I had no information, incriminating or otherwise. My fearful thoughts had pinwheeled endlessly. Terror robbed me of sleep, pushed me toward alcoholism, and finally convinced me to find a Sunday manager for the diner. Or maybe I should say Becky convinced me.

"I'm worried about you, Ed," she'd said. "All you do is work, come home, and sneak belts of whiskey to pass out. You never relax. That's no way to live. It's a way to die, though. You're committing slow suicide."

"You've never seen me drinking anything other than beer."

"You smell like a distillery even before your nightly six-pack. My dad was a whiskey drunk. You remember that. You smell just like he did. The few things you say don't make much sense."

"I'll cut back. Give me a few days to taper off."

"You're going to do more than cut back, mister. The first thing is to stop working seven days a week. And if you can't stop drinking after two beers, you better go to an Alcoholics Anonymous meeting. My dad would sponsor you. AA saved his life."

"You're making too big a deal out of this, Beck."

"I am not! I may as well get divorced if you're going to be a distant, drunken workaholic."

Becky had never mentioned divorce before. It jolted me into a cold sweat. But it also helped me see things from her point of view.

I decided to find a manager for Sundays. Maybe the job would become weekend manager if I found the right person. It turned out the ideal candidate was right under my nose. I offered the job to Anita Kirkwood, my most reliable employee. She agreed to start her Sunday duties immediately. Becky and I saw a play in downtown Chicago that first Sunday afternoon. We had dinner on the drive home at a great Italian restaurant in Kenosha. We split a bottle of wine during the meal, and I didn't have a nightcap at home. I slept pretty well too.

Over time, I learned my longtime worries about being swindled from within at the diner were exaggerated. My employees were honest, and Anita was great. The receipts from Anita's first Sunday matched mine and then, to my astonishment, began trending to new heights. The best surprise came when I checked the receipts from her first six weeks against my own averages. Anita grossed more money on Sundays than I ever had!

"How did this happen?" I asked her.

"I'm probably nicer to customers, especially since that murder. You've been kinda crabby, Ed."

"You sound like my wife. She says I've been awful."

"That's harsh. But crabby, yeah, you sure were. Did you notice the fresh-cut flowers I've been bringing in? And the Sunday papers from Milwaukee and Chicago? I think it makes Eddie's more like home. My customers want to stick around."

"*Your* customers! I hope they remember I *own* the place. But maybe you've got the right attitude. Want to try managing the joint both Saturday and Sunday? I'll schedule you from Wednesday through Sunday."

"That means I'd have two days off every week, Monday and Tuesday."

"You'll be the assistant manager when I'm here too."

"You haven't said anything about a raise."

"How about a twenty-five percent raise in your base pay and ten percent of the weekend net?"

"Done!"

It was a great raise for Anita, but it still helped me. Once I started enjoying my free time, and had more of it, my drinking became less of a problem—then not a problem at all. It wouldn't work for everyone who was drinking too much, but it helped me.

I even tried to joke about it. But Becky wasn't a good audience.

"It's not like I was an alcoholic," I said once. "Alcoholics go to meetings. I was a drunk."

"Real funny. Keep joking, and you'll be laughing alone."

Fear of coming home to an empty house kept me focused. It wasn't hard to do.

As the owner of Eddie's, I benefited most from having a weekend manager. My diner income was better than it had ever been! I made almost as much money as I had running the diner and taking bets. I spent less money too. And it was all legal.

I had also started keeping the books on a computer program and found it easier to track supplies and order only what would sell in any given week. It helped me identify waste and freed up more money for me. And Becky too.

I soon replaced her low-rent laptop with a top-of-the-line model. Becky was pleased, of course, but also a savvy wife.

"I love my new computer!" she said. "It's funny how quick you bought it after you began using my old laptop to keep the books. You finally realized I wasn't bitching over nothing."

"Simply a coincidence, my dear. The new model was on sale, if you'll recall."

"Yeah? That same sale is run every few months. I read the newspaper ads more than you."

She had me dead to rights, of course. It still made me smile when my thoughts wandered—a frequent occurrence whenever Muffin sought the sunshine on my lap and sacked out. It kept me at the desk chair longer than necessary, but it's hard to displace a purring feline.

·∵·

For many weeks, it was impossible for me to relax. Detective Ida apparently still thought I might have killed the young man whose remains were strewn along our rural road. Maybe she was getting pushed by her boss. I don't know. But it sure was damned uncomfortable, especially because of my gambling activities. I'd been watched at the diner by at least one undercover cop and probably tailed by others as I made bookmaking treks after work. I figured they were still watching me.

A lot of time had passed without me being arrested or charged with anything. I'd needed a lawyer again, which wasn't cheap, but Milwaukee attorney Peter Fitzpatrick scuttled efforts by Ida and the sheriff to give me a lie detector test about the dismembered body or grill me about sports wagering.

I learned that even though Fitzpatrick wouldn't sue a newspaper, he loved battling local cops and federal agents. There would be no lie detector test, he said, nor would there be any gambling talks with the feds.

"You don't have to tell them a thing," Fitzpatrick told me. "Make 'em arrest you. Even if you get arrested, don't say anything unless I'm in the room with you."

"Are you nuts? I can't go to jail!"

"They're blowing smoke. They won't do anything to you. We'll sue Howard County for false arrest and imprisonment. I nailed 'em for the same crap two years ago. They popped a schoolteacher for sexually assaulting a student. He was innocent. By the time it was over, he was rich too."

"Maybe you're right."

"Keep your trap shut. If you don't talk, they've got nothing."

It was good advice. I'd have been given the same by Angelo Calacia, if I'd been goofy enough to call the gambling boss in Kenosha, who hated phone calls. He'd already ordered me to stop taking bets. And it was pretty obvious that he never wanted to hear from me again. Still, it helped to remember what Angelo had said when I started working as one of his bookies.

"Sooner or later, a cop will get curious about ya. A customer rats you out, maybe cuz he goes broke, gets hauled into divorce court or jailed on somethin' serious. He'll make a deal for himself by giving you up."

"What do I do?"

"Coupla things. Don't mention my name. Ever. Don't answer questions. Tell the cops you want a lawyer. Then dummy up."

"Can I give my name?"

"That's about all ya should say. Some guys try to talk their way out of trouble. Cops live for that. All they have is what some rat says. Talkers give 'em evidence."

∴

I once felt like a good citizen for reporting roadside litter to the highway department. But it would have been better if I'd kept quiet—better still if I'd never spotted plastic trash bags among the weedy drainage ditches.

It didn't seem to matter that I hadn't killed anyone or cut a dead body into pieces. Also ignored were the odds against a murderer reporting his crime. I was officially a person of interest because I lived in the area and operated a diner that featured fresh-cut meat.

News reports about innocent people serving long prison terms had scared me silly. I learned that dirty cops in Chicago sometimes beat confessions out of suspects, especially if they were poor, Black, and had a rap sheet. Some cops flat out lied about what they'd seen, or planted evidence on Black men. Although I was a white business owner with nothing more than traffic convictions, I still had been worried.

Why? I couldn't account for all the hours between the diner's closing and my returning home for the night. It was time I'd spent as a sports bookie, a federal crime.

I was certain Ida knew plenty about the gambling. I could even imagine hearing her drawl about my predicament: "Y'all could find yourself in US court for gambling and racketeering. It'll lighten your load if you help me out on the homicide."

I'd already told her everything I knew about the bloody remains. And I was innocent. Still, time had passed slowly. It was nerve-racking waiting for the legal hammer to fall. But it didn't.

∴

It had been weeks since I'd spoken to Ida. My arrest now seemed less likely.

I spent some of my free time reading news online. I searched for reports of dismemberment killings and wondered whether Ida was looking too. I especially wanted to know whether she was aware of a murder being investigated in Iowa. It was far north in the Hawkeye State, less than fifty miles from the Minnesota border. Bagged body parts had been found along rural roads near Mason City.

I wanted to know whether there was a connection to the killing near my home. A nearby homicide occupies your mind. Especially if you're a "person of interest."

I wanted to call Ida. But was that wise? I had to talk to somebody about it.

Angelo would have asked me if I was nuts. Then he'd have told me to let the cops do their own work. I didn't even want to ask my lawyer. I'd learned his meter was running even during a ten-minute phone call. It felt like I was on his go-broke plan.

I finally asked Becky about calling Ida. At first she looked at me as if I'd lost my mind. But she didn't speak until she'd given the idea some thought.

"She's a country girl," Becky said. "I think she's a decent person. All she wants to do is catch a killer. She's not after you. You didn't kill anybody. Ida needs you as a witness, doesn't she?"

"Yeah. Maybe you're right."

"Just don't get carried away, Ed. Don't get too friendly. And for God's sake, don't say anything about gambling."

"Jeez, Beck, I thought you forgave me."

"I do forgive you. But Ida's a cop. Don't ever forget that. When she sounds warm and friendly, be wary."

"What do you mean?

"If you're relaxed, you might slip and say something that helps her investigation. Or starts another. I'm sure that's her plan."

I said nothing more. The look on Becky's face was deadly serious. It made me nervous. The last thing I wanted was to talk with Ida while Becky watched and listened. I'd be edgy enough without her fretful gaze, head shakes, rolling eyes, and hand gestures. I'm a man, not a marionette or a ventriloquist's dummy.

I called Ida a few days later. It was a Wednesday, I guess, and I made the call from the diner's basement during the midmorning lull. I used my cell phone and kept my voice down. She answered her office phone on the first ring.

"This is Ida Mae Rollins."

"Hello, Detective. This is Ed Norwood. How are you doing?"

"Well, Mr. Norwood, it's nice to hear your voice. I was just fixing to call you."

My heart sank. I sat hurriedly in the chair at my desk.

"What is it now? Have more questions? Still trying to jam me up with a lie detector test?" I spoke quickly and a little angrily. My voice might have been heard upstairs.

"Take it easy, Ed. You don't have to shout. I just wanted you to know the cops in Iowa are looking at a similar dismemberment murder."

"That's why I called. I read about it online. Is there a serial killer?"

"Why do you think that? You've killed others?"

I nearly hung up the phone in panic but somehow sensed Ida might be kidding me. I decided to tease her too.

"You better check my travel records before arresting me. I've never been anywhere near Mason City, Iowa. My parents took me to the Iowa State Fair when I was a boy, but that's in Des Moines."

"Why did you mention Mason City?"

"You know why. That's where cops are looking at the dismemberment killing. They found some remains of a man. I read about it on some newspaper's website."

"Why do you read that kind of stuff? I've got to do it as part of my job. What's your excuse?"

"I was hoping to further prove I didn't kill the guy who lost his head in George's field."

"Lost his head? You've got a sick sense of humor, Mr. Norwood. Only a cop or a thrill killer would say a decapitated murder victim 'lost his head.'"

"I'd make a lousy cop. If I was a thrill killer, you'd already have me locked up."

Ida chuckled, but so briefly it sounded like a cross between a cough and a sneeze.

"So you know about the death in Iowa?" I asked.

"More than what was reported in the press. There's some details that won't be shared with anyone outside law enforcement. I guess the county sheriff in Iowa isn't a blabbermouth like mine."

"Why do the details matter so much?"

"If someone we're looking at says something known only by the killer and cops, we're going to make a quick arrest."

Since we were talking so amicably, I asked Ida whether she'd heard anything from Martha Thomas.

"Mrs. Thomas was really worried about her son," I said. "But she was kind to me."

"Mrs. Thomas is like my mama, churchgoing and forgiving. She's a good-hearted woman. Wish I could help her."

"How's she doing?"

"She seems like a survivor. This can't be easy for a mother."

"Can't you find her son?"

"Well, as you know, the remains are still unidentified. I talked with Mrs. Thomas after we got the DNA test results. She doesn't know where her son is, and neither do I. DNA testing proved the remains are not those of John Michael Thomas."

"You've got a tough job, Detective."

"It's worse when you tell someone the remains were positively identified as a loved one. I'm sure Mrs. Thomas wants closure. All crime victims *say* they do—not that it ever happens or does any good."

"Why do you say that?"

"Closure usually means a murder was solved and the killer was convicted. There's no such thing as closure for a survivor's tormenting thoughts."

"Still, it must be awful living with the unknown, always fearful of phone calls and police visits."

"It's a terrible burden," Ida said. "But at least Mrs. Thomas still has hope."

CHAPTER 13
CHANGING SCENERY

Some of Martha Thomas's longtime neighbors were uncomfortable with the young and growing families who'd settled into the working-class bungalows of Milwaukee's south side. They rented flats on National Avenue or bought low-priced homes along the thoroughfare and its intersecting streets. Some of the newcomers bought dwellings that had been foreclosed. Others took advantage of estate sales.

The newcomers to Martha's neighborhood were darker skinned than the area's traditional residents, first-generation Germans, Irish, and Polish. Many didn't speak English. And the nearby markets didn't initially have the groceries they wanted—sometimes exotic but uniformly spicy foodstuffs that wafted new aromas into the old neighborhood.

Martha's missing son, John Michael, had been friendly with their new neighbors. He defended them whenever he heard a racist crack. It was his nature to stick up for underdogs.

Martha once had to intercede in a heated argument between her son and a slightly older man with a shaved head. It happened on the sidewalk in front of her home. She'd once heard John Michael describe the other man as "a skinhead white-power freak."

"Yer a traitor to your own kind, man!" the skinhead snarled. "Them mud people are chasing our white brothers and sisters outta their homes."

"Is this about skin color? That's ignorant. They're immigrants like you and me. We're all immigrants in the US, except the Native Americans. We took away *their* land and lives."

"Yer just a bleeding-heart liberal, ya pinko fag. Like the other college pansies."

Both young men balled their fingers into fists as Martha came out her front door. She wasn't worried about John Michael getting hurt. He'd been a Golden Gloves boxer. He might seriously injure anyone he fought.

"Excuse me, boys," Martha said sweetly. "John Michael, I need your help inside. You and your friend can talk later."

"He ain't a friend, Ma. And he started it."

"I'll see ya 'round, man. This ain't over," the skinhead said as he walked away slowly.

Martha noticed that the white thug's blue jeans rode low on his hips. To her, it was like the street style favored by the black- and brown-skinned newcomers. She wondered what other traits they shared, and whether they ever noticed. Then she turned her attention to John Michael.

"You both were shouting like hooligans," Martha said after she and her son were indoors. "The police would arrest both of you for disturbing the peace. Two wrongs never make a right."

• ⁖ •

Martha remembered that day as one of the neighborhood's longtime residents shuffled by on the sidewalk. And despite what she'd said to John Michael, she would have loved to hear him stick up this day for the new neighbors.

Her conversation with Al Wotowicz began when he asked a question. It appeared he was heading home from a nearby supersize tavern that cashed payroll checks for a shot-and-beer clientele.

"Whadda ya think about them five kids and their loud music two doors away from ya?" Wotowicz said gruffly. "The cops oughta bust 'em. They gotta be sellin' dope."

Martha looked up from the roses she was deadheading, checked the condition of Al's bloodshot eyes, and hazarded a reply.

"They seem like nice kids, Al. The older boys carry their mom's groceries into the house. One of them offered to help me with some packages."

"So what? He was connin' ya. Never did a decent thing in his life, I bet."

"He's also helped weed my garden and trimmed the bushes. And he wouldn't take the ten bucks I tried to give him."

"I know why he wanted to carry packages from your car. Prob'ly he wanted to see what ya got worth stealin'. Don't let them beaners get inside, Martha."

"Nice talking to you, Al. I hear my phone ringing inside."

"I don't hear nuttin," Al said, resuming his walk toward the three glass-and-metal domes of the Mitchell Park Horticultural Conservatory. Martha knew he lived on the east side of the Mitchell Park attraction, which most people simply called "the Domes." She was glad Al's home wasn't closer.

Martha grabbed the day's mail from the weathered brass box fastened to the wood siding. Arnie had hung the mailbox after he and Martha bought the only home they ever owned—or, as Arnie had joked, "rented from the bank." His parents didn't trust banks or mortgages, and neither had he. Not entirely.

Martha carried the mail to her kitchen table, which had bright lighting from a faux chandelier Arnie had bought from a building supply house. He'd hung it securely from a ceiling beam and done the wiring too. Martha remembered his handyman efforts whenever she flicked the light switch.

"We won't blow a fuse with this light, sweetie," he'd said so often it grew tiresome.

Martha now often wished she could hear Arnie bragging about the light, even just once. She imagined him smiling as she admitted never having to replace the kitchen circuit's fuse.

Most of the mail was junk, even the important-looking envelopes marked "open immediately" and "urgent." It still bothered her that the mail was delivered in the afternoon instead of the early morning, as it had been for years. Delivery time changed with the neighborhood, it seemed. Martha sometimes wondered whether the postal service downgraded her route because of the neighborhood's changing demographics. She once discussed it with Helen Vorhees.

"Maybe it's not as racist as it looks, Martha."

"There can't be any other reason. Haven't you ever noticed all our mail carriers are white?"

"I've seen a Black mail carrier before. Maybe our route is desirable. The post office is a union shop. Carriers with seniority get the routes they want."

"That might explain the white carriers, but not the late deliveries."

"Maybe African Americans and Latinos want their mail later in the day. They usually get night-shift jobs. Maybe they deal with bills in the afternoon, before work."

Martha took a closer look at her mail after she'd changed out of her garden clothes, washed her face, and freshened the little makeup she wore.

Most of the mail went straight into the trash. But there also was a plain white envelope she hadn't immediately noticed. Her name and address were neatly typed on the business-sized envelope, and a USPS Forever stamp was in the top right corner. There was no return address, nor did the postmark disclose where the mail had been processed.

Despite the impersonal typing and missing return address, it still looked like a personal letter. No business would use a single Forever stamp. Martha couldn't remember the last letter she'd received, other than the impersonal family news messages among the ever-dwindling number of Christmas cards.

Martha grabbed her reading glasses from the nearby counter. Then she carefully sliced the envelope with an opener, which was kept among the bills in a handmade tabletop mail caddy—one of Arnie's woodworking projects.

Inside the envelope was a carefully folded piece of white business stationery. It was undated, typed, and single-spaced. It looked as if it had been written on a computer in a small and common typeface and then printed out.

"Dear Mom," the letter began.

Martha gasped, then looked at the bottom of the page. In the neat handwriting she recalled from his homework, her boy had ended the letter by signing with a pen, "I miss you. Your loving son, John Michael."

It took a few minutes for her heart to settle. A cup of coffee from the warming carafe helped. She slowly read the full letter.

"I am sorry I haven't written earlier. There are many things I cannot tell you, but I want you to know I am alive and well.

"It is important that you keep the contents of this letter entirely to yourself—if you want me to stay in touch and find my way home. I am especially sorry you thought I might have been murdered! I read about that killing online. I know the Howard County Sheriff's Department still hasn't identified the victim.

"DO NOT tell the cops you heard from me, especially not that lady detective. Your sheriff couldn't find his way out of an unlocked closet, but Ida Mae Rollins might. I've heard about her through friends. They say she's smart and tough. I will write again, unless it's reported in the news that I'm alive.

"You MUST keep this our little secret. I've gotta go for now."

In the hours since Martha read the letter, she tried to take a nap, prayed for guidance, and thanked God her son was alive. At least he appeared to be alive. Martha couldn't help fearing he had been forced to write the letter—or had signed a blank piece of stationery that someone else later typed on.

Martha watched the evening news and then made a simple supper. Tomato soup and a grilled-cheese sandwich calmed her stomach. She'd also made up her mind about the letter. She knew what she'd do with it.

Martha wanted Ida to know John Michael was alive. The detective had been kind to her. But it would be a mistake confiding in Ida, who couldn't be expected to keep a secret. The information would be included in a written report. Others would see it, beginning with the sheriff. Then it would be printed by the obnoxious Calvin Krebs in the *Howard Register-Press*. Then a wire service and various websites would spread the news from Texas to Timbuktu. Martha had to keep the letter secret, in a safe spot.

Martha put the letter in a locked strongbox kept beneath the floor of a hall closet. A section of the closet floor could easily be removed, though it wasn't noticeable. Arnie had built the secret spot.

"It's our hidey-hole," he'd explained to Martha. "We can put jewelry, important documents, and maybe some cash in it."

The hidey-hole descended a foot from the closet floor to the lath work of a plastered ceiling above a stairway to the basement. The strongbox perfectly filled the space. Martha kept her vacuum cleaner on the closet floor to complete the hidey-hole camouflage.

Martha admired Arnie's ability to take what was readily available, though not immediately apparent, and tweak it into something useful. He'd discovered the dead space below the closet floor by accidentally losing his grip on Martha's vacuum, which clunked as it hit the floor. He then removed the vacuum and rapped on the floor with his knuckles. It sounded hollow.

Arnie used a pry bar to lift a section of the floor. It had been nestled in place. It looked as if it had been created intentionally by the builder, or perhaps a previous owner had been a carpenter.

"I've gotta admit it, honey," Martha said when Arnie unveiled his creation. "This is really clever."

"It's just a hidey-hole. Any guy would think of it if he'd heard the hollow sound I heard."

It turned out Arnie was too modest.

Burglars hit their home during Arnie's life, but they never found the hidey-hole. They'd stolen a TV, some spare change kept in a desk drawer, and cheap jewelry from a dresser, but little else. They even passed up the expensive bicycle Arnie kept in the back hallway.

"They must've been in a hurry," Arnie had said. "I'm lucky they left my bike."

Martha came to regret that bit of good fortune. Within the month, Arnie was killed while riding his bike to work.

CHAPTER 14
STILL WORKING

Ida brought her work home. Solitude and silence encouraged contemplation not easily achieved at the sheriff's department, a place of jangling telephones, ceaseless emails, law enforcement fax documents, and booming voices.

TV at home provided a kind of companionship, even with low volume. It was an escape from the frustration of the dismemberment killing, now considered a cold case. The only time it made news was when the *Howard Register-Press* reported that the investigation was stalled or printed editorials criticizing Sheriff Clark.

The sheriff was especially annoyed by the most recent editorial. It was printed in the Sunday paper, the week's biggest seller. "Clueless Sheriff Fumbles Murder Probe" was the headline on the paper a red-faced and fuming Sheriff Clark plopped on Ida's desk.

"Have you read this?" he asked. "Can't you make any progress? Do you think we need to ask for help from state police or the Milwaukee PD's homicide dicks?"

"I don't think that's necessary, sir. The cops in Racine, Kenosha, and Milwaukee counties are aware of the killing. I talk with their lead investigators often. But it's hard to make progress without the identity of the victim."

"Goddamn it! Can't you squeeze that gambler? I'll bet he knows about a regular player who couldn't pay up. Sometimes those deadbeats go missing."

"That's a good idea, sir," Ida said. "I'll get on it."

"I'm up for election in a few months, girl. The paper says I'm clueless and a do-nothing sheriff. I don't want them telling voters those lies. It'll never end."

"I understand, sir," Ida said, controlling an urge to sigh and roll her eyes.

But later in the day, while at home and ironing her uniform, Ida thought again about the sheriff's suggestion. Perhaps he had a good idea. It sometimes happened, though not with great frequency.

Ida spent a full day thinking about the sheriff's suggestion, and then she made a decision. She first considered surprising Ed Norwood at the diner as he locked up for the night. He'd be alone and off guard. If she acted as though he was on the verge of facing gambling charges, he might remember whether a gambler had suddenly stopped betting. If he named a missing person, their dental records and DNA might be useful.

"Still think Norwood will give me a name, sir?" Ida finally asked the sheriff.

"Wasn't he working with that Milwaukee lawyer, that Fitzpatrick?"

"Yes, sir, he was."

"Maybe it's not a good idea. Fitzpatrick's guys know they've got to keep their mouths shut. Why don't you take a run at the wife?"

"You mean Becky Norwood?"

"Have coffee with her. Just a general woman-to-woman chat about the case. See if she's heard anything, seen anything. Once she's comfy, act like you know all about her husband's bookmaking."

"I'd be stretching the truth, sir."

"Nothing says a cop has to be a hundred percent truthful in a murder investigation. Act like the gambling is no big deal. Say that her husband won't be charged. She might mention some names."

"I don't feel good about this, sir."

"It doesn't matter how you *feel*, girl. This is an *order*. Get it done and report back to me."

Becky was surprised when there was a knock at the front door early the next morning. She hadn't heard the unmarked patrol car as it rolled up the driveway, or footsteps leading to the doorway, or the squeak of her screen door opening. Just a firm rapping on the door. It was a metal door with a dead bolt lock and a security peephole that Becky approached cautiously.

Becky's heart sank as she peered at her visitor. *What now?* she thought while unlocking the dead bolt. *Was Ed arrested?*

Ida smiled as Becky opened the door.

"Hope I didn't wake you up," she said. "I know you teachers spend your summers trying to catch up on sleep."

"I was talking to my boyfriend on the phone," Becky said with a grin.

"You're joking, right?"

"Of course I am. Ed isn't perfect, but he loves me."

"That's what my mama always said about Daddy. Did I ever tell you about them? Lula Belle and Earl Wayne? That's when I was living on the Budslick family farm in southern Illinois. Just outside of Cobden."

"Cobden? That's the name of a town?"

"That's right, ma'am. I played softball in high school with the Appleknockers."

"The school team?"

Ida nodded. "We grow apples down there. You knock them off trees to harvest. We were apple knockers."

"Feel like some coffee, Ida? I just made a pot, and we've got some cookies too."

"I've got a warrant to consume those cookies, ma'am."

"It's Becky, remember?"

"And I'm Ida. Just plain Ida."

After the two talked about their childhoods, the unusually dry Wisconsin weather, and the difficulties of their jobs, Ida felt the timing was right to talk about Ed's gambling. She eased into it slowly.

"That husband of yours seems like a good guy. How did you meet?"

"We were students at the University of Wisconsin–Oshkosh. He was a business major, and I was studying to be a teacher. He worked in a paper mill for a year while I finished my degree. We saved a lot of what he made in the mill. It was in Neenah."

"I'll bet that's where he started betting on football."

"I wish he'd never got started. He made good money in the mill."

"He was doing a lot better down here, though. There isn't much we don't know about Ed taking bets on sports."

"I shouldn't talk about this," Becky said. "Ed is paranoid about getting arrested. We've got a lawyer."

"Ed doesn't need to worry," Ida replied. "That gambling is too small and too distant to worry about. We know Ed got out of the business. The feds are after bigger fish, not guppies like Ed and his pals."

They continued talking easily. Becky said a few more things about Ed's gambling, but nothing that would cause him trouble. At least that's how it felt at the time. She couldn't remember everything she'd said, but Ida probably did.

After Ida again assured her that Ed wasn't going to be charged with gambling crimes, Becky smiled happily. Then she patted Ida on the hand. "Thank you for telling me."

"I could use another cup of coffee. Anything left in the pot?"

"Coming right up."

In the late afternoon, Becky thought more about her talk with Ida. She was having second thoughts. She worried about Ed's reaction, too, especially if he heard it first from Ida.

He'd never asked her to keep the details of his bookmaking a secret, but why would he? It was hardly the kind of thing she'd share with Caroline, fellow teachers, or any of their parents. Ed no doubt thought she'd keep his admission confidential, even without asking.

Becky wondered whether she'd deliberately been tricked by Ida, but there was nothing to be done about it now. She decided to tell Ed about Ida's visit, but she would emphasize that he wasn't going to be arrested for gambling. The other details would only make him nervous and more paranoid.

Ed pulled into the driveway just before five o'clock. Becky gathered Muffin in her arms, then met Ed at the door with a smile and a kiss.

"How're my two girls? Has Mama been good to you, Muffy?"

"She's been looking out the front windows all afternoon. I think she was waiting for you. She didn't start purring until you came in the door."

"Give me that kitty," Ed said and cuddled the cat against his chest. "Anything happen around here today?"

"I had a visitor."

"One of your boyfriends?"

"It was Detective Ida. She said to say hello to you."

"What the hell did she want?"

"She told me she was talking again to everyone she'd met while investigating the murder. She wanted to know if I'd seen or heard anything. Stuff that might help her ID the victim. You know, no big deal."

"Maybe not to you, but I'm a person of interest."

"Ida said she'd be talking to you too."

"She can talk all she wants. I've got nothing to say."

Becky took a long, deep breath and softened her gaze. It was now or never, she thought.

"Ida told me that you're not in any danger of being arrested for gambling. She doesn't want you to worry."

"How did that come up?"

"She told me the FBI and sheriff's department knew all about your gambling. But you're not a big-enough fish to go after. They want big fish, Eddie. Isn't that great news?"

"I don't know, Becky. They need little fish to catch the big ones. What did you tell Ida?"

"Nothing she didn't know. She knew about that one customer of yours who wasn't paying up."

"She knew about Lennie Spivak?"

"That's what she said."

"Look—I don't want to start a fight. But it's hard to believe she just started spilling her guts. Are you sure she didn't bluff you into saying too much about Lennie?"

"I don't think so but maybe I did," Becky said. "Anyway, the big thing is you can stop worrying about the feds busting our door down."

"But what about the IRS? They don't need anything other than our bank records and tax returns. Did Ida say I was in the clear with the tax people?"

"No, not specifically. But she said you are in the clear. Stop worrying. I'll get you a beer if you're able to put that cat down long enough to have a sip."

"Maybe you're right. A beer sounds good."

Ida felt a little guilty about how she'd tricked Becky into talking about her husband's gambling business. But she was trying to solve a killing, and the first step was finding out who'd been murdered. It also wasn't exactly true that the feds had no interest in Ed. If they thought he'd talk about his connections, the feds would jail him in a heartbeat. But since he had a lawyer and had refused to talk earlier, Ida suspected he wasn't going to be charged.

That didn't mean her visit with Becky had been useless. Ida had been able to confirm the suspicions she'd had about the extent of Ed's gambling. He wasn't a kingpin or a major player. And that's the extent of what she told the sheriff. This was *her* investigation, not his.

Her plan was to learn everything about Lennie Spivak. All she had was a name and no assurance it was legitimate, but still, it was worth running through an online search engine.

She hit pay dirt after typing "Lennie Spivak of Milwaukee." Ida had never heard of the man, but others probably had—especially bowlers. It appeared Lennie was a great bowler, perhaps one who could have bowled professionally. The region's biggest newspaper had many listings for Lennie Spivak among bowlers who'd scored a 700 series. It looked like a weekly occurrence for Lennie, who bowled in two different leagues in Milwaukee.

It made Ida think fondly of her father. He'd been very proud of the single 700 series he notched in twenty years of league bowling.

Ida figured Lennie was well known in the Milwaukee kegling crowd. Maybe someone knew why the reports of his 700 series scores had stopped. The summertime gap in scores was understandable. Most leagues run from fall to spring. But that didn't explain the absence of Lennie Spivak's scores from recent newspapers.

Many of Lennie's scores came from an old-fashioned place in West Allis. Dairyland Recreation was a two-story brick building on the main road crossing the city's small downtown. It held a pool hall and a shabby lunch counter on the street level, which was hidden behind dusty shutters that Ida suspected were rarely opened.

As Ida opened the door, she was met by a cloud of tobacco smoke. There was a subdued murmur from a knot of male onlookers sitting on stools facing a busy pool table under a fluorescent light. A tall and lean man was stretched over the table to make a shot as another gaunt man held a pool cue, rubbed his chin, and affected a disinterested gaze.

The poolroom chatter stopped as the men noticed Ida, who was dressed in full uniform—including a duty belt that holstered her handcuffs, police radio, and handgun.

Out of the corner of her eye, Ida saw one of the spectators slide from his stool and walk slowly into the men's room. *Probably a warrant out on him*, she thought.

"Everyone can take it easy," Ida said to the room. "I thought there was a bowling alley here."

"It's upstairs," said the man with the cue stick.

"I'm looking to hold a fundraiser," Ida said. "The manager here?"

"The *owner's* upstairs."

The upstairs lighting was dim, except for the lights above lanes being cleaned by a greasy-haired, potbellied man dressed in jeans and a dirty white T-shirt.

"You the manager?" Ida asked.

"You kidding? He's behind the counter, has a cigar in his mouth. See him?"

"Yeah. Thanks."

Ida remembered the smells of a bowling alley—oil used on the lanes, polish rubbed into the shoes, and the ever-present smoke. She smiled and approached the counter.

The man behind it carefully placed his cigar on the edge of a black plastic ashtray. "Can I help you, Officer? There ain't no trouble, is there?"

"No trouble," Ida said. "No worries."

"Wanna rent some shoes and roll a few games?" the man asked with a smile.

"I'm not dressed for it right now. I'm looking for a bowler. Thought maybe you'd know him."

"That all depends. Who exactly are ya?"

"Ida Mae Rollins. I'm a detective with the Howard County Sheriff's Department. Who exactly are you?"

"Ace McGuire. I used to be a ranked middleweight. Maybe you heard of me?"

"Sorry. I don't follow boxing."

"A lot don't nowadays. The kids all watch that mixed martial arts crap."

"Guys, mostly. Some of our deputies are big into MMA."

"You sure you don't have a warrant?"

"I'm looking for Lennie Spivak."

"So am I. The bum owes me money. Figgered he'd come 'round once leagues started, but I ain't seen him."

"You got a picture of him somewhere?"

"We don't have no photos," McGuire said and took a puff from the cigar's slobbery end.

"What's he look like?"

"Average, I guess. Like any other bowler we get here."

"You know where he works?"

"He was selling cars in a cruddy lot on Blue Mound Road. Place was called House of Wheels or something like that."

"Ever look for him there?"

"Once. No luck. Who's got time for a stakeout? I don't make money when we're closed."

Ida walked out of the rec center cognizant of her own smell. She took a deep breath of fresh air, then another. It made her even more aware of the surrounding stench. Her uniform would smell like a filthy ashtray until it was washed.

Ida used her smartphone to search for the House of Wheels. It was far west of Milwaukee's lakefront and properly known as Frankie Fortuna's House of Wheels. She decided to visit the next afternoon. It was a Friday near the end of the month, a critical time to make a sale. Ida believed the owner would be present for the final say on any deals that were proposed.

Ida was in plainclothes when she drove her Mustang to the House of Wheels. She didn't want to be seen getting out of an undercover car, a midnight-blue four-door sedan with black-wall tires, tinted windows, spotlights near the side mirrors, and several small antennae. Although considered undercover, the overall look screamed cop.

Ida pulled onto the dusty gravel lot. Balloons were tied to the side mirrors of cars marked "Special" and "Low Miles" and "Cream Puff" and "No Offer Refused."

"Good afternoon, miss," said a barrel-chested man in his fifties. He straightened his tie, pushed thick, curly black hair away from his well-tanned forehead, and smiled.

"Are you Frankie Fortuna?" Ida asked.

"The one and only," Fortuna said and grinned.

"I'm looking for one of your salesmen, Lennie Spivak."

"Smokin' Lennie? What for? The rabbit die?"

"I've never met the man, sir. My name is Ida Mae Rollins. I'm a detective with the Howard County Sheriff's Department. I'd like to talk with Mr. Spivak."

"So would I, miss. Took off without giving notice. He owes me money."

"Why'd you call him Smokin' Lennie?"

"The only time he wouldn't have a cigarette or cigar in his lips was when he sipped a drink. Probably not when he slept, either, but I doubt he got much sack time."

"Why do you say that?"

"Guy looked like shit his last weeks here. Then he disappeared."

"You got an address for him?"

"It's in the office."

There was a wall of photos in the office, under a "Frankie's Team" sign. As Frankie jotted an address from his card file, Ida spotted a grinning Lennie Spivak.

Lennie was a burly, pie-faced man in his forties. He wore an impossibly loud checked sport coat and an open-necked shirt that couldn't have been buttoned without strangling Lennie. He had thinning dirty-blond hair worn in an ugly comb-over. His hair looked as if it were secured with varnish.

Ida took the address from Frankie, then stuffed it into a pocket.

"Thank you, Mr. Fortuna. If I see Lennie, I'll say you're looking for him," Ida said, knowing there was no chance of it happening. Lennie Spivak didn't look anything like the murder victim. There was no reason to waste another minute in a pointless search.

CHAPTER 15
OUT WEST

It was a quiet and private place. Nestled near the top of the mountain, with a panoramic view of Casper, Wyoming, the rental cabin was ideal for a couple who did not want to be disturbed. The nearest neighbor was a half mile away. The high-desert setting of Casper was especially tranquil and still at night—aside from darting headlights, winking traffic signals, and a virtual Christmas tree of city lights.

Daytime, also, was quiet in the cabin. Twittering birds and squirrels scrambling across the metal roof were the dominant sounds. An occasional heavy truck crunched along the mountain road. The kitchen coffee maker gurgled in the early morning, and cell phones chirped later in the day. He rarely used the radio, TV, or stereo. Work was his focus.

She spent her daylight hours styling hair, a trade easily transferred from town to town. She earned a living by driving down from Casper Mountain to the downtown salon. While she worked, he searched various websites for payday possibilities, including drug connections, gay hookups, and rich men looking for threesome action. At times, he thought of what had happened since early summer, when he left Wisconsin. His thoughts would drift back to the US 20 route that finally brought them to Casper. The highway crossed Illinois, Iowa, Nebraska, Wyoming, and points west to the Pacific Ocean.

Iowa had taken more time to cross than they'd anticipated. An overnight stay in Fort Dodge was planned for a low-priced motel. But his laptop led to another stop north of US 20. It was an opportunity for a windfall.

A personal ad caught his eye. "Generous fortysomething white male looking for fun times with attractive couples. I'm fit, good-looking, and sensual with males and females. You should be too. Call my cell and ask for Ronnie."

She used the laptop to make the call. Ronnie answered on the second ring. That was a good sign. He probably had a cell phone that was only for liaison purposes, she guessed.

They both spoke on speakerphone to Ronnie, who was obligingly candid. It makes no sense to confide in a stranger, but most people will. Ronnie said he was self-employed as an investor, his wife worked nights, and he often was lonely, bored, and *frustrated*. His wife was a registered nurse at a medical center near Mason City. It was a demanding job, he said, and it often required overtime shifts that left her too exhausted for bedroom playtime.

"She can't find out about this," Ronnie said. "We have a good life together. She earns enough to support us, but doesn't need to. We save what she earns, or she spends it on herself."

"How is that possible?" he asked.

"I bought stock after the market crashed in 2008, stuff that looked underpriced. My investments doubled in time, then doubled again. I sold when it was soaring, then bought again with blue-chip dividend stocks."

"Must be nice," she said.

"I'll never work again. Don't need to," Ronnie chuckled. "What did you say your names were?"

"We didn't. But she's Lynne, and I'm Mike."

Ronnie described his sexual interests, which weren't especially unusual or disgusting. At least not so much to Mike. For Lynne, it was a different story. Sex with men was revolting to her, but she could play along if necessary—and it usually became necessary when amorous men looked closely at her face, sexy hairstyle, and well-developed body.

Ronnie wanted to meet for a drink and "consider the possibilities." He suggested a roadhouse more than an hour north of Ames, off Interstate 35. They agreed to meet Friday night. Ronnie said his wife would be working all weekend, sleeping in the nurses' dormitory, and probably wouldn't check his whereabouts.

"She'll call me on my main cell phone, if at all."

"Sounds safe," Mike said.

"It will be. And just so you know, if you're not interested, or I'm not, we can just walk away. No hard feelings."

"I'm sure you'll be feeling hard, Ronnie," Lynne purred.

"That's my kind of woman. I hope you dress like a high-class hooker."

"Count on it," she replied. "Sweet dreams until Friday. Wet dreams too."

Lynne and Mike knew that Ronnie probably wasn't his real name. That didn't matter. Things that did matter they'd learned from experience. It mattered that Ronnie was a wealthy loner with only a wife at home—when she was home.

Friday night was warm and clear. Lynne sipped a second Tom Collins, her lipstick leaving a red kiss on the glass. Ronnie had moved next to her in the lounge's horseshoe-shaped booth, far from the piano and sparingly lit.

"You look hot," he said.

"Thanks, handsome. Why don't we get a bottle and a hotel room? I'd like to see what you've got," Lynne said, sliding her long fingernails up and down his crotch. "It feels like Little Ronnie wants to come out and play."

"Maybe you should say Big Ronnie," Mike said. "We don't want anyone insulted."

Ronnie laughed, a big horsey chuckle that showed his teeth. "I'll get the check," he said, grabbing a credit card from a field of gold and platinum plastic in a bulging wallet. "We'll ride together in my Lexus. Just bought it. Has a great back seat."

"Think my SUV will be safe here?" Lynne said. "It's not much, but it's all I've got."

"I've left my car here overnight," Ronnie replied. "More than once. It's a safe spot."

Lynne and Ronnie sat in the back seat as Mike drove the car out of the lounge parking lot.

"I'm going to need five hundred dollars to get through the weekend, stud," Lynne said to Ronnie while pulling down the fly of his suit's trousers. She played with his bulging member as Ronnie moaned with pleasure.

"Find an ATM," Ronnie mumbled to Mike.

Mike easily watched the ATM's keypad in the driver's side mirror as Ronnie punched in his PIN. The digital snooping device he carried in a pocket copied the secret numbers. Even if the numbers Mike saw slipped from memory, the PIN was recorded and ready to use when needed.

Ronnie likely noticed nothing about Mike. He was too busy groping Lynne. But after driving for nearly half an hour Mike pulled off the road and into a parking lot at a package liquor store. Ronnie collected himself and calmly bought a bottle of scotch. A short drive later, he got a room at an upscale hotel near Clear Lake.

"I used cash for the bottle and the room," Ronnie said, flashing a swollen wallet. "They didn't get a license plate or the make of the car. I fibbed about both on the registration. Gave 'em a phony name too."

Ronnie and Lynne walked to the second-floor room while Mike filled a small cooler with ice. Ronnie began massaging Lynne's buttocks as they waited inside the doorway to their room. They kissed deeply as Ronnie held the door open for Mike.

Ronnie was out of his clothes and pulling at Lynne's skimpy dress moments after the door was closed and locked. The fat wallet in his suit coat's breast pocket was out of sight, out of mind. For Ronnie. But not for Mike. As Ronnie backed Lynne onto the king-size bed and pulled her panties to her knees, Mike grabbed the billfold and shoved it into his hip pocket.

Ronnie didn't see anything other than Lynne, who was gasping for breath and begging Ronnie to slow down.

"Let's have some scotch, tiger. I want to lose *all* my inhibitions," she said. "Pour us a strong drink Mike."

Mike slipped the powdered roofies into the glass of scotch he then handed to Ronnie, who drained it in two gulps and returned his attention to Lynne.

"Sit on the edge of the bed, tiger," Lynne said as she knelt between his legs.

In what seemed only a few moments, Ronnie settled into a paralyzing chemical fog.

Mike and Lynne quickly emptied Ronnie's wallet. They took the cash he'd withdrawn from the ATM, along with his bank card. They found a panel in the billfold that hid a stack of hundred-dollar bills. They also took his credit cards in case he used the same PIN on all of them. Many people do.

"He didn't want us to know about the hidden cash," Mike said. "That's why he went to the ATM—to fool us. He was trying to limit his losses if he got robbed."

"Not a bad move," Lynne said. "But I'll bet we get cash advances on all his cards."

"Many people use predictable PINs, like 1234. Ronnie probably thought he was clever to use 4321," Mike chuckled. "What a yutz. What a buffoon."

It was a profitable evening for Lynne and Mike. The only remaining problem was Ronnie.

"He isn't a bad guy," Mike said. "Let's leave him in the room. He'll find his empty wallet on the bed and have a terrible headache. He'll go home and keep his mouth shut."

"What if he doesn't?" Lynne said. "Security cameras will have our pictures. And Ronnie probably saw stuff the cops could use."

"What stuff?"

"He probably made a mental note of the Wisconsin plate on the SUV. And I think you said something about heading to Wyoming."

"Maybe I did. But he'll be too ashamed to tell the cops he was robbed. He's a big shot. He was cheating on his wife. Let's just leave him on the bed."

"Too risky. We can't take any chances of him talking."

"What, then?"

"You know what's next. Get your big duffel bag," Lynne said. "Let's get him into the car and get out of here."

"You're sure about this?"

"There's no other way. And bring my makeup bag when you get the duffel. I need to brush my teeth and use mouthwash. I can still taste that pig. Ugh!"

Summers were brief but pleasant in Wyoming. The days were mostly sunny and arid, the evenings cool and dry. It had snowed on Casper Mountain shortly before they drove into the region. Longtime residents of the area—cowboys, refinery workers, oil field roughnecks, meatpackers, and health-care professionals—were already talking about the soon and sudden onset of a typical winter.

Mike often had a beer at the convenience store at the foot of the mountain. It sold "last chance" overpriced gas and grocery goods that were marked up to whatever the traffic would bear. A small bar was a good place to hear what people thought about the president, the governor, and their congressmen. All were considered crooks.

But the weather was the dominant topic.

"Think it's ever gonna rain? My cattle need fresh grass," said a rancher known as Red.

"More likely we'll get snow, 'specially on the mountain," replied bartender-clerk Anabelle.

"You mean like a few months ago?" Mike asked. "That normal here? We almost got in a wreck getting here from Casper."

"That was nothing. We don't call it a snowfall unless we get more than a foot. That was a dusting."

"When does the snow start around here?"

"Late October if we're lucky. But it melts too. We get warm days sometimes in the winter."

"Kind of like the Midwest? That's where I'm from."

"Figgered you wasn't from 'round here. You sound funny," Red said between gulps of beer from a longneck bottle. "Ain't nothin' like the Midwest. Snow on the mountain in late August ain't unusual."

It was something Mike told Lynne that night.

"We've gotta think about where we're going next," he said. "We ain't roughnecks or cowboys."

"I'm figuring we'll go south, like when I was on my own."

"Think we'll be OK here for a few more weeks? The locals say the snow sometimes starts before Halloween."

"They're right. This ain't my first mountain home in the West."

"We need to score some coke too."

"What do you think about New Orleans? It's a great town for drugs."

"Isn't it too pricey? Will we be able to make that kind of money?"

"Don't look at me," Lynne said. "I spend my days with a bunch of fancy ladies. Find us a rich guy on that computer of yours. All you've got to do is troll the apps and chat rooms for hooking up. Someone like that Iowa dude, Robbie."

"You mean Ronnie."

"Whatever. He was just another asshole to me."

CHAPTER 16
WHAT'S UP?

There was something about Caroline's tone of voice that troubled Becky. She'd called early Saturday morning, at a time when Ed was driving to Chicago for a restaurant equipment trade show. Becky was alarmed by the phone, fearing Ed had been in an accident on the dangerous and overcrowded Kennedy Expressway. Her initial relief at Caroline's voice gave way to new concern as they spoke.

"I just need to talk with someone," Caroline finally said.

"Come on over. I've got a fresh pot of coffee."

Becky wondered whether something had happened to George, who had a carpentry job on a project in Memphis. It was a big job and paid well, especially with overtime, but he came home only once a month. It would be steady work for a year, though, and he'd told Caroline he'd be able to stay home for six months when the assignment ended. The big paychecks made it look worthwhile to Caroline.

Caroline came through the kitchen door without knocking. Her eyes were red rimmed. It appeared she had been crying more than a little.

Becky handed Caroline a mug of steaming coffee and put a platter of cookies on the kitchen table. "Is something wrong?" she finally asked.

"Oh, Becky, I don't know what I'm going to do. It's Maddy. That girl is going to ruin us. She seems to know whenever we start getting ahead. Then she wants help."

"Not again."

"I'm afraid so."

"But you said she'd be doing better the last time Maddy took off. You agreed to trade your SUV for her beat-up pickup truck. That was really generous."

"I know. She ought to be grateful, but, but I really …" Caroline said, halting in tears.

"What is it, honey? Is she asking for more money? A lot more money?"

"She talked me into sending a big check to the private mailbox service she uses. Maddy's mail is sent to her wherever she's staying. I never know where she is until she comes home and tells me about her latest adventures."

"Don't send her money, Caroline. She's an adult. You're not helping her, not really. You're enabling her to fail."

"I already put a check in the mail. I *had* to."

"What? I don't understand."

"Maddy won't forgive me because of something that happened a long time ago. We had a family problem with my dad. I didn't want to believe what Maddy was telling me."

"Oh no, it wasn't …"

"I'm afraid it was. She wasn't even a teenager. I accused her of making it all up to get her way. She'd always been a very difficult child."

"But still, Caroline, she was just a child …"

"I know that now. This sin is on me. And it gives Maddy power over me."

"Why? I don't understand."

"George doesn't know a thing about it. I threatened Maddy to keep her from telling her father. I told her it would ruin things between him and Grandpa—they were best buddies."

"George still doesn't know?"

"No. Maddy keeps telling me that she'll tell him all about it unless I give her what she wants."

"So, what if she does? She's a grown woman now. She needs to paddle her own canoe, like Eddie says."

"George adores that girl."

"You're in a tough spot. You're keeping something from George. Ed would go nuts if I did that."

"Don't be judgmental. You don't have a daughter. How do you know what you'd do if it happened to you?"

"You're right," Becky said. "I'm sorry."

"It's OK."

After they finished the coffee and cookies, Caroline helped Becky wash their dishes and put everything away. As they worked, Becky couldn't stop thinking about what Caroline had said.

"You didn't send her more than you can afford, did you? You and George will be OK, right?"

"It's not that big a deal. I worry too much about money. What's a thousand dollars? But still, it won't be much fun when George finds out."

Becky nodded.

"If things get too tight, Ed probably could hire you to wash dishes," she said and grinned.

Caroline snapped her with the wet dish towel and laughed. They hugged at the kitchen door, and Becky walked her toward home. It gave Caroline time to think about their conversation.

She hadn't been fully honest. She'd sent Maddy a check for more than she'd told Becky. It wasn't as much as Maddy had wanted, but it still was $10,000. It would take George many weeks of overtime to make that much money. And it put another dent in their savings.

Maddy had angrily resented begging her mother for money. It was really *her* money anyway. As an only child, Maddy someday would be the sole heir to her parents' estate. She'd been shown their will and assured that her later years would be comfortable.

She didn't want to wait that long. Her mother was too tightfisted with money. Her father made good money. It wasn't fair to make her wait for her share!

It never occurred to Maddy to cut her expenses. She believed she wasn't earning what she deserved. Especially recently. Maddy expected better pay from her summer in the West. But the hair salon didn't pay well. And the tips weren't generous. She'd done much better elsewhere, including in various salons between Milwaukee and Chicago. The roommate she'd taken on to split expenses for food, housing, and transportation hadn't earned what they needed, while her own expenses had nearly doubled. There'd been grand plans for big scores through her live-in partner's online schemes, but most vanished like campfire smoke. Without some real money, and soon, there'd be no trek south for warm weather and better opportunities.

It was a good thing that she'd be driving her mother's SUV for the foreseeable future. It was under warranty, registered in her mother's name, and insured by her mother. Her mother's gas station credit card paid for gas and oil changes.

Maddy knew the $10,000 from her mother would soon be available. She'd endorse the check and take it to the nearby branch office of her nationwide bank. But it wasn't going to be enough to get a good start on life in the South. She really needed more money. Just another $5,000 would help a lot!

She finally decided to call her parents' credit union to get what she needed. Harriet Needham, the woman who handled the Connellys' savings and checking accounts, was a family friend. She'd often remarked to Caroline and Maddy that they looked like sisters and sounded just like each other.

It was an interesting recollection for Maddy. She knew her mother handled financial matters by phone and mail. During Maddy's last stay at home, Caroline had said she hadn't been inside the credit union in recent years.

"Harriet takes care of me when I call," she'd said. "She's great! The money goes wherever I want."

It sounded perfect to Maddy, who was more talented with the phone than her tech-savvy partner. She knew enough about the digital world, however, to make it look as though the call came from her mother's cell. She placed a midmorning call to the credit union.

"Good morning. This is Harriet Needham. How may I help you?" said a stressed-out voice.

"Hi, Harriet. It's me, Caroline. Why so formal?"

"I'm sorry, girl. This place is a madhouse! Something's happened in the markets. My customers are cashing out stocks and buying CDs. Cash is still king."

"It sure is. That's why I'm calling. I'm going to surprise Maddy with an early Christmas gift."

"What a good mom! How is that girl doing?"

"She's fine. Spent the summer on a mountain out west. She's heading south for the winter."

"Wish I was, Caroline. Wisconsin winters aren't easy on my old bones."

"Mine either!"

"What would you like me to do?"

"I need you to send an electronic transfer to Maddy's bank. Make it for five thousand dollars."

"Sure. No problem. Are you sure you want to do that much? It looks like you recently moved ten thousand dollars from savings into checking."

"That was for a down payment on the RV I'm buying for George and me. That's a surprise too."

"I'll do the transfer, but you've really cut into your savings."

"You can't take it with you, Harriet!" Maddy laughed.

Harriet laughed, too, then dispatched the money to Maddy's account.

"Thanks, Harriet. Have a good day."

"You too. Say hello to Maddy for me. Bye-bye."

⁌⸱ ⸱

With her own savings, the check from Caroline, and the electronic transfer from the credit union, Maddy had a new account balance of $19,204. It was enough to buy a new wardrobe for wintering in the south, plus months of living expenses. But first she'd have to deal with her mother.

Maddy didn't worry unduly about her mother's reaction to a bank statement that would show a $5,000 electronic transfer to Maddy. It wouldn't be like Caroline to call the credit union before calling Maddy.

The expected call from Caroline came as Maddy and her partner packed their belongings into the SUV. They'd be out of their mountain home by dusk.

"Hi, Mom! What's up?" Maddy said.

"That's what I want to know. What do you know about a five-thousand-dollar electronic transfer from our savings account?"

"You refused to give me what I really need. All you had to do was give me all the money when I asked for it."

"Your father and I aren't getting younger, Maddy. He wants to travel and take it easy before he's sixty."

"You're making too big a deal out of this, Mom. That money's going to be mine after you're gone. I just decided to take it now. Think of it as a loan from my inheritance."

"As if you'll ever pay it back!" Caroline shouted. "You don't know the value of a dollar. Never have. I'm sick of this!"

"You want to know about sick? Think about what Grandpa did to me! You swept it all under the rug. Said I was making it up. I should tell Dad what you did!"

"You better not, or—"

"Or what? You can't do a thing about it. There are other things I could tell Dad too. You went to the fitness center a lot when I was home, but the stuff in your gym bag looked like what a slut would pack for a date. I looked through it one night."

"You little bitch. I ought—"

"And your hair, makeup, and perfume were better when you got home than before you left."

Caroline slammed the phone down and poured herself a glass of wine. What exactly did Maddy know? Or was she just bluffing?

Caroline knew she couldn't risk calling her bluff. Maddy knew it too.

It was an uneventful trip down the mountain. In less than an hour, the SUV was on the highway, Maddy's partner at the wheel. Maddy had decided to shop for her winter wardrobe by making stops along the route to New Orleans. It would break the monotony of a long and boring drive.

She didn't know whether the latest styles could be found in Denver, Kansas City, and Saint Louis, but she planned to check. There was enough money for overnight stays in the best hotels, fine dining, and cocktails. Maddy saw the approaching winter and new year through rose-colored glasses.

CHAPTER 17
MR. LUCKY

At first, I worried about Becky's coffee klatch with Detective Ida. But after I slept on it for a few nights, my fears seemed silly.

I knew from earlier conversations with my lawyer, Peter Fitzpatrick, that a wife couldn't be compelled to testify against her husband in court. That eased my concerns.

It also helped knowing that Becky could share only a few little things I'd told her, including the tale of deadbeat Lennie Spivak's disappearance. I hadn't told Becky that Lennie didn't look anything like the young man whose remains were strewn along the roadside near our home. Lennie was a red herring, nothing more.

I'd told Angelo Calacia about Lennie's disappearance and another problem a few weeks before spotting the bagged body parts in roadside ditches. Angelo's only concern was my bad judgment.

"Waddaya thinkin'?" he'd snarled. "Are ya fucked in the head? You shouldn't take bets without gettin' the money up front."

"I usually don't, but—"

"There ain't no *but* to this. Get the money first. There ain't no friendships in gambling. This ain't charity."

There were a few others I'd carried, too, but not for long. And not for a lot of money. Even before Angelo put me out of the bookie business, I'd ended the risky practice. Angelo was right. Friendships and gambling don't mix.

I hadn't told Becky about the other gambler I'd brought to Angelo's attention. Thad Elliott, a construction worker, had lost money on baseball bets. I carried him for a couple of weeks hoping his luck would change. It always had.

"Yer stupid. Losers keep losin'," Angelo had said. He also said he'd have someone looking for Lennie and Thad.

I wasn't especially concerned about either deadbeat. But after the murder, I thought more about Thad. He was in his early twenties, about six feet tall, with a muscular build. His brown hair was collar length. He worked as a laborer on a high-rise project near the Hoan Bridge in downtown Milwaukee.

That was all I'd told Angelo. He wanted to know more.

"Where's his family?" he'd asked. "He'll get the money after his mother is threatened."

"I don't know where he's from. This shouldn't have happened. I'm sorry."

"Sorry doesn't cut it. He'll be taken care of. I'll take care of that other shithead too. My guy will find them."

"Thanks, man."

"Can the grateful act. I need more weight in your envelope. This ain't a request. It's an order."

"I'll do better. Don't worry."

"You better be worryin' right now. Goodbye."

I'd dipped into our savings to save my skin and decided never to carry anyone again. The only thing Angelo cared about was his money. Once that was squared away, everything was OK.

I'd almost stopped worrying about Angelo by the time I reported roadside trash to the highway boss.

In the following days of murder hysteria, I began to wonder about Thad Elliott. He hadn't tried to bet a game for a week, nor had he called me again looking for another extension on the money he owed.

I was sick of his whining and excuses, but after I'd learned the sickening details about the murder near our home, my feelings changed. I would have loved to hear Thad Elliott's voice.

But he didn't call. And when I looked for him at the jobsite, he had disappeared. I tried to forget about him after Angelo put me out of business, but I just couldn't. I wasn't going to risk another interrogation session with Ida. It made me feel a little guilty, but it was more important to protect myself.

CHAPTER 18
NEW BUSINESS

New Orleans didn't work out as planned for Lynne and Mike. They were right about mild winter weather on the bayou. But Mike's online prowling of hookup sites didn't yield a suitable sugar daddy or any strong prospects. Sex was too easily available in New Orleans through old-school tactics— barroom pickups, prostitution, telephone escort services, massage parlors, and straight-up propositions in the French Quarter.

They rented a furnished apartment in Metairie, which wasn't as close to the French Quarter as they'd intended. But it wasn't as costly, and the expense of commuting to Lynne's job was minimal. Mike usually drove her to work in the old neighborhood, at the almost prohibitively upscale Le Hair Affair, while he moved about coffee shops, French bakeries, and taverns. Free Wi-Fi was available everywhere, but Mike never worried about his laptop searches becoming anyone else's business. He spent a few bucks every month from Lynne's salary and tips for state-of-the-art VPN protection.

Lynne expected a financial contribution from Mike, but it wasn't happening fast enough for her.

"We're supposed to be a team. I'm paying all the bills. What the hell are you doing all day long?"

"It's not easy finding the right guy. He's got to be a loner with money. We can't be messing with family men. When a breadwinner goes missing, the news is full of 'Where's our daddy?' crap."

"Are you really trying? After I'm done with work, sometimes you smell like sex."

"I've got my needs, Lynne. It never bothered you before. I don't bug you about partying with the other stylists."

"I've got my sexual needs too. You knew from the get-go I hate the idea of sex with a man. When a man touches me sexually, I go berserk."

"That's weird, you know. Sex is sex. Doesn't matter to me if it's with a guy or a girl."

Mike wasn't being completely honest. He'd kept it a secret while living at home, but he enjoyed sex with another man. It began while he was in college, using drugs for the first time. One thing had led to another.

For Mike, sex was no more special than an intensely pleasurable physical act. It was something he pursued without inhibitions. He didn't understand why Lynne wasn't the same.

"I don't see why it's such a big deal," he said. "What's wrong with men?"

"You know why I hate it. My grandpa molested me. He made me keep it a secret, and when I finally told on him, my mother wouldn't believe me. I never did tell my dad."

"I guess I understand. But I thought we had a good thing going. We get along OK. Why can't we fuck every now and then? You make it look real when we get a guy."

"We're together for business. Only for business. When's the next big score?"

"I'm looking," Mike said. "It's not easy finding guys who carry a roll of cash and a stack of plastic. They tend to be missed real soon—and missed a lot."

"You made it happen in Wisconsin and Iowa. If you don't come through soon, we're going our separate ways."

⁕

Mike knew the approaching holiday season would work against him. Even satyrs stayed closer to home as Christmas drew near. He needed either a new approach or a new plan.

Mike had spent the afternoon in bed with Kim and Brendan, a no-strings-attached hookup he made over drinks. Mike was attracted by each, but especially by Brendan. He began to wonder if his bisexuality wasn't really a chickenshit way of easing into the gay world. The other man had played college football, and his thick black hair was only slightly graying. Kim often fell into the background as the men enjoyed each other.

"What do you do for money?" Brendan asked.

"I could probably do this for money. Want to pay me?"

"I'm thinking you could help me move some product. There's a guy in Texas who does import-export work with Mexico. A guy he knows in Juárez."

"Drugs?"

"Heroin. Big market now. It's cheaper than buying opioids on the street. Big drug companies and doctors get 'em hooked. We just help them scratch the itch."

"What would I need to do?"

"Drive the stuff to Chicago. Guy who lives near Gary, Indiana, has a warehouse that we use for distributing."

"I can do that if it's worthwhile."

"Would ten thousand dollars do it?"

"For one trip?"

"Yeah. Maybe you can move into a little dealing too. Buy some product, cut it fifty-fifty, and sell it in bars and coffee shops. You come across as a good guy. You're a natural for sales. You'll make a small fortune in no time."

"What's the risk?"

"You're on your own if you deal. If you get arrested, I don't know you."

"What about driving the stuff to Chicago?"

"As a driver, there isn't much risk. Especially for you. You look really straight, like a former Boy Scout."

"What will I be driving?"

"I'll provide a rental car—some bland fleet sedan a salesman would drive."

"I guess I could try it."

"Let me give you a little more convincing. You and I need another go in bed."

⁕

Lynne didn't like the dangers of dealing drugs, but the chance for big money changed her mind.

Mike would be taking the risk, not Lynne. But they'd both enjoy his big payday and might not need to stay involved with drugs. They both thought the New Year and the soon-to-follow Mardis Gras party scene would yield horny rich guys looking for discreet three-way fun.

That was weeks away. Mike grew impatient, but not as much as Lynne. Brendan finally called Mike two weeks before Christmas.

"I've got a shipment ready to move," he said. "It's packed in old suitcases in the trunk of the car I rented. You need to hit the road before dark."

Mike was told to dress like a traveling salesman—white button-down shirt, necktie, office-casual pants, and a sport coat draped over the passenger seat.

Mike met Brendan for coffee at a strip mall. Brendan slipped the keys across the table and nudged toward the silver-colored sedan near the front window. The rental paperwork said the car was leased by Toolco, a fictitious tool-and-die supplier created by Brendan. Mike also was given a three-ring binder filled with Toolco's supposed products—all depicted on high-gloss paper from online images posted by legitimate supply houses.

"One last thing," Brendan said. "You have a driver's license?"

"Of course," Mike said. "Clean record too. What do I do next? Just start driving?"

"Take the interstate north. Most guys make their way to Interstate 57 and cut across Illinois to Chicago. You should take the long way. Follow I-65 through Indiana. When you get near Gary"—Brendan handed Mike a Toolco business card—"call the number on the back."

Mike looked at the penciled note. "What then?"

"My guy will know what the call's about. Don't mention any names. All you gotta say is 'I'm here.' He'll give you directions to the warehouse. Just go there, open the trunk, and get away after he unloads you."

"When do I get paid?"

"This is your road trip envelope," Brendan said as he handed over a Toolco mailer. "Two Gs. You'll need meals, but don't let the car out of your sight. You'll get the rest of the money when you get back."

"What about a hotel?"

"I wouldn't risk it. Get a catnap at a truck stop or rest area. My guy's expecting you to call tomorrow night between seven and nine. Once you've unloaded, you're safe getting a room for the night."

"I understand. No problem."

"Don't screw this up. I'll have more runs for you if you do a good job this time."

Mike grew more relaxed as the miles slipped away. By the time he passed Indianapolis, he felt confident. He maintained the speed limit, obeyed all traffic laws, and blended into the northbound flow. If he needed to talk with the police, Mike was prepared to describe the wonders of Toolco and show his three-ring catalog of goods.

That wasn't necessary.

Mike finally napped in a truck stop near West Lafayette, then gulped a fast-food meal. He'd timed the drive to arrive in Gary just after six, but he was delayed by the typically murderous Chicagoland rush-hour traffic at the I-65 interchange with I-80/94. He called the number after stopping for gas and learned he was within two miles of his destination.

Mike drove into a well-lit warehouse parking lot at 7:40 p.m. A man in his forties, heavyset, with thinning black hair slicked straight back, pointed to an open garage door into the warehouse. Mike drove inside, where another man was waiting.

He was younger and Black. He wore a red sweatshirt, several heavy gold chains around his neck, charcoal-gray warm-up pants, and expensive basketball shoes. He looked like an athlete, perhaps a former boxer. He had a soft-spoken, friendly manner.

"How was your drive, man?"

"It went good. No worries. Let me get the trunk open."

It took less than a minute to unload the trunk.

"We got what we need," the man said. "You're outta here."

Mike worried as he drove away. He'd seen too many movies about drug kingpins and their blazing guns. It helped to know the heroin load was delivered safely, but he still had most of his $2,000. It could easily be stolen at gunpoint.

His mood changed as he merged onto I-65 and drove south from Lake County into Indiana farmland. It was the easiest job he'd ever done.

He might make enough money through his partnership with Brendan to break away from Lynne.

That would serve her right, he thought. She'd been a total bitch since they'd left Casper Mountain. Now that there was a chance he'd be bringing home most of the money, why did he need Lynne as a partner?

Her hatred of men would never end. She actually enjoyed killing men who wanted sex from her. "It's like I'm a black widow," she said.

Mike helped her conceal the killings, but he never felt right about murder. No matter how often Lynne said they got what they deserved. He was frightened of her, fearful she'd eventually consider him a risk to her freedom. She'd terminated such risks.

The first killing had come as a shock to Mike. He'd talked in an online chat room with Lynne, who'd called herself Lady Love, and a construction worker who called himself Hammer Time. They talked about three-way fun a number of times and finally agreed to meet in person at a tavern between Milwaukee and Howard.

They hit it off immediately. Lynne kissed and fondled each and suggested riding to her home together.

"I've got my mom's SUV. We can party at my place. I'll bring you guys back here later."

"I've gotta work tomorrow," Hammer Time said.

"Don't worry about work. I've got plans for you boys."

Mike decided it was his own sexual interest in Hammer Time that probably saved him from Lynne in that first meeting. Once naked and visibly aroused, Hammer Time was interested primarily in Lynne and had fondled his way between her legs. As he neared entry, Lynne struck. Hammer Time looked stunned when she plunged deep into his upper back a knife she'd been hiding under her pillow. Then she cursed and spat at him as she stabbed repeatedly.

Her obscene chant and his cry of pain didn't last long. The noise likely couldn't have been heard outside the barn that held Lynne's hayloft apartment. Certainly not in her parents' home. It was a good walk between the house and barn.

"Jesus Christ, what the hell?" Mike said.

"Shut up, or you're next. You're in this as deep as me. You helped get him here."

"I didn't know you'd kill him. I wanted to party—that's all."

"Enough of that! We've got to get rid of this guy. There's a hoist below. We can cut him up above the floor drain and dump him in the ditches. He won't be found until harvest."

"Cut him up? Are you nuts?"

Lynne pulled a handgun from her bedside table and aimed it at Mike. "You were talking about working in a grocery store in high school. They wanted you to apprentice as a butcher, didn't they?"

Mike said nothing. But he helped Lynne drag the body. And it wasn't as troubling to cut apart a man as Mike might have thought, if in fact he'd ever thought about it. Which he hadn't.

Turned out it wasn't a great deal different from butchering a cow or deer, he realized.

It was even less troubling in Iowa. By that time, Mike had been threatened daily by Lynne. She knew Mike's greatest fear was his mother discovering her son's sexual interest in other men. She knew his parents, Martha and Arnie, were devout fundamentalist Christians. Marriage and lovemaking occurred only between a man and a woman in their world, especially for Arnie, who devotedly clung to those beliefs.

"Just keep doing what I say, and you won't have any trouble," Lynne said as they crossed Iowa. "Chicken out or skip on me, and I'll tell Mommy you like boys. It didn't take me long to find her phone number and address on your computer."

It was a frightening threat for many months. But it had lost its initial and sustained horror for Mike. Gay marriage was now a reality across the nation and much of the world. In New Orleans, a most tolerant community, homosexuality was treated as normal behavior. Rarely did a week pass without Mike being propositioned by another man, sometimes successfully.

In time, Mike suspected his mother would be far more understanding than his father would have been. He'd still be her son, her only child.

There might be a way, he finally decided, to break free of Lynne and live off the proceeds of drug dealing. She was in no position to tell the cops about anything, Mike realized.

Even if he somehow got arrested, he had the upper hand with Lynne. He'd tell the cops everything she'd done and offer enough details to prove it. She was a killer, not him. All he'd done was conceal corpses, though in a manner most would find distasteful at best.

All he needed was a good bankroll, Mike realized as he drove the rental car south into Louisiana. He'd move drugs for Brendan whenever asked, and use some of his profit to buy heroin and sell it in the French Quarter's bars.

Suddenly the future looked sunny and bright. He'd be making some real money, keeping Lynne off his back, and probably getting his rocks off regularly with Brendan and Kim.

That's just what he had in mind when he visited Brendan to collect the $8,000 he was owed. It was especially pleasing to find Brendan and Kim naked when he entered their apartment in the Garden District.

"Your money is in the envelope on the coffee table, stud," Brendan said. "Kim and I want some of your sweetness."

Kim drifted into sleep after the bedroom party cooled off, but Brendan wanted to talk business. He and Mike grabbed beers from the fridge, then sat at the kitchen table.

"You did a good job," Brendan said. "But I've got someone else who wants the Chicago work. He's a Chicago guy with connections. He can grow the business."

"What about me?"

"Want to make a few runs to Saint Louis? I'd like to move into that market. If you like it, maybe you can be a distributor for Missouri, southern Illinois, and western Kentucky."

"How would I go about that?"

"Set up in a small town and deliver the stuff to your customers. The local cops won't see a thing. There ain't enough of them."

"My customers, though. Who would they be?"

"I can get you started with contacts in Saint Louis, Springfield, Carbondale, Paducah, and Cape Girardeau. You'd take orders and deliver the stuff."

"Sounds like it might work. I'll think it over."

"Don't take too long. I'm gonna do this with you or without you."

CHAPTER 19
WE NEED TO TALK

I knew it was the right thing to do after talking with Becky.

We sat in our rockers in the living room, a purring Muffin deep into the late-day sunshine on my lap. The dinner dishes were rinsed and stacked in the dishwasher. I was on my second beer. Becky had just taken a sip of her favorite California red, an affordable version of an expensive French wine. It was a long and serene moment until I broke the silence.

"I need your help, Beck," I suddenly said.

"What? What's wrong?"

"You remember about Lennie Spivak?"

"Oh my God! He's dead! You think that guy in Kenosha killed him, don't you?"

"I don't know if he's dead. Lennie still is missing. Maybe he's alive. But there's another guy I didn't mention. I think Ida should know about him too."

"Who?"

"A guy named Thad Elliott. Last spring, he had breakfast in the diner most every morning. After Thad finished his food, he went to his job. He worked construction on that high-rise near the Hoan Bridge."

"Why would you tell Ida about him?"

"Thad bet baseball games with me. I carried him a little, but he got behind. I told my guy in Kenosha. I guess that's when Thad stopped coming to the diner."

"You need to tell Ida. Maybe it's important."

"I can't say anything about Kenosha, not a word. If I do, I'll go missing."

"Tell Ida you got tough with Thad and told him to pay up. Then he disappeared."

"Ida knows I'm not scary. Why would Thad take off because I was angry?"

"Just take your attorney when you talk with Ida. He'll make sure you don't say too much. All Ida really needs is the guy's name. He's a missing person she doesn't know about."

"It'll cost a fortune, Beck. We're not rich people."

"We're not poor either. Think of it as an investment in your future. It will ease your conscience. That's worth something."

"I'll think about it. Maybe you're right."

⋅•ៈ ⋅ •

I called Ida after I'd talked to my lawyer, Peter Fitzpatrick. He told me it was a mistake to trust a cop—any cop.

"You're the client, and you're paying the bill," he said. "But it would be best to stay quiet."

"What if I keep quiet and Ida somehow learns Thad's the murder victim? Once she's got a name, it won't take Ida long to figure out where he worked."

"So what?"

"I'm sure the other guys on the job knew he was gambling. In his case, losing. He came into the diner with some of them. Ida will find out I was his bookie. It'd be better if she heard it from me."

"Why? You didn't kill anyone, did you?"

"Of course not! But if I'm honest now, they might believe what I say later, if they find it was Thad who was killed."

Fitzpatrick still didn't like the idea, but he agreed to accompany me to the sheriff's department if I insisted. I did.

"Stay on a tight script and don't talk about your guy in Kenosha," Fitzpatrick said as we drove from downtown Milwaukee to Howard. "That man's more dangerous than you think. I'd heard of him before we met. That should be a warning to you."

"How did you happen to hear of Angelo?"

"Another client. I can't say any more without violating his attorney-client confidentiality."

"Stop me if I'm saying too much, OK?"

"You want a signal or something?"

"That'd be good. Something other than 'Don't say *that*!'"

"What if I touch my nose with my left index finger?"

"That'll work."

My conversation with Ida took longer than I'd expected. To start with, she asked me a lot of basic information. Maybe she was checking to see whether my story had changed. But all I'd ever done was tell her the truth. It's easy to remember the truth.

"You said there was something new to tell me," Ida finally said.

"Lennie Spivak was a customer who disappeared. So was Thad Elliott," I said. "He bet on baseball games with me and got behind. I let him bet on a few more games on credit, which was a big mistake. I finally said he better pay up or else."

"Or else what?"

"I didn't say. I was angry, though, and—" I stopped after seeing Fitzpatrick touch his nose.

"What else did you say?" Ida asked.

"Nothing. Thad knew he better pay up, though."

"Did he?"

"I haven't seen him since. He must have taken off. He was working for A. G. Meyer on that high-rise near the Hoan Bridge. I stopped by and asked the job superintendent about him. He said Thad was gone."

"What was the super's name?"

"I don't know. I didn't ask him. All I said was 'I'm looking for Thad Elliott.' He said Thad stopped reporting for work."

"Was this conversation at the jobsite?"

"Yeah, in a trailer they use as an office."

"I'm gonna visit that office myself," Ida said. "Can you—"

"I think that's all my client has to say, Detective," Fitzpatrick said. He then looked at me and touched his nose. "I've got a court appearance in downtown Milwaukee in an hour. We're leaving."

"I've got what I need—for now," Ida said.

"Look," Fitzpatrick barked. "For your report, I'm asserting my client came here on his own free will. He wants to help your investigation. He didn't kill anyone. If you want to ask anything else, arrest him."

"I'll think about it," Ida said as her eyes grew fiery and her nostrils flared.

Fitzpatrick and I walked quickly to his car. Not a word was said until we were outside Howard city limits.

"I'm not sure that was a good idea," I said, "pissing Ida off."

"This isn't my first rodeo. They've got nothing. If they did, you'd already be staying in the crowbar hotel."

"What if I think of something that might help Ida?"

"Look, Ed. I played ball with you today. Get a new lawyer if you want to share anything else with Ida that I haven't approved. Nothing's going to happen to you unless you say too much. I won't let that happen."

I worried that night about the meeting with Ida. I took a shot of whiskey and drank more beer than I had in many months. A purring Muffin camped out on my lap as I settled back into my recliner.

Once the alcohol kicked in, I got more confident that Fitzpatrick was right. I didn't have anything to worry about if I kept my mouth shut.

Or did I?

CHAPTER 20
NO WAY OUT

While on a weekend visit to southern Illinois, Ida noticed a bearded young man in a baseball cap. She was impatiently waiting in line to buy milk, chicken, ground chuck, elbow macaroni, red beans, tomato sauce, and toiletries at the big-box store in Anna. Her mother was waiting at home, expecting homemade chili and a few groceries. The visit had been a great distraction from Ida's stalled investigation.

The young man's collar-length brown hair looked familiar. What really caught Ida's attention became visible only as he shoved his purchases over the scanner at the nearby self-checkout station. There was a small star tattooed on the back of his left hand. John Michael Thomas had the same tattoo, on the same hand. And the man checking out was also in his early twenties, about the same height and build as the missing Milwaukee man.

Could it be? Ida wondered. *How could it not be?*

She had to move quickly. As the young man walked to the exit toting a plastic bag in each hand, Ida stepped out of line, leaving her shopping cart, and headed for the door.

"I forgot my money," she told the clerk. "I'll be back later."

"Yeah?" the clerk said and turned to the customer who'd been in front of Ida. "Whatever. I'll have to get someone to put her stuff away. The meat will spoil before she gets back. *If* she gets back."

Ida didn't need to trot, but she walked rapidly. She saw the man put his bags into an SUV parked two rows distant from her Mustang. Her pulse quickened as she opened the door, settled behind the wheel, and started the engine. It took a few moments to approach the SUV, which was either black or dark navy blue in color. It was a late-model vehicle, a popular model but not especially noteworthy. More interesting was the license plate. It was a long way from home in Wisconsin.

It also was interesting that the SUV wasn't headed toward Interstate 57, which Ida had consistently used to begin her return trips to Wisconsin. Nor did the vehicle make a right-hand turn into the northbound lanes of US 51, the onetime main road between the Gulf of Mexico and northern Wisconsin.

The young man instead drove west on Highway 146, rolling slowly through the sleepy town of Jonesboro.

Ida quickly phoned her mother as she drove.

"Mama, it's me. I won't be making chili tonight. I'm following a man."

"Aren't you a little old for that? It sounds like something you did in high school."

"I can't explain it now. It's police business. You better fix yourself something to eat from the fridge."

"Ida! What's goin' on?"

"Bye, Mama."

Beyond Jonesboro, there were few westbound destinations in Illinois. The SUV was more likely headed into Cape Girardeau, Missouri, via the Bill Emerson Memorial Bridge crossing the Mississippi River.

Ida followed the SUV at a distance. She swung the Mustang north after the SUV turned toward the business district surrounding the football stadium of Southeast Missouri State University—home of the Redhawks, various signs said.

Ida followed as the SUV headed northwest from Cape Girardeau and into another county. Five miles later, she threaded the narrow streets of downtown Gillespie, a onetime factory town. The small downtown was surprisingly busy with Saturday-night traffic and pedestrians. Apparently the twenty-four thousand souls in Gillespie liked to party through the weekend.

The SUV pulled to the curb outside a building that housed storefronts for a tavern, pizza business, and "Head Quarters," a unisex hair salon that was still open. Ida parked on the opposite side of the street from the SUV and watched the young man carry his shopping bags to a locked door. He used a key to enter a foyer containing mailboxes and leading to a stairway. Ida saw nothing else after the door slammed shut.

Then she waited and watched the darkened windows above the storefronts. In a few minutes, the lights went on above the hair salon. After a few more minutes, a stylish young woman with an expensive hairstyle walked out of the salon to the nearby door and stairway. She used a key to enter, then apparently climbed to the same apartment as the young man. No other lights were switched on upstairs after her ascent.

Ida took a chance and pulled her Mustang away from the curb, briefly worrying the SUV would move before she returned. She circled a few blocks before parking in the vantage point she wanted. It was still on the opposite side of the street from the storefront businesses, but more distant and near the entrance to a parking lot. She watched both the SUV and the doorway to the upstairs apartments. An hour passed.

As Ida began to doubt her suspicions, the doorway opened, and the stylish woman emerged with the bearded man, who was now wearing a different baseball cap. They walked past the SUV and then crossed the street and entered an Italian restaurant.

Ida decided to take a closer look. It was a little risky, she knew, because the man might have noticed her in the big-box store. If she could see him, he could've seen her.

He paid no attention when Ida sat on the other side of the restaurant's lively bar. Nor did the woman. They both were engrossed in whatever the young man had summoned on the laptop computer he plopped on the bar. Ida sipped slowly at the Virgin Mary she'd ordered, nibbled the drink's requisite celery stalk, and pretended to be busily texting on her phone. They couldn't possibly have heard the click of her phone's camera as she captured mugs taken in profile and dead on.

Ida planned to finish her drink, which was going down slowly. It gave her time to watch another young man—also bearded but with many tattoos on both forearms—as he approached the young couple. The men shook hands enthusiastically, then walked together to the men's room. Ida knew women visited public restrooms together. There was safety in numbers. But men usually went solo.

The two men returned to the bar together, again shook hands, and smiled as they spoke quietly. Ida surreptitiously snapped another photo.

Tattoo Arms then departed. Ida ordered another drink and read news headlines on her phone. When another young man approached the couple, she snapped another photo. The men then went into the bathroom together for a short period of time. The newcomer then left. It happened four more times, with Ida getting a photo each time.

There were a few possible explanations for the bathroom treks. Bladder issues weren't likely, but it could be homosexual activity. The young man she'd followed from Anna might be turning tricks. It was possible. But Ida thought it more likely he was selling drugs, especially after the roll of bills he used to buy two more drinks appeared larger than it had been when he paid for the first round.

What she had wouldn't prove anything in court, not alone. But the photos and her observations might prompt the local police to take a closer look at the laptop-using young man who apparently lived above Head Quarters.

Ida left a five-dollar tip, then walked out of the restaurant. She walked to the door leading to the upstairs apartments' stairway. Luckily, it had been propped open. Ida used her phone's camera to get a picture of the mailboxes. She'd earlier written down the street address on the notebook in her purse, along with the license plate number on the SUV. She had photos too. It all constituted credible proof of residency.

She called the Howard County Sheriff's Department from her car, asking the dispatcher to check the registration on the SUV. The owner was listed as Caroline Connelly of Howard, Wisconsin. Ida thanked the dispatcher but said there was nothing more to be done in the matter. At least not by the dispatcher.

Ida suspected Caroline Connelly's vehicle was being used by her daughter, Madeline "Maddy" Connelly, and John Michael Thomas. But why were the two Wisconsin residents in Missouri? Drugs could be sold anywhere. Why go to the trouble of moving to another state? Where else had they been? For what reason?

Ida planned to find out. She began by calling the Gillespie County Sheriff's Department to report having witnessed drug sales in a downtown bar. She fully identified herself as a law enforcement officer.

"Let me connect you with our drug squad," the dispatcher said.

Ida pondered the unlikeliness of a drug unit in a small rural town. But not for long. Detective Ernie Carmelo answered on the second ring.

"Drug enforcement and prevention, Carmelo speaking," a husky voice said.

"I'm Detective Ida Mae Rollins from Howard County, Wisconsin. I'm with the sheriff's department in that county. I just witnessed drug sales. Thought you might be interested."

"Where? How long ago? Who?"

Ida was invited to the nearby office immediately after offering to share her snapshots, observations, and notes.

A few minutes were wasted as Ida explained why her weekend trip to southern Illinois had detoured into Gillespie. Then Carmelo looked at the pictures on her phone and took copious notes.

"I recognize the guy with the tattoos and the other locals," he said. "They're dopers. The couple is new in town, driving an SUV with out-of-state plates. We pay attention to new people. Gillespie ain't a tourism hot spot."

"They appear to be living above a hair salon, a place called—"

"Head Quarters. Like I said, they've been noticed."

Ida then texted her evidentiary photos to Carmelo, who also wanted her local contact numbers.

"Call me on the cell," Ida said. "You can also have my mama's number. I'm staying with her."

"I'm going to act on this tonight. You'll hear from someone tomorrow."

Ida was grateful for the twist of fate that had led her to cross paths with two persons of interest in a stalled murder probe.

"Thank you," she said to the stars while driving from Gillespie to Cobden.

Ida knew it was a blessing, but it wouldn't be her last one of the day. The next came in the form of a phone call as she crossed the Mississippi River.

"Scuse me, Detective," said a woman caller. "I understand you've been looking for my boy."

"It's possible. To whom am I speaking, ma'am?"

"My name is Wanda Elliott. Thad Elliott is my son. He dropped out of high school and moved north to work construction. He said the money was better up north. I live near Louisville."

"Kentucky?"

"Yes'm. Why are you askin' after Thad?"

"I've been looking for a man by that name. He had been living in Milwaukee, working construction for A. G. Meyer."

"That's the company that called me. They gave me your name and number, Detective."

"What do you mean? Why did they call you?"

"After you visited the jobsite, a supervisor checked company records. They have some back pay for Thad. I'm listed as next of kin on his personnel records. I told him to send me a check. I'll give the money to Thad when I see him."

"When will that be?"

"I have no idea. Why are you trying to find him? Is he in trouble with the law?"

"It's a long story, ma'am. Do you have time to talk?"

Ida carefully and sensitively explained she was investigating a murder. She said there was no strong indication the victim was Thad Elliott. But she'd learned from a former bookie that Thad owed money and had suddenly stopped reporting for work.

"It's probably nothing, ma'am. But I've got to check."

"Maybe I'm just gettin' jittery with age, but now I've got a real bad feeling, Detective."

"Like I said, it's probably nothing. I've got a question, though. Did Thad see a dentist regularly? When he was a boy?"

"Every year. He needed fillings, probably because of all the sodas he drank."

"Can you get the dentist to send dental records? Tell him it's for the police."

"Give me the address and phone number for the cops. I'll call the dentist first thing Monday morning."

●‥•

Ida called Sheriff Clark before going to bed in Cobden. She knew he was hungry for developments in the murder probe.

"I've learned a couple things today, sir."

"Stuff worth a midnight phone call?"

"Could be. I talked with a Kentucky woman. Her son went missing from a construction job in Milwaukee around the same time as our murder."

"Did you ask for dental records?"

"Of course. His physical description is similar to our dead guy. The guy's name is Thad Elliott."

"You said 'a couple things.' What else?"

"I think I've found John Michael Thomas."

"The guy we first thought was killed?"

"Yep. And he appears to be living with Maddy Connelly, the daughter of George and Caroline Connelly."

"In Cobden? How can that be?"

"They're across the river in Missouri. Some little town called Gillespie. I saw him buying groceries and tailed him. He was driving an SUV with Wisconsin plates."

"That's interesting," Clark said. "You've maybe found a guy we thought was murdered. Not only is he alive—maybe he's driving an SUV registered to one of our witnesses."

"That's right, sir. Caroline Connelly owns the SUV."

"She's the lady whose dogs dug up the head, right? And the young man we thought was killed is living with a young woman who probably is the daughter of the witness."

"That's it exactly."

"Connections with Howard County and proximity to a crime scene. Can't be just coincidence."

"I don't think so either, sir."

"What are you gonna do next?"

"Kind of got lucky on that, sir. I got their pictures on my phone's camera. They were in a bar and looked to be selling drugs. I talked with a guy from the sheriff's department down here. He leads the drug squad. I gave him the location and photos. It looks like our guy was selling drugs in the men's room near the bar."

"How does this connect with our murder?"

"It doesn't, not yet. But maybe they're connected to Thad Elliott."

"Sounds like a long shot, Ida. And we don't know if Elliott is our dead guy."

"We'll have the dental records Monday. And you never know what the drug squad might learn about Thomas and Connelly."

"Are they gonna make a bust?"

"One of their guys recognized the drug buyers in my photos. He's going to pick them up for possession and squeeze them for what they know about our couple. He thinks it'll be enough to get a search warrant for their apartment."

"Good work, Detective. Think they'll arrest our two?"

"Depends on what they find. I like our chances, though."

Ida got a call from the Gillespie County Sheriff's Department early Sunday afternoon. The apartment above Head Quarters had been raided just before dawn. A large quantity of Mexican heroin had been seized, along with drug paraphernalia, a hollowed-out dictionary containing $9,500 in cash, and a laptop computer thought to be filled with records of drug transactions as well as numerous emails and various online connections.

Arrested without incident were a woman who identified herself as Lynne Connelly and a man who said his name was Mike Johns. Each had legitimate-looking Wisconsin driver's licenses. Both immediately asked for lawyers and refused to answer any questions.

"They're jailed without bond, Detective Rollins," the Missouri officer said. "They'll get a bond hearing tomorrow, but if an amount is set, it'll be too much for those two. Odds are they'll be here for a long time."

"Any chance I can get a look at the two and have access to that computer?"

"We'll need you to testify about the drug sales you witnessed. You can look at the computer and make copies of anything you might need. Does that work for you?"

"Sure does. When can I get started?"

"You can start as soon as you get here. We never close. Call first, though. I'm done for the day."

"Who do I ask for?"

"Ask for the shift commander. You can look at the laptop in the detective bureau. It just can't leave the building."

CHAPTER 21
LUCKY ENCOUNTER

Ida had planned to spend time with her mother in Cobden, but it now looked like she'd do police work for a few days in nearby Gillespie, Missouri. Maybe a lot more. She'd need to witness a bond hearing for the drug suspects, inspect their confiscated laptop's contents, and work with the drug squad's information technology specialist to further search and copy digital data for her own sheriff's department.

She'd also need to meet the sheriff and deal with any complications that arose. It sounded time-consuming, to say the least. Ida called the Gillespie County Sheriff's Department to get some of the work done right away. She wanted to inspect the seized laptop and had plenty of time. Why not do the work on an otherwise lazy Sunday afternoon? Ida asked permission from the weekend shift commander, a position typically filled by an officer being groomed for promotion.

Ida hoped he wouldn't be the typical overly cautious type. He was. Their phone call quickly went sour. The shift commander insisted that Ida wait to inspect the laptop. He said it couldn't be done before Lynne Connelly and Mike Johns were charged in court with drug crimes.

"It's all about preserving the integrity of the chain of custody, ma'am," Lt. Bedford Stonewall icily said.

"My rank is detective, sir," Ida said just as icily. "Your drug squad guy said I could look at the laptop."

"He doesn't control weekend operations. That's *my* job."

128

Ida thought about calling the local sheriff for help but learned he was taking a long weekend in Branson, Missouri. She suspected it would be like talking with a vacationing Sheriff Clark, who spent his time off boozing and fishing. Ida decided it would be better to wait patiently than risk infuriating a drunken sheriff. She knew cops held grudges forever. She'd held some too.

Ida used the time to phone Martha Thomas. She expected to leave a message because Martha liked to garden in the afternoon. But Martha answered after the second ring.

"Thomas residence, Martha speaking."

"Hello, Mrs. Thomas. This is Ida Mae Rollins from the sheriff's department."

"Oh my God. What's happened?"

"I'm in Missouri. I found a guy who looks a lot like your son. He's with a woman who might be the daughter of two of our murder witnesses."

"He's OK?"

Martha hoped she didn't sound suspicious. Did her tone of voice betray that she already knew her son was alive?

"Of course," Martha added, "I guess you don't know if it's John Michael."

"No, I don't. Don't get too excited. This guy *looks* like your son, but I'm not sure it is."

"How did you find him?"

"They're both in jail on drug charges."

"What happened? What did John Michael do?"

"Again, I'm not sure it's your boy, Mrs. Thomas. I wish you were closer. I'd like you to get a look at him."

"I can get someone to take me to Missouri. Are you in Saint Louis?"

"Further south, a place called Gillespie. It's near Cape Girardeau."

"Where can I meet you?"

"I'll be at the county courthouse in Gillespie. It's on the town square— you can't miss it. There's a court hearing set for one thirty tomorrow afternoon. We can meet for lunch. Call me on my cell in the late morning, and we'll get together."

"OK, Detective. I'll see you tomorrow morning."

"It's Ida, remember?"

"That's right. And I'm still Martha, OK?

"OK."

Martha immediately worried that Ida had learned of her boy's occasional letters. She didn't have the heart to lie to Ida, but it wasn't really lying to withhold information. Or was it? She'd ask Reverend Driscoll on Sunday. Maybe he'd even agree to drive her to Gillespie. He might have some wisdom on the finer points of lying, she thought.

Martha also suspected that Ida wasn't telling her everything she knew or suspected. Why in the heck was Ida hundreds of miles from home on a Missouri drug case? Was John Michael also suspected of a crime in Wisconsin? What crime?

●ᵇ∙ ●

Ida left the air-conditioned comfort of her bedroom and looked in the barnyard for her mother. The afternoon sun was scorching, the air thick and sticky. She'd grown up without air-conditioning, but the day's draining humidity still caught her off guard. It was drier and cooler in Wisconsin.

Ida found her mother scattering corn to the chickens she kept for eggs. She was also chattering happily to her birds.

"That was a long phone call," her mother said. "Who were you talkin' to? I was starting to worry about you."

"It was police business. That drug case over in Gillespie. The call took longer than I expected. Can I stay here a few days?"

"I wish you'd *move* back here. Quit that dangerous job and keep me company. Why don't you come back home?"

"I like what I do, Mama. I'm careful. You worry too much."

"Someday you'll have kids to worry about too. You'll see what it's like, that is, if you ever have kids."

"Please, Mama. I ain't even married. I've got time, lots of it."

"Let's have some coffee."

After two cups of coffee and a muffin slathered with butter, Ida made another phone call. This time she talked to Wanda Elliott.

"Mrs. Elliott? This is Detective Ida Mae Rollins from the Howard County Sheriff's Department. Remember me?"

"No mother forgets when the police call about a child. What's happened? Have you found Thad?"

"Nothing new has happened. I'm just calling to remind you about sending Thad's dental records to my sheriff's department."

"I saw our dentist's assistant, Dixie, after church. She said the records could be sent on the computer. She'll do it in the morning."

"Email or fax?"

"Maybe. I don't know nothin' about computers."

"Dixie has the phone number of the Howard County Sheriff's Department?"

"Dixie has all those numbers you gave me. She's a sharp girl, with a college degree. I'll call and make sure it went OK."

"I'll call the department too. Sounds like it's under control."

"I'm sure worried about this, Detective. I've got a dark feeling that won't go away. D'ya believe in a mother's premonition?"

"Please call me Ida. And no, I don't believe in premonitions or dreams or haunting dreads. You shouldn't either. All I'm doing now is collecting facts."

"I hope you're right, Ida. And please call me Wanda. You sound like maybe you grew up 'round here."

"I was born and raised in southern Illinois. That's where I'm calling from. I'm home with Mama for a few days."

"That kinda gives me a good feeling. You're not just another fast-talkin' Yankee. They ruined our little town. Built a highway bypass to their big mall near the river."

"You must mean the Ohio River?"

"That's right. It's bigger and bluer than the Mississippi."

"Not as long, though. Or as muddy."

Wanda chuckled a little, then remembered why she was on the phone. It wasn't a laughing matter. Ida finally broke the resulting long pause.

"You sound like a nice lady, Wanda."

"You do too, Ida. Maybe next time you'll call me with good news. I hope so."

"Hang on to that hope."

Ida made one more call before ceasing police business until Monday morning. She called Deputy Scott Brooks in Howard. He was manning the detective bureau until Ida returned, because of both his aptitude for the work and his ambition to be promoted.

"Hey, Scotty. It's Ida."

"Ida who?" he laughed.

"You ain't got my desk yet. I need you on the lookout for a fax or email from the dental office of Clayton Price. It's in Kentucky. Or you might get a phone call from Dixie. She works for the dentist."

"Dental records, right? To compare with our John Doe?"

"That's right. The records are for Thad Elliott. He went missing around the same time we found the body parts. Don't mess this up, Scotty."

"Home cooking hasn't sweetened your disposition. You sound grumpy as hell. Is that good?"

"I'm doing great. Get those dental records to the medical examiner. Tell him it's from me on our John Doe."

"Chain of command is coroner to medical examiner. Shouldn't this go to Clyde Sternberg before Dr. John Azarian?"

"Do you want to be a detective or a desk sergeant? Get that stuff to Azarian. Get confirmation for it too. I need it for the file."

"Hey, there's something else."

"Yeah? What is it?"

"You got a fax from the cops in Iowa. They recovered a head and hand in the river near Mason City. I called and talked with a detective sergeant."

"That was smart. What did he tell you?"

"The officer was a female. Detective Sergeant Amber Kilquist. She sounded kind of like you, but nicer."

"Iowa people are friendly. What did she say? They find anything more that resembles our murder?"

"The head and hand were neatly severed, probably by someone with butchering experience. Some kids found the body parts snagged in brush under a bridge. They were playing on the riverbank. The water's real low because of the drought they're having."

"Sounds like our John Doe, doesn't it?"

"It sure does. But they've already got a tentative ID. Amber gave it to me after I agreed not to use it for anything other than our investigation. It's not for publication, obviously."

"Like I'd tell that asshole Calvin Krebs anything. If he walked in with his hair on fire, I wouldn't tell him."

"I'll get him on a DUI one of these days, Ida."

"Forget Krebs. Who got killed in Iowa?"

"Guy's name was Ronald Bernard Foster III. He lived in Hampton, Iowa, which isn't too terribly far from where his remains were found."

"What else?"

"Guy was wealthy and played the market, I guess. Married guy with a working wife. Was known to travel for golf and fishing when his wife was at work."

"Think he actually did much golfing or fishing?"

"I asked. Amber said she has her doubts. She says he preferred bedroom sports."

"How did that come up?"

"Amber said their department's IT guy was looking through Foster's laptop and desktop computers. I guess the guy was kinky—into threesomes with young men and women. Called himself Night Rider online."

"Amber said that?"

"Yes, ma'am. Foster used that name on websites for people wanting to hook up. It looks as though his last rendezvous was with a couple who said they were passing through Iowa."

"They have names?"

"Nicknames. She called herself Lady L; he was Master M."

"Well, I'll be dipped. Isn't that something?"

"Does that help you out some, Ida?"

"I don't want to jinx myself, but it just might. Call me right away if you hear anything more, Scotty. You're doing great."

"Just trying to do the job like you would."

⁂

Ida drove to Gillespie earlier than necessary. She wanted to see the city in daylight and get a parking place near the courthouse. Gillespie looked dingier than it did at night. But there was plenty of parking and green space near the courthouse, probably from dead businesses that had been bulldozed to the ground.

Ida walked through the courthouse and found the offices of the prosecutor and the clerk of courts as well as several courtrooms. She decided a cordial trip to the sheriff's department would be smart, considering the chilly reception to her phone call a day earlier. As she walked toward the department's office, Ida's cell phone vibrated and tweeted.

"Hi, Ida. It's Martha."

"Are you in Missouri? I'm at the courthouse, but there's a big restaurant right across the street. It's called the Jury Box. The folks here say it's cheap and good."

"I've got a sensitive stomach. What do they serve?"

"I'm told they serve everything. And they actually serve jurors during trials. They have a private room and do some catering too. You should be OK."

"I'll try it. When should I be there? Pastor Driscoll drove me here. Can he eat too?"

"Sure thing. Meet me near the front door at eleven thirty?"

"See you, Ida."

Ida stashed the cell phone in a pouch on her service belt, which also held handcuffs and a chemical spray for stopping dogs and subduing combatants. The phone holster was in the place where most officers carried a service handgun. Ida preferred a shoulder holster when she wore her badge and an official Howard County Sheriff's Department jacket, polo, and khakis—kept ready to wear on the hanger in her car. Ida knew she looked better in civilian clothes, which flattered her athletic figure, but she wanted to avoid any chauvinistic doubts about her law enforcement credentials.

She strode into the sheriff's office ready for anything—whether it was professional headbutting or overly friendly interest of the personal kind. The first officer she met was the abrasive Lt. Bedford Stonewall.

"Nice to talk with you again, Lieutenant," Ida said.

"Have we met before, Officer?"

"It's *Detective*, sir. I called you yesterday. I wanted to look at the computer that was seized with the drug arrests of Lynne Connelly and Michael Johns."

"Was that you? You sounded like a lawyer."

"I need to see your sheriff, Lieutenant. Could we do it now?"

"Yes, ma'am—er, I mean sir."

Sheriff Bingham "Bing" Thompson sat behind an immense wooden desk that was on a raised platform. He towered over Ida as he stood quickly, offered a pink and plump right hand, and boomed a hearty welcome.

"Y'all are from up north, I hear," Thompson said in a voice likely heard outdoors. "So, Detective, I hear you're going to help us with our druggies. Sure do appreciate your being a witness and having photos of the drug customers."

"Glad to do it, sir. Your drug squad leader also told me I could have a look at the computer they seized. It might help us solve a homicide."

"Well, I s'pose that'll be all right. Can you wait till we get the druggies charged in court? Later this afternoon?"

"Perfect, sir. Thank you very much."

"Are you free for lunch, Detective? Maybe we could swap stories? There's a place right across the street, the Jury Box."

"I'm meeting a friend there for lunch in less than an hour. I grew up across the river in Cobden."

"I thought you sounded like a down-home gal. Shucks, I'll have to get a rain check, I guess."

"Could we meet tomorrow for breakfast? Or maybe lunch."

"Let's make it for lunch tomorrow. I'd like to know how my guys treat you. We've got some ol' rednecks that need new attitudes."

After lunch, Ida led Martha and the pastor into the busy courtroom. She quickly noticed a familiar, if not friendly, face. The lean and mean Lt. Bedford Stonewall looked like the lead dog in a pack of court officers, most of them near retirement and obviously well fed.

Surprisingly, Stonewall nodded hello to Ida and presented what he probably considered a smile. Ida thought he was simply baring his teeth. Then he walked closer and beckoned Ida, Martha, and the pastor to the front bench—normally reserved for law enforcement use.

"I'm sorry we got off on the wrong foot, Detective," Stonewall said in a soft southern drawl. "I was out of line. I won't hassle you anymore."

"It's OK, Lieutenant. You were just doing your job. Tight security protects our work. I've forgotten about it. You should too."

Ida noticed that his eyes had brightened, and the standard law enforcement smile broadened. She wondered how he'd managed to keep such a great smile since his nose had been broken at least once. Maybe the perfect white teeth were implants? But it was obvious that the thick brown hair was his own, not the type issued by artificial-hair professionals. It sure wasn't a hilarious toupee—not that any weren't.

"I'm sorry, Detective, but I'm heading back to my post. I'm much obliged by your kindness," Stonewall said before spinning on his heel and walking into position between the judicial bench and the secure doorway used by prisoners.

As he walked away, Ida noticed his narrow waist and broad shoulders. She didn't know a single thing about Stonewall's earlier police assignments, but she'd have bet they included stints on the SWAT and tactical squads.

"Looks like he could be a brawler," Ida quietly said to Martha.

"We'll be safe, right?"

"I'd bet on it."

The judge took the bench just before one thirty as the felony prisoners were led into the courtroom. Mike Johns was in the middle of five prisoners secured together with belly chains. All wore orange jail uniforms, black jailhouse flip-flops, handcuffs, and ankle shackles. Lynne Connelly wore the mint-green jail uniform and pink flip-flops issued to females, but she was also handcuffed and shackled. A jail matron accompanied Lynne into the courtroom.

Martha gasped when Mike looked at the courtroom crowd. Even though his hair was much longer, and he wore a full beard, she immediately recognized her son. There was no mistaking his eyes.

"That's John Michael," she said to Ida. "Oh God, now what am I going to do?"

"You should listen carefully to the accusations. He's going to need a lawyer."

The rest of the hearing was a blur for Martha. She didn't fully understand the conditions of her son's $50,000 bond, the gravity of the charges, or the nature of his relationship with Lynne Connelly. She'd never seen or heard of her. Martha suspected her son had been led astray by Connelly, who also was jailed in lieu of a $50,000 bond.

Ida could see that the man identified as Michael Johns almost instantly recognized his mother. He had maintained a hardened blank expression as he shuffled to the table used by defense attorneys. But his eyes opened wide as he caught sight of his mother, then quickly sat next to the public defender who represented felony suspects who hadn't arranged for legal counsel.

To Martha, the stoop-shouldered slump reminded her of the little boy who'd broken a neighbor's window. John Michael had been no more than seven at the time and ashamed that he'd been throwing rocks at birds, despite numerous warnings. He'd hidden under a table, easily seen by Martha, and wept at the thought of punishment.

"I've got to talk to him," Martha said to Ida and Pastor Driscoll.

"They won't let you," Ida said. "You'll have to work with the jail to schedule a visit."

"But I'm his *mother*. Doesn't that matter?"

"I'm not sticking up for them, but the officers and jailers don't know you. He's got a different name than your boy, as far as they know. And even if you convince them you're really his mother, it won't matter. They'll follow their procedures."

Later in the afternoon, Ida learned that even with the apparent cooperation of the sheriff and Lieutenant Stonewall, the task of reviewing the contents of the seized laptop would be no simple matter. Ida would be given access to the machine only when it wasn't needed to build the Missouri drug-dealing case against the defendants. Investigators from the sheriff's department and the prosecutor's office had top priority.

Ida was told she could have access at seven o'clock in the evening and would be able to work until five the next morning. That didn't seem like something she'd be able to do without great strain and the risk of carelessness. She might miss things. She might fall asleep with her face on the keyboard. She'd need coffee—a lot of it.

Her work also included Martha, who, even with the help of Pastor Driscoll, seemed to be on the verge of a mental collapse. Ida had no professional obligation to the mother of a crime suspect, but they'd met when the mother thought her boy had been murdered. Ida was nothing if not compassionate.

Still, it was unsettling when her phone jangled at 7:20 p.m.

"This is Ida Mae Rollins."

"It's Martha. You sound tired, Ida."

"I've got a full night of work ahead of me. I can get it done, but it's gonna take a long time."

"I'm calling to see what you found out about the jail's visiting policy."

"Lieutenant Stonewall told me the jail allows visitors on Tuesday and Thursday afternoons. But they won't let you see your son unless he puts your name on his visitors list."

"How would he know to do that?"

"The lieutenant said the jail staff would explain it. Check with the jail in the morning. Don't phone. Go there in person."

"Thanks. I guess maybe this is goodbye. I'm trying to find a lawyer for John Michael. I've talked to a few already. They told me to say nothing to the police—any police."

"It's good advice, Martha. Someday when this is all over, you and I can talk again."

"I hope so, Ida."

"Me too. Bye-bye for now."

"So long."

CHAPTER 22
IN THE MORNING

It was almost six in the morning when Ida heard the unmistakable sounds of another police officer shuffling in the hallway near the evidence room. Metallic clatter from a big key ring, the hissing and popping of a police radio, and the squeak of rubber-soled shoes on a tile floor.

Ida braced herself for the arrival of some hillbilly-stormtrooper type as she looked away from the laptop and her notes. She peered at the locked door of the evidence room. A key scraped inside the lock, and the door opened wide. Ida was barely visible inside the half walls of the workstation she was assigned.

"You in here, Detective?" a male voice asked.

"Yes, sir, I am. I'm just wrapping up for the night. I'll be outta your way in a minute."

"Don't hurry, Detective. I'm not here on business. Thought maybe you'd like to have breakfast with me. My shift starts at seven."

Ida finally realized she was talking to Lieutenant Stonewall, who was dressed for a workout and carrying a gym bag filled with his police gear. He wore gray-colored fleece sweatpants, white basketball shoes, and a maroon-colored T-shirt decorated with a fanged canine and the block-lettered words SALUKI FOOTBALL.

"You going to the gym?" Ida asked.

"Just got done. I work out hard on Mondays, Wednesdays, and Fridays. Free weights and stair-climbing. Tuesdays and Thursdays I just run or swim or ride a bike. Cardio gets a good sweat going."

"How come you smell so minty fresh?"

"We've got indoor plumbing, ma'am. Even a hillbilly cop likes to shower."

"I didn't say you were a hillbilly."

"I could see it in your eyes, Yankee."

"Smile when you say that, mister. I was raised right by that football shirt's home. I almost went to Southern Illinois University."

"I would've remembered you. I've got a bachelor's degree in political science. Planned to be a lawyer. Still might do it someday. Mind if I sit down?"

"Suit yourself."

Stonewall pulled a chair next to Ida's desk, then settled into the cushion and chairback. His hazel eyes twinkled, perhaps with mischief, and the creases near his eyes and lips hinted at a smile. He took a deep breath and exhaled with a sigh.

"OK, Detective. Where did you grow up?"

"Cobden. I'm an Appleknocker. How did you get that football shirt?"

"Bought it online. I still have some of my training gear from SIU at home, though."

"Training?"

"Played football all through school. Linebacker. Led the team in tackles my junior and senior years."

"Ever try pro ball?"

"Too small and slow. All the scouts said so."

"Must have been disappointing."

"Not so much. Undersized guys get torn apart in the pro game. I've still got my health, even if my nose looks kinda funny."

"It's not so bad. Where did you say you were from?"

"I didn't. Grew up on a farm southeast of Murphysboro. My daddy bought gas in Cobden. My brothers and I would ride in the back of his pickup with our dogs."

"I'll bet my daddy would have liked you, Lieutenant."

"I wish you'd call me Stoney, Detective."

"Only if you call me Ida."

Ida walked into her mother's kitchen about an hour after her breakfast. She dropped her rucksack with police gear on the floor near the door, stretched lazily, and yawned.

"I'm gonna get a little sleep, Mama. I spent all night staring at computer files."

"Whatcha grinnin' about, little girl? What else happened at work?"

"I had breakfast with another cop. We were talking about our work and stuff."

"What's his name?"

"Why do you think it was a man?"

"I've seen that look before. Before things went bad between you and Bill."

"This guy's a lieutenant, Mama. Lieutenant Bedford Stonewall. But his friends call him Stoney."

"Does that include you?"

"For now it does. I'll tell you more later. I've got to get some sleep and then meet the sheriff for lunch back in Missouri. He agreed to meet me at one. Wake me up at noon, OK?"

"OK, Ida. Just be careful with Stoney. I don't wanna see you abused by another mean ol' cop."

"I won't let that happen, Mama."

◦ ∴ •

Sheriff Bing Thompson was a big man in more ways than one. When Ida walked into the Jury Box before one o'clock, she couldn't quickly spot the sheriff, though he was in a brightly lit corner booth. He was holding court with a small group in front of the booth—a deputy, three lawyer types, and a rumpled older man wearing a paisley tie over a frayed yellow shirt. The shirt appeared to be straining the buttons covering a bulging belly.

"I can't tell you everything you wanna know, Les," Bing said. "You gotta be patient. It'll all come out in court, at trial."

"Don't gimme that bull, Bing. I don't have a year before we go to press. There's hardly anything in the criminal complaint."

"It's all you're getting, big guy. The complaint is public record. The law doesn't require me to share any investigation details."

"I was just hoping you were feeling generous, Bing. Can I call you after lunch?"

"Fine. But you ain't gettin' anything more."

Ida moved into the semicircle fronting the booth and smiled at the sheriff. She'd showered, moussed her hair into its spiky best, and hung small hoop earrings from her lobes. She'd also used a little makeup and a touch of coral-colored lipstick. Ida had figured the sheriff would be more accommodating with a good-looking woman. With her police gear tucked inside a shoulder bag, Ida looked like a civilian. An attractive one, she hoped.

"Howdy, Detective," Bing drawled. "Boys, get on outta here. The lady and I have police business."

"You can call me Ida, sir. And by the way, your people have been really helpful."

"Mighty glad to hear it, Ida. Please call me Bing. Everyone else does."

"What do you recommend for lunch, Bing?"

"Eating somewhere else, maybe in downtown Cape. Since we're stuck here, the chopped steak ain't bad. Get it with hash browns and maybe some biscuits and gravy, like me."

"A girl's got to watch her figure more'n a man. Can I get chopped beef with a side salad and cottage cheese?"

"Ever seen cottage cheese being made? The smell alone would kill you."

"I like it, sir."

"Now, stop that 'sir' crap right now. If we're gonna be friends, it's Bing."

After they'd ordered and sipped some tepid but strong coffee, the sheriff got down to business.

"How're my men treatin' you? I hear Stoney gave you grief over the weekend. He gets a little gung-ho as shift commander. I figure he wants to be sheriff someday and gets all official when he's in charge."

"He didn't know me from the man on the moon. Probably thought I was a lawyer."

"Think he oughta apologize?"

"Already did. He helped me get set up in the evidence room, looking at the druggies' laptop. Surprised me this morning and took me to breakfast."

"Did he skip the gym?"

"He went early. Real early."

Bing considered what he'd just heard, stroked a meaty palm over what once had been a full head of hair, and squinted at Ida. Then he sipped the last of his coffee and waved at the waitress, who dashed to the table with a fresh-brewed pot.

Ida gulped the last of her java just before the waitress poured another cup, this time steaming, and then sipped carefully.

"Who was the older fella talking to you before?" Ida asked.

"Tubby guy in crummy clothes? That's Les Strock, a reporter for the *Gillespie Gazette*."

"I'll bet he's a pain in the ass."

"Les ain't a bad fella. Nosy as heck, but that's his job. He can't print what he ain't been told."

"Other sheriffs should remember that," Ida said, resisting the urge to tell Bing about her blabbermouth boss.

"Sometimes Les digs up stuff that helps my men. We read his stuff carefully. And away from his job, he's a good guy."

"How so?"

"We fish together down near Branson. He's got what he calls a deer shack, but it's a nice cabin. Has a little boat too."

"Ain't that risky for you? Socializing with a reporter?"

"I watch what I say. But ol' Les gets a loose tongue after a glass of whiskey. He's told me stuff that put a few bad guys in jail."

"On his say-so?"

"Course not. I get a detective to check out his tips. Most are just what he said."

"Wish my pain-in-the-butt reporter was like that. Calvin Krebs hates our sheriff and me too."

"Goofy name, ain't it?"

"The whole package is goofy. He's a pinhead with razor-cut hair. Way too aggressive to be any good."

"Squirt with a Napoleon complex?"

"You got it," Ida said.

"Your coffee need a little warmer-upper?" Bing asked as he waved to the waitress again.

As Ida nodded, her cup was being refilled.

"This coffee is much better," she said.

"Ain't half bad till it chills off."

As they finished their coffee, Bing asked why Ida was so far from Wisconsin. Her testimony in the drug case wouldn't be needed before the preliminary hearing. That was weeks away.

"Those two druggies are using aliases. Lynne Connelly is Madeline 'Maddy' Connelly of Howard, Wisconsin. Michael Johns is John Michael Thomas of Milwaukee."

"How do you know?"

"From records checks with my department on her. The guy's mother identified him when he came into the courtroom."

"You got a drug case against them?"

"No. They might be mixed up in a murder in my county."

"Figured it was something big," Bing finally said.

"I suspect they were involved in murders in Wisconsin and Iowa. Can't prove it yet."

"Iowa too?"

"Some kind of sexual perversion is involved, I think. I'm looking at the laptop to see if there's a positive link between your two druggies and the dead guys."

"They shoot 'em?"

"Stabbed repeatedly, then cut apart."

"Sexual thrill killing?"

"Maybe."

"Ida, if we dig up anything that helps, it's all yours."

"Thanks," she replied. "I'll share what I get too."

Bing banged his coffee cup down as the waitress plopped his heart-attack special on the table. "Guess I shouldn't eat both hash browns and biscuits 'n' gravy with chopped steak, but I love it."

"Enjoy it while you can, Bing. That's a meal my daddy would love."

"My kind of guy."

"He's dead," Ida said. "Heart attack. I try to eat healthy."

"None of us gets outta here alive, Ida. I wanna enjoy my food."

After finishing lunch and declining dessert, Bing settled back in his seat, waved for the bill, and stroked his chin. He was either contemplating or rubbing hash brown grease off his face.

As they walked out of the Jury Box, Ida considered both Bing and Sheriff Clark. Bing looked like a rube; an old country boy who'd somehow made it big. His appearance wasn't as professional as Clark's, but Ida suspected he knew more about police work than her sheriff. A lot more.

She now realized it had been silly to think that maybe he was inviting her to a meal as a prelude to romance. She couldn't picture Bing as having ever been romantic, though she did notice the wedding band on his massive hand. Ida wondered what kind of woman would tolerate both police work and getaway weekends for fishing.

Bing broke the silence as they strolled into the courthouse.

"Anyone else helping you with your investigation?" he asked.

"I'm alone. Lieutenant Stonewall's been helpful, though. I'm searching through a laptop, basically."

"Not my kind of thing. I'm old school. But Stoney's got some computer ability, and our IT officer is one of the best in Missouri. He helps the Saint Louis PD regular."

"You mean Freddie Sherman?"

"That's the guy. Doesn't look like the sharpest knife in the drawer, but he's the best."

"I wasn't even sure he was a cop. No uniform, and I didn't see a badge either."

"He's a detective lieutenant. I gave him that rank to keep him. Now I can pay him what he's worth. With his overtime, he makes more than me! But he's worth it."

Ida couldn't imagine her sheriff allowing anyone to make more money than he did.

"Who does the detective lieutenant oversee?" Ida asked. "The whole bureau?"

"He doesn't oversee anyone. That rank is s'posed to supervise, but Freddie ain't got people skills."

"I kinda noticed that."

"Was he insulting? Hit on you?"

"Nothing like that. He mumbled and never looked me in the eye. I told him what I was looking for, and he just said something under his breath, sighed, and left me on my own."

"That set you back?"

"Not really. I know my way around computers. He's meeting me tonight at seven. Said he'd have some ideas for me."

"Lemme know if it doesn't help," Bing said.

• ᵕ ⁚ •

Ida went inside the courthouse after lunch. She watched the last of the felony first appearances and then waited for any bond hearings that weren't posted on the court calendar. Most judges tackled last-minute stuff as it developed. The court calendar posted near the entrance wasn't a complete guide to what would happen inside.

"State of Missouri versus Michael Johns," a bailiff announced as the security door swung open. Lieutenant Stonewall escorted the shackled, chained, and cuffed prisoner into the courtroom. At the same time, the public door opened for Martha Thomas and a well-dressed man carrying a leather attaché case.

Ida immediately recognized but otherwise ignored the combatant defense attorney. Instead, she nodded a "hello" to Martha. She didn't nod back. Instead, she stared intently at the back of her son's head—an unkempt, uncombed mass of overgrown hair.

"If it pleases the court, I've been retained to represent Michael Johns for the purposes of a bond hearing. I'm attorney Peter Fitzpatrick of Milwaukee."

"Are you licensed to practice law in Missouri, sir?" Judge Carleton Callow asked.

"Definitely, Your Honor. I'm a graduate of the University of Iowa College of Law. I'm licensed to practice in that state, Missouri, and Wisconsin."

"Very well, counselor. Please proceed."

Forty minutes later, after establishing his client's genuine identity and opening the door to a new charge of obstruction, Fitzpatrick negotiated a property bond. It allowed Martha Thomas to post her home for her son's release. But as a condition of the bond, he would be prohibited from leaving Missouri, required to undergo random and frequent drug and alcohol screenings, and ordered to appear for all court hearings.

He smiled and gave his mother a thumbs-up as Lieutenant Stonewall led him back to jail.

As Martha left the courtroom, Ida approached and said, "Good luck, Martha."

"Thank you," she replied with a tight smile.

Nothing more was said until Martha and her lawyer were in the hallway, a wide corridor with stone flooring, marble pillars, and limestone-block walls. Oil paintings of judges hung on the walls.

"What was *that* all about?" Fitzpatrick finally asked.

"She's a detective with the Howard County Sheriff's Department. She was kind to me when I thought John Michael had been murdered."

"Stay away from her. She and that dumbass sheriff, Peter Clark, squeezed one of my clients like you wouldn't believe. Anything you say will get twisted to hurt your son."

"I understand. Can I still say hello?"

"Nothing more than that. Not even about the weather. If you can't keep quiet, you'll need another lawyer."

Ida walked out of the courthouse at four thirty. The shadows grew longer from the trees bordering the lawn and adjacent parking lot. It was a warm day, and the shade felt good. Ida thought about the heat in Wisconsin, which at times felt uncomfortable but was nothing compared to the heat and humidity of Missouri and southern Illinois.

"Hey, Ida!" a voice called from behind.

It was Lieutenant Stonewall, in full uniform, jogging to catch her on the sidewalk. He was carrying his gym bag too, and despite the sweltering conditions, he wasn't breathing rapidly or heavily perspiring.

"Stoney! What's up?"

"Freddie Sherman said he's got some ideas for you. Wants you to meet him in the evidence room at six."

"I guess that'll be OK. I don't have enough time to see Mama even if I wait till seven."

"Wanna have a snack at my place? It's close enough to walk."

Ida wondered what Stoney had in mind. She was attracted to him and sensed the feeling was mutual. And she was both pleased and worried about looking her best, as she did today. Did Stoney think she was open to seduction?

"I guess a snack would be OK. A walk would do me some good too. I've been sitting all day."

It took several minutes to walk the three blocks to Stoney's neighborhood. It was a tree-lined street, deep in the shade, with flower beds and green lawns surrounding the Victorian-era homes.

"Well, this is the place," Stoney said as he opened the gate on a wrought iron fence. The walk led to a large white home with green shutters and a front porch that spanned the width of the wood-sided structure.

Three mailboxes were posted near the front door, the one on top labeled "Stonewall."

Stoney opened the door with a quick twist of his key and then led Ida to a carpeted stairway. "I've got the whole second floor," he said. "But it's not as big as you might think."

He used another key to unlock a dead bolt on the apartment door. It looked very secure, as did the frame. Ida suspected the place was basically a gun safe with a kitchen table, futon, and Saluki football posters on the walls. She was in for a surprise.

"Stoney, this place is beautiful," she said after taking a quick look at the polished wood flooring, Oriental rugs, and framed watercolors in the living room. There was a TV, too, and an old-school component stereo atop a record cabinet packed with vintage vinyl LPs.

"I dig classic rock," Stoney said. "Pick something out, and I'll play it. Or we can just chill and talk. I'll get us some cheese and crackers."

"Let's just talk," Ida said. "Where'd you get the paintings?"

"I go to art fairs. Couple good ones every year in Saint Louis."

"They look nice on your walls. How long have you been living here?"

"Since I joined the department," Stoney said from the kitchen. "I dropped out of law school and looked for police work. My uncle knew Sheriff Bing and told him about me."

"Didn't you go to a police academy?"

"Nope. Sheriff Bing interviewed me. A few weeks later, he offered me a job. I was teamed up with a patrol officer for six months. Then they took the training wheels off."

Ida laughed as she walked into the kitchen. She'd imagined a clutter-strewn hovel with Stoney preparing a feast of spray-can cheese and grocery store crackers—round ones from a red box.

Another surprise was waiting. The kitchen was immaculate, aside from several cracker boxes and the chunks of cheese Stoney was slicing on a cutting board. It looked like she'd be savoring brie, gouda, blue, and swiss cheese on a sampling of gourmet crackers.

"Don't tell me you cook too?" Ida said as she looked at the neat glass-fronted cupboards and inspected a wine rack filled with six bottles—four red and two white. All with French labels.

"Did you buy this stuff in Gillespie?"

Stoney laughed as he arranged the crackers and cheese on serving china.

"I shop in Cape Girardeau," he said. "They've got just about everything you'd find in Saint Louis.

"Want some sweet tea, Ida? I'd offer wine, but you're on duty. I've got an assignment tonight too. Our tactical unit has something planned. I'll need my wits about me."

"Tea would be great. Don't get yourself hurt tonight."

"I'll try not to. Hey, do you think maybe we could have a real date some night before you go back to Wisconsin?"

"That's a definite maybe, Stoney."

"Just maybe?"

"OK, you got me. That's a big ten-four. Maybe tomorrow or the next day. It all depends on what Detective Lieutenant Sherman can do for me."

"Don't worry about Freddie. He's the best."

CHAPTER 23
DIGGING DEEP

The walk from Stoney's home to the sheriff's department went quickly. Ida felt a nearly forgotten spring in her step. And she couldn't easily remember a time when the birds had sung so beautifully. Was it when she and Bill were newlyweds? Had it been that long ago?

"Lovely evening, isn't it?" Ida said to a young woman pushing two babies in a side-by-side stroller. "They're twins, aren't they?"

"Yes they are. Janice and Judy."

"How can you tell them apart?" Ida said before getting self-conscious about the grin she wore. She hated the wrinkles a smile put on her face.

"I shouldn't say this, but sometimes I can't tell my girls apart. Isn't that horrible? My name is Hollis, Hollis Hathaway. You live around here?"

"I'm Ida. Just Ida. And I'm visiting from Wisconsin."

"Came here to warm up?"

"Something like that. Nice meeting you. I've got to run."

"Bye-bye. Enjoy your stay in Missouri."

Hollis and the babies rounded the corner and were out of view as Ida neared the courthouse and sheriff's department.

Ida used the keypad to open the department's secure door. She punched in the four digits she'd been given by Stoney, then followed the "To Detectives" signage painted on walls above red arrows pointing the way.

"Detective Lieutenant Sherman in here?" she asked a hulking Black man wearing a shoulder holster and shuffling through papers on a desk. A placard identified the big guy as Investigator Larry Foster.

"Sure thing, ma'am. Mind if I tell him who you are and how you got in here?"

"Stoney gave me the code for the day. I'm Detective Ida Mae Rollins from the Howard County Sheriff's Department in Wisconsin."

"*Wisconsin*? I almost froze to death one summer in Madison. My daddy had me stay with him for the summers after he left Mama. I'll get Freddie for you, Detective."

A few minutes later, Freddie arrived, dressed in camouflage shorts and a golf shirt opened from the collar deep into his hairless chest. A red baseball cap worn backward and filthy high-top tennis shoes completed his look. If he had a gun and badge on him, Ida couldn't see either.

"Hello, Detective," Freddie said, "I guess you're looking for me."

"Just call me Ida, please."

"Hey, whatever. Bing says maybe you need some IT help."

"You've got a laptop seized in a drug case. The druggies might be connected to killings in Wisconsin and Iowa. Maybe you can find digital links from the dead guys to your druggies."

"Bing told me all that. Got any names for me?"

Ida gave him the real names of the Missouri drug suspects, Madeline "Maddy" Connelly and John Michael Thomas, both of Wisconsin and known online as Lady L and Master M, respectively. Ida said they might have used other screen names, too. Then she explained that the dead man in Iowa was Ronald Bernard Foster III, known online as Night Rider.

She also provided the full identification of Thad Elliott, a Kentucky native who was missing and may have been killed in Howard County. Had there been any online communications with the suspects and Elliott to arrange threesome action? Kinky stuff?

"I started looking through the emails last night and read until I was dizzy," Ida said. "Didn't see much I could use."

"Let me have a look," Freddie said. "Whose laptop is this?"

"It belongs to the male suspect booked under the name Michael Johns. That's an alias. Connelly is calling herself Lynne, but it's really Madeline."

"Sex perverts use fake names. They hide stuff too."

"The male suspect also had a laptop at his mother's home in Milwaukee. Nothing on that one. I didn't see anything, and neither did the crime lab."

"Sonny boy kept secrets from his mom," Freddie said.

They walked to the workstation Ida had used the previous night. Freddie sat at the desk chair backward, hanging his arms over the chair back and flicking his long fingers around the keyboard. He resembled a pianist. Ida couldn't recognize anything he typed, but a maze of windows opened at Freddie's command. He arranged the windows neatly as tiles, then studied each as if going through flash cards. Very occasionally, seemingly as an afterthought, he jotted terse notes.

One hour later, Ida had what she was looking for. Freddie had found multiple communications between the suspected killers, the dead Iowa man, and the missing Kentucky native. There was a record of threesome dates being arranged and finalized. The get-together plans promised satisfying male-male action, as well as heterosexual relations.

"This is amazing, Freddie. How did you do it?"

"If I told you, I'd have to kill you," he said and grinned at a wisecrack used by cops everywhere. Ida had used it herself.

"Can you make me a copy of all this?" she asked. "I'll eventually need the laptop too, but this will give me enough to get started."

"Want it on a CD or a memory stick?"

"One of each should do it. Can you have it by the end of the week?"

"You can take it with you tonight. I'll copy my notes and give you those too."

For the Missouri prisoner booked on drug charges as Lynne Connelly, the world turned upside down after her codefendant was released on bond. She'd learned from her public defender that her codefendant's identity, John Michael Thomas, came out when his mother used her home to post a property bond.

Madeline "Maddy" Connelly had remained in jail, unhappy and angry. She'd already admitted her real name to her lawyer. She knew it was only a matter of time until her true identity surfaced and a charge of obstructing justice was piled on top of her existing charges.

"I've gotta get out of here!" she said to her state-paid lawyer, John Richards.

"You don't have money hidden somewhere, do you?" Richards asked. "Don't you have family somewhere? Maybe they can get you out."

"My mother is in Wisconsin. My dad's working as a carpenter in Memphis. His address and cell number are in my wallet, which the jail seized and locked up. My mom was really angry the last time we talked. She's always been tough on me."

"She's still your mother. What if I called on your behalf?"

Maddy thought quietly, then ran her fingers through a still-stylish hairstyle. "This mop should have been cut and colored last week," she said. "Get me outta here!"

"Give me the number, and I'll call. I'll put you in the best-possible light. I'll bet she comes through for you."

"What if she doesn't?"

"You won't be any worse off than you are now."

"Go ahead. Call the bitch," Maddy snarled.

•⸴∶ •

Caroline Connelly had thought little about Maddy since their last phone call, a stormy shouting match that ended only when Caroline hung up. She'd instead focused on George, who had always been a good provider and was especially valuable in that role now that he was working steadily and earning as much overtime as possible. They talked on the phone every night, after which, she knew, George would turn off the light and immediately go to sleep.

Sexually, George had never been a perfect fit with Caroline. He wasn't impressively endowed, and he sought sex only a few times a year. Caroline had more demanding physical needs, which she'd found a way to meet. His name was Jerry Maldonado.

They'd met at the fitness center in Howard, caught each other's eye and flirted openly for months. He was only twenty-six and still had the chiseled physique of a top athlete.

They finally ended up in his bed, a long and sweaty session that filled Caroline's needs. She was visually turned on by the contrast of Jerry's darkness against her fair skin. And she was physically rewarded by his endowment and endurance.

Caroline's fitness routine no longer was limited to the gym. She still loved George, but she *needed* Jerry.

The phone rang as Caroline got ready to visit Jerry.

It's probably Becky, she thought. *It'll be OK to let the call go into voice mail.*

But she took a final look at her cell as she climbed into the pickup truck she'd taken in trade from Maddy.

"Missouri Public Defender" had placed the call, according to the phone's listing for Recents. She checked the resulting voice mail, worried that it might somehow be connected to George. Memphis wasn't too far removed from the Missouri Bootheel, and George sometimes made long drives for supplies on workdays.

"Mrs. Connelly, my name is John Richards. I'm a public defender in Missouri. Your daughter asked me to call you. It's an urgent matter. Please call me."

Caroline went back into the house and grabbed a notepad and pen to write the number Richards left in his voice mail. It was a slightly different number from the one recorded by her phone. She figured it was a direct line to a desk phone and placed the call.

"This is John Richards."

"I'm returning your call, Mr. Richards. This is Caroline Connelly. Has something happened to my daughter? An accident? Is she hurt?"

"She appears to be in good health," Richards said. "But she's in trouble with the law, jailed in lieu of bond."

"In loo? What's that mean?"

"She needs money to get out of jail. Let me describe the situation, right from the start. Have you got fifteen or twenty minutes? Were you headed out or something?"

"It'll have to wait. What did Maddy do?"

"She's *accused* of dealing drugs. She'll get charged with obstruction, too, when the cops learn she used an alias and fake IDs."

Caroline felt her pulse race as she considered what she'd just heard. Her face felt hot, and a trickle of perspiration dripped from her hairline onto her nose. Already she was angry with Maddy.

"Mrs. Connelly? You still there?"

"Yes, sir. Why are you calling me? My daughter and I are on the outs."

"Look—she's in the county jail in Gillespie, Missouri, on a fifty-thousand-dollar bond."

"That's not my problem," Caroline said. "And I don't have fifty thousand."

"You probably could post a property bond. Do you own a home?"

"My husband and I do."

"Maybe I should talk to him. Is he available?"

"I don't know where he is," Caroline said. "As far as I'm concerned, that girl can rot in jail. She's already looted our savings account."

"Listen—think it over. I'll call you back tomorrow after you have a chance to cool off. Anything you want to tell her?"

"Yeah, there sure is," Caroline sputtered. "Tell her to go to hell."

John Richards was surprised by Maddy's reaction to the blunt message from her mother. She didn't blow up angrily or weep miserably, though he was prepared for either. Instead, Maddy acted as though it was nothing more than a temporary setback.

"You can try my dad next," she said calmly.

It was the type of reaction he'd often seen with career criminals, most of them self-centered sociopaths.

"But you don't know where he is. Your mother said she didn't either."

"That's a lie. That bitch knows everything about my dad. She's cheating on him with some stud she met in the gym. She has to know his whereabouts at all times to avoid getting caught."

"That's more information than I need, Miss Connelly."

"Maybe call that dickhead who lives near my parents. He runs a diner close to Milwaukee. Place is called Eddie's. Catchy name, huh?"

"Is his name Eddie?"

"Hey, you're sharp, counselor. You get that from law school? Just naturally quick?"

"Very funny, miss. Let me remind you I'm your only shot at getting out of jail."

"Once I do, you're history. My dad'll get me a real lawyer."

"Any idea what Eddie's last name is?"

"Norwood. He's got a nice wife, named Becky. But she's a good friend with my mom. Don't call her. She won't say anything until she checks it with my mom."

"Eddie will?"

"He's too busy cooking and running the diner's cash register to do much thinkin'. Tell him you can't get hold of my mom and need to call my dad about me. Say it's urgent."

"He's got your dad's cell number?"

"They drink beer and barbecue together. He's got my dad's number."

As the attorney visit ended, Maddy was led from the private conference room by a jail matron. She looked over her shoulder to make a last comment to Richards.

"Call Eddie early in the morning. At the diner. They're super busy, and he'll give you the number so he can get back to work."

CHAPTER 24
ONE PHONE CALL

There are no dull moments at Eddie's. From the time I unlock the door to the moment I walk out late in the afternoon, the diner is busy with never-ending tasks. That's good for a guy like me. The less idle time I have, the better.

First there's the frenzy of getting ready to open—brewing coffee by the gallon, moving eggs, bacon, ham, potatoes, and other fixings to the keep-ready bins near the grill. Then there's the final wipe of the counter, a check to ensure the washrooms are tidy and supplied with paper towels and toilet paper, lowering the blinds to keep glaring sunlight out of my eyes, and making sure all hands are on deck.

Just when it seems we'll never be ready for business, I look at Anita, and she gives me a thumbs-up gesture. It's time to post the Open sign and unlock the door. A few breakfast customers have been waiting patiently, others puffing a final cigarette in a car before entering the smoke-free diner. Suddenly the place is alive with chatter, laughter, and clattering plates. It's a blessing to have the bacon spattering noisily and the hash browns sizzling on the grill. The cooking din makes it impossible for me to be distracted by conversations—especially those pertaining to sports. I still miss booking games, probably always will.

Things were moving nicely as nine o'clock loomed into sight. I heard the telephone ring, an old-school clanging that might wake the recently deceased. Anita grabbed the call while serving a ham-and-eggs platter to a workman in coveralls.

"Call for you, Ed! I've got the grill."

"This is Ed Norwood," I said to the caller. "Can I help you?"

"Sorry to interrupt you, Mr. Norwood. This is attorney John Richards calling from Missouri. Have you got a cell number for George Connelly?"

"Can't you just call his home? His wife has the number."

"I don't get an answer on her landline or cell. This is urgent. About his daughter."

I gave him the number and went back to work. I didn't give it another thought until I started driving home from work. Then I put it out of my mind. Why would George object to receiving an urgent call?

When I got home, Muffin failed to meet me at the door—an endearing doglike habit. Becky was nowhere to be seen either, nor did she respond to my customary "Hey, Beck, I'm home."

She was upstairs, where I'd expected she was using the computer. Instead, I found her sitting in the rocking chair petting Muffin, who appeared unconscious and blissful on Becky's lap. A normal feline state.

Becky looked at me with a frown. "I didn't hear you until you started up the stairs."

"Everything OK? You look unhappy."

"I just got home from Caroline's. She's so angry with you I don't know if we're still friends."

"Me? What about?" I asked, though a sinking feeling in my gut suggested a link to the lawyer's phone call.

"What were you thinking? How could you give a lawyer George's phone number?"

"He said it was about Maddy—that it was urgent and he couldn't reach Caroline."

"That's a lie. Caroline said she was home all day and neither phone rang. Until George called, that is."

"Oh God …"

"George is driving home from Memphis. It might cost him the best job he's had in years. And it's all because of you!"

"I didn't mean any harm, Beck. Why is he coming home?"

"Maddy got arrested for selling drugs. She's in jail in Missouri. The judge set a fifty-thousand-dollar bond."

"That's a lot of money."

"It sure is. It's more than George and Caroline have in savings. Maddy pretty much cleaned them out, Caroline said."

"What are they going to do?"

"George is going to use their home and post a property bond. He can't stand the thought of his little girl sitting in jail, Caroline said."

"She's a grown woman. George should slow down and think about it."

"That's what Caroline said. The lawyer called her a day earlier and asked about posting bond, she said. I guess she turned him down."

"What a mess. I feel terrible."

"I would too. But that lawyer eventually would have found George without your help. Maddy is a clever girl. I'll bet it was her who gave the lawyer the diner's number."

"I was wondering why he called *me*. I should have asked, but it was during the breakfast rush. I just wanted to get off the phone."

CHAPTER 25
FAMILY BUSINESS

It was nearly dawn when George approached the far southern suburbs of Chicago. He'd battled sleep for hours but kept gulping coffee and heading north on Interstate 57. He bought an extra-large cup every time he found an exit with an all-night eatery. But even coffee isn't enough when sleep insists. George finally stopped for sleep in a truck stop near Interstate 80. He slumped nearly to the floor of his pickup, wishing such vehicles were still made with bench seats.

Sunlight woke George after a few hours. He left his windows barely open, locked the truck, and walked into the restaurant. He used the washroom, a clean and bright facility with full showers needed by long-distance truckers. George instead washed his face and upper body in a sink, then brushed his teeth and combed his hair. It looked grayer than ever in the harsh light, he noticed, and it was time for a haircut.

After eating a short stack of pancakes with sausages, George bought a large take-out coffee and walked back to the truck. He called Caroline after getting into the pickup and pulling his phone off the charger.

"George! Where are you?" Caroline said sleepily. She obviously hadn't left the bed, though it was nearly nine.

"I'm still trying to figure out what happened to all our money. Run that by me again, will you?"

"Let's talk when you get here. I don't want you driving when you're upset."

"I ain't upset. Just worried."

"Me too, George."

"I'll be there around noon. Try to get out of bed, OK?"

Caroline shooed the dogs outdoors, cleaned and put away the kitchen clutter, and then darted around the house with a feather duster and vacuum cleaner. The place was a showpiece of domesticity by noon. Caroline finished the transformation by defrosting a pound of ground hamburger in the microwave and forming four large patties that would be ready for grilling when George arrived. Chopped onion and green pepper were mixed into the hamburger as she formed the patties.

She knew George would be hungry after hours behind the wheel and the scent of sizzling burgers would be a useful distraction. Caroline knew exactly what she'd tell George—and what she'd avoid. She planned to lay much of the blame on the financial carelessness of their credit union, hoping to prevent George from pursuing the $10,000 check she'd written and mailed to Maddy.

The plan worked perfectly. By the time George had admired the condition of the house, followed his nose into the kitchen, and then gobbled a pair of freshly grilled burgers, his mood was pliable, if not wholly pleasant.

"So how much are we out? What's the bottom line?"

"We've still got some money left, George. Maddy didn't get all of it."

"How much did she get? Just tell me."

"I'm afraid to say. You'll blame me for not watching our account carefully."

"Tell me."

"It was fifteen thousand."

"Jesus Christ! That's more than half our savings! Who did you say worked the electronic transfer to Maddy?"

"Harriet Needham. I've already talked to her about it. She started crying when I told her what had happened. Harriet said she thought she was talking to me. She said she was sorry."

"Sorry? Sorry? We ought to sue her and get the money back. We can get her wages garnished, I'll bet."

"That *might* work. Right now we've got to think about what to do with Maddy."

"There's nothing to think about. We're gonna get her out of jail. No daughter of mine is going to prison. She's probably taking the fall for someone else."

Caroline didn't like the idea of using their home to post a property bond for Maddy's release, but she agreed to get the needed paperwork from their safe-deposit box. She wasn't looking forward to seeing Harriet, but it was a much better plan than allowing George to pay a visit. She couldn't allow Harriet to provide George with her own version of what had happened to their savings, especially not about the big check Caroline had willingly mailed to Maddy.

She couldn't let George catch her in a lie. He wasn't a sophisticated or well-educated man, but he had common sense and a good understanding of people. She remembered something he'd mentioned to Ed when they talked about the way the cops were investigating the murder near their homes.

"What kinds of things do the cops check?"

"That Detective Ida keeps asking me the same questions," Ed said.

"Well, you're a person of interest. At least according to Calvin Krebs."

"Fuck Krebs. Half his readers probably think I'm a killer, maybe more."

"They're probably comparing your answers. If you give a new answer to an old question, they get suspicious."

"Huh?"

"My daddy said it like this: 'Truth doesn't change. Lies are hard to remember.'"

"I guess you're right."

"There's another thing he said too."

"What's that, George?"

"When ya catch someone in a lie, you can bet it's not the first one they ever told. And it won't be their last."

Caroline shivered as she recalled those words.

She didn't want George to start asking questions about her health club visits. It would take just a quick stop at the check-in desk to learn Caroline Connelly's workouts were no more than sporadic.

Caroline also didn't want George going to Missouri without her. There was no telling what Maddy might tell her father if she wasn't there to supervise.

It took less than fifteen minutes at the credit union. Harriet was startled to see Caroline, who'd phoned and told her off in no uncertain terms after getting scammed by Maddy. It wasn't easy, but Harriet still forced a smile and spoke pleasantly.

"Can I help you, Caroline?"

"Just need to get into our safe-deposit box. Won't take me more than a few minutes."

"How've you and George been? I've thought of you."

"We're OK, I guess. He's home now, and we're planning to hit the road for a few days."

"Sounds fun. Where are you going?"

"Missouri."

"I hear Branson is fun."

"That's what I hear too."

Caroline pulled the paperwork from the box and stuffed it into her shoulder bag, a big black leather satchel once used primarily for workout gear. More recently, it was used to carry lingerie, makeup, and heels for her bedroom exercises with Jerry. He liked a high-glamor look, and Caroline happily obliged.

She thought about taking the entire contents of the box in her bag. She and George would be taking their financial business elsewhere, but that was a long-term security action. For the near future, it would be safe to leave the stock certificates and essential papers in the box. Safer than carrying the stuff while driving to Missouri.

"Got what I needed, Harriet," Caroline said as she returned the credit union's key and signed a time-of-entry-and-departure registry. "Hey, I should have asked earlier. Have you talked to that husband of mine lately?"

"George? I can't even remember when we last talked. It's been maybe ten years since I've seen him. Why do you ask?"

"I just want to make sure we're not both trying to do the same thing."

"Makes sense to me. Sometimes a married couple will bump into each other right here. Happens around Christmas, usually."

"That's funny. Hey, I've gotta run. See you next week, maybe."

"I hope so." Though it probably would be a visit to sever all Connelly ties with the credit union. Probably a visit with Harriet's boss, who'd be asked to fire her.

As Caroline drove away from the credit union, she noticed the Check Engine light glowing on the dashboard of the old pickup truck. She decided to stop for a quick visit with Becky. It would give her a chance to apologize for blowing up about Ed's telephone mistake, which had been an innocent screwup. It also would allow the engine to cool, perhaps resetting the warning light.

More importantly, it would give Caroline a chance to ask a favor.

Becky was sitting in the glider on her front porch when Caroline pulled into the driveway. She smiled and waved a friendly hello as Caroline approached, also smiling but slowly shaking her head.

"Becky, I'm such a fool," she said. "You're about the best friend I could have, and I blew my top over nothing."

"It's OK. I went off on Ed too."

"Ed was just trying to help. He thought it was urgent."

"We're still friends, then?"

"Always."

"Want some lemonade? Just made it fresh with real lemons."

"Sounds great. Can I have it with ice and a shot of vodka?"

"Sure thing! I'll make mine that way too."

After a few minutes of sipping and chatting about nothing, Caroline took a deep breath and opened up.

"George wants to get Maddy out of jail. The lawyer said a property bond probably could be posted as bond, but the judge has the final say."

"You're willing to risk your home?"

"I'm dead set against it. But George is crazy about that girl. Thinks she can do no wrong."

"She's a grown woman, not a girl."

"I know. But George is bullheaded about this. We're driving to Missouri at the crack of dawn. Can you let our dogs out and feed 'em until we get back? It's a lot to ask, 'specially since I had such a big mouth yesterday."

"It's no problem, Caroline. But I'll need a key. I'll bring in the mail too. And make sure the dogs are locked inside the house at night."

"There's a key under the ceramic frog in the garden next to my kitchen door."

"The cute one with the big smile?"

"Yep. That's my little froggy."

"How do I get the dogs back in the house?"

"Nothin' to it. They know when it's seven o'clock. All you gotta do is open the kitchen door and pour kibble into their bowls and fill the water dishes. Once those dogs hear food being served, nothing can stop them."

"They're a lot different than cats. Sometimes I have to find Muffin and carry her to her dish."

"I'll let the dogs out when we take off. You won't have to do anything until it gets near seven. We might be gone for a few days. Can you put the dogs out in the morning?"

"What time?"

"They ain't fussy. Whenever it works for you."

Becky offered another lemonade, to be polite, and wasn't surprised when Caroline refused.

"I've gotta get home to George. I'll call you if we're going to be gone for more than three days."

CHAPTER 26
WHEELS OF JUSTICE

Ida sat patiently by the dryer in Cobden. The clothes she'd worn on Saturday for a planned overnight visit with her mother were spinning dry, along with the uniform she always carried on the hanger in her car. Then the cell phone on her hip jangled and throbbed. The name Lt. Bedford Stonewall was on the screen.

"Hi, Stoney. What's up?"

"It's about the druggies," he said. "The woman's parents are in town. They stopped by the jail. They met with Sheriff Bing. He said they identified themselves as George and Caroline Connelly."

"Thanks for calling. That's more proof that your drug suspect is Madeline Connelly of Howard County."

"The parents told our sheriff they wanted to post bond for their daughter. Said there's a bond hearing this afternoon at three."

"Thanks. I'll be in court for that. I need to see how her parents react when they spot me."

"They know you?"

"I interviewed them about that dismemberment killing. Their dogs uncovered a human head on their farmland."

"They're suspects?"

"Not yet—probably not ever—but I think their daughter and the male druggie were involved. Can't prove it, though. Not yet."

Ida walked into the courthouse nearly an hour before the bond hearing was scheduled. Her plan was to sit quietly in the courtroom and get a good look at George and Caroline as they waited for Maddy to be brought from the jail. The plan changed when she spotted the couple talking with Maddy's attorney, John Richards, in the hallway.

It was apparent to Ida that George didn't recognize her. But it was even more obvious that Caroline did. She physically flinched, then flashed a half-hearted smile and waved hello.

"George, you remember Detective Ida, don't you?" Caroline said.

"Oh, yeah, I guess I do. You asked me about that skull my dogs dug up, didn't you?"

"That's right, Mr. Connelly. I'm Detective Ida Mae Rollins of the Howard County Sheriff's Department. Are you here for Lynne Connelly?"

"She's our daughter, Maddy," Caroline said. "I guess she started calling herself Lynne."

"You're a long way from Wisconsin," George said. "What brings you here?"

"I was visiting my mama in Cobden, across the river, and witnessed drug dealing."

"Excuse me, everyone," John Richards said as he stepped between the Connellys and Ida. "I need to talk privately with my client's parents."

Ida watched as he led George and Caroline into an empty courtroom. The heavy oak door closed with a thud.

"That woman is the enemy," Richards warned George and Caroline. "Don't talk to her. You might have said too much already."

"But I got to know Ida a little bit back in Wisconsin," Caroline said. "Won't it seem suspicious if we act like we don't know her?"

"You've already positively identified my client as your daughter. If you keep talking, there's no telling what harm you'll do to her defense. You never know what might be important to a cop."

"Can't I even say hello?" Caroline asked.

"Nothing more than that. That detective knows the rules. She won't be surprised or hurt if you dummy up."

Jail had not been as dreadful a time for Maddy as it was for John Michael. She'd been locked up before, under various names, on charges ranging from disorderly conduct to retail theft. She usually posted bond after a first court appearance, then moved to another state. Warrants were issued, but she changed identities whenever she jumped bond.

The longest time she'd been in a cell was ten days after being arrested for public drunkenness in an Atlanta suburb. With work release. And the women's section in the county jail was not altogether uncomfortable.

The jail in Gillespie was more primitive, but Maddy discovered the food was better than what she'd been served in Georgia.

Maddy was released from the Gillespie jail late in the afternoon after her parents were allowed to post a property bond.

"You realize that your parents are taking a substantial risk, don't you?" Judge Callow asked the defendant.

"Yes, sir, I do. I'm very grateful too," Maddy said. "I need to get back to work. I'll need money to beat the bogus charges against me."

Defense attorney Richards rose to his feet as she spoke.

"Your Honor, if it pleases the court, my client has been advised to hold her declarations of innocence in abeyance. This isn't the time or place."

"Try sitting in jail and see how long you can keep quiet, counselor," Maddy snapped.

"That will be enough, miss," Callow said. "Don't make me reconsider the wisdom of the bond. It's a privilege, you know, and a property bond wouldn't even be considered if this was a violent offense."

"I'm sorry, Your Honor," Maddy said. "It won't happen again."

As conditions of her bond, Maddy was ordered to remain in Missouri, undergo frequent and random drug and alcohol tests, and avoid all contact with her codefendant. The prosecutor also warned that she might soon be facing an obstruction charge for using an assumed name.

"They haven't got anything on me," Maddy told her parents as they walked away from the courthouse. "John Michael was selling drugs, not me. They're blowing smoke with that obstruction crap too."

"Blowing smoke?" Caroline asked. "What's that mean?"

"It's just a threat. Lynne is a common nickname for Madeline, probably more common than Maddy."

"But why change names now? It looks suspicious."

"I did it for professional reasons. Marsha said I needed a more adult name. She owns the salon where I've been working. Now I've got more clients than any of the other girls."

Maddy climbed into the rear of her dad's crew-cab pickup, fastened her safety belt, and slumped into the soft leather seat.

"Let's go by my apartment, OK? I want to see if my stuff is safe, make sure the SUV is locked up, and see Marsha. The salon is right below my apartment. Marsha's my landlord too."

"She's probably gonna fire you and evict you," George said.

"What for? *I* didn't do anything. John Richards said he'd drag Marsha into court if I get fired *or* tossed out."

"So you're gonna stay here and keep working?" Caroline asked. "Like nothing ever happened?"

"Weren't you listening, *Mother*? The judge said I can't leave Missouri. If they can't find me, I'll get charged with bail jumping. Then you'll lose your house."

"Sounds like you've got it all figured out," George said.

"I had plenty of time to think in jail. Oh, by the way, thanks a lot for bailing me out, Dad."

"You're not gonna be stuck in jail, honey. You're still my little girl."

"I knew *you* wouldn't let me down."

Maddy looked at the vanity mirror on the passenger seat side. Her mother was touching up her makeup, or so it appeared. But she more obviously was looking directly at her daughter. It was a burning-hot glare.

Ida pulled her Mustang into the parking lot at the Bavarian Haus, a supper club on the main highway south of Gillespie. Stoney said it was the only nearby place with anything resembling fine dining. "Even the money crowd from Cape drives out here," he'd said.

It might have been true since the lot was full, mostly with expensive late-model vehicles. Stoney's oversized pickup truck was illegally parked near the door, but the sheriff's department license frame and window sticker would deflect a ticket or tow.

Stoney was waiting under a forest-green canopy. It shaded a wooden double door with gleaming brass handles and art-carved scenes from a woodland hunt. It looked suitable for display in a museum, Ida thought.

Stoney looked pretty good too. Perhaps a little underdressed in boots, jeans, and freshly pressed white shirt, but certainly presentable. She wished it had been possible to wear something more feminine, but the sheriff's department polo, jacket, and khaki pants would have to do. Fortunately, she'd quickly spiked her hair, switched to a dangling pair of earrings, and added a dab of lipstick. A touch of perfume completed her minimakeover.

Ida confidently strode across the parking lot.

"Hello, cowboy," she said with a grin.

"About time you showed up."

"Say what? Listen, Lieutenant, the time is exactly seven. That's what we said, right?"

"Simmer down, girl. You're right."

Ida felt a warmth from Stoney's eyes. He'd also briefly touched her elbow as he opened the door, a courtesy to ensure she wasn't bumped by the dense wood. Ida would later tell her mother that when Stoney touched her arm, it felt like a tiny strike of lightning.

Stoney ordered for them and asked for an expensive bottle of Riesling. Ida rarely drank, but she agreed to have just a glass—which is what Stoney said he'd allow himself when driving. The rest would be corked and taken home, he explained. The wine was delicious, as were the appetizers and the German entrée for two that Stoney ordered, a heavily sauced cut of beef with a name Ida couldn't pronounce. They split a piece of bavarian cream chocolate cake for dessert and finished the night with the strongest, most aromatic coffee Ida had ever tasted.

As they lingered near Ida's car, Stoney fumbled for words and suddenly took Ida's right hand into his own. It was a massive, powerful hand, but his touch was gentle.

"I guess what I'm tryin' to say," he finally stammered, "is there might be something special between us."

Ida felt faint and worried that she might topple and send her service pistol and handcuffs skidding across the pavement. Instead, she leaned into Stoney's chest. She thought they might kiss.

"I'd love to kiss you, Ida. But I've been hurt before. I don't wanna go too far, too fast."

"My heart was broken too, Stoney. I thought my marriage was forever, not just a couple years. Maybe you're right. If we wait a little bit, things will be more special."

"We're young. We've got plenty of time."

As Ida drove across the Mississippi River and aimed toward Cobden, she struggled with her thoughts. It had been a lovely evening, but Ida worried she had opened the door to heartache. She didn't really *know* Stoney—didn't have a clue about his family or anything other than what he'd volunteered about his background. Maybe there was something awful about his past. Maybe he was another Bill, sweet at first and whenever he got his way, but sullen when a woman took charge of her own life.

And what business did she have falling for a man who lived nearly five hundred miles away from her job? Their schedules would always conflict, he'd get annoyed if she spent more time with her mother than him, and the goofiness of a love affair would interfere with law enforcement. By the time Ida drove through Cobden and pulled into her mother's driveway, she'd decided to nip things in the bud. She just didn't have time for love. Not now. Maybe never.

Her mother looked up from the television as Ida walked into the house.

"What're you smilin' about, little girl?" she asked. "You look like the cat that just ate the canary."

"Oh, nothin', Mama. Just thinking about work, I guess."

"The kind of work you do? Smiling? Don't fib to me. What's goin' on?"

"Oh, Mama. I had dinner with a real man."

As Lula Belle rose from her chair to hug Ida, the detective's cell phone interrupted.

"Your boyfriend?" she said with a grin.

"I wish it was, Mama. This is police business. I've gotta take the call. It's coming from the Howard County Sheriff's Department."

CHAPTER 27
FORK IN THE ROAD

"Hello, Ida. Sorry to call so late," Deputy Scott Brooks said. "I knew you'd want to hear what I've got immediately."

"Don't be silly, Scotty. It's not even eleven o'clock. What's up?"

"I hope you're sitting down. This is big. I mean really big."

"Tell me about it."

"It's just huge. You won't believe it."

"Scotty, if you don't tell me right now, I'm gonna drive back to Howard. I'll shoot you right between the eyes. Spill it!"

"OK, it's like this. We got the dental records of Thad Elliott."

"Yeah, so?"

"It was a match. The guy who was killed and cut apart was Thad Elliott. That comes from the medical examiner. We should get confirming samples of his DNA too."

"Thanks, Scotty. You better tell the sheriff I'll be coming back to town. I've got enough to get arrest warrants for two suspects. I better not say who they are over the cell—you never know who might be listening. You already know who they are."

"Are you talking only about our murder? What about Iowa?"

"This might help their case too."

"That's great. Good work!"

"It wouldn't have happened so fast without your help. I'm gonna ask Sheriff Clark to promote you to detective."

172

"That'd be great, Ida. Anything else I can do for you?"

"Somebody's got to call Thad Elliott's mother, Wanda. That falls on me, though. She knows who I am, just another southern girl."

"That's a tough call to make, I bet."

"Nothing worse," Ida said. "But I won't call her till tomorrow morning. That'll give her a chance right away to call everyone who needs to know. She won't be all alone in the dark, crying and thinking about the little boy she brought into this world."

"I wouldn't have thought of that. How did you learn all this stuff?"

"Mostly from mistakes and remembering what I did wrong. I try to put myself in their shoes before I give them bad news."

Ida woke before dawn, slipped quietly into the kitchen, and quickly prepared a pot of coffee before her mother stirred. It gave her a chance to double the strength of what would otherwise be a timid brew. After a few deep sips, Ida was as alert as her mother's barnyard rooster.

Lula Belle padded into the kitchen in badly worn slipper socks and a housecoat Ida remembered from childhood. The sight inspired a mental note of future birthday and Christmas gifts Ida could afford—and that might be appreciated and used.

"Something's wrong with this coffee, Ida. You make it like I do, don'tcha?

"Yes, Mama. Your taste buds are out of whack. Maybe you're getting a cold."

"Nonsense. Mothers don't get sick."

"Just enjoy your coffee, Mama. I'll make you some toast."

Ida cut four thick slices of bread from a fresh loaf, dropped two in the ancient toaster, and kept an eye on Lula Belle—who looked unusually perky for a quarter to six in the morning.

"Ida, I don't know what I was talkin' about. This coffee is good. Really good."

"Glad you like it. What are you gonna do today, Mama?"

"I'm thinkin' I'll scrub the kitchen floor, take some rugs out to the clothesline, and beat 'em clean."

"That sounds like two days' work. Don't overdo it."

"Don't be silly. I worked a lot harder takin' care of your dad, you, and your sisters. But if you wanna help, I'll let you beat the rugs."

"Can't do it, Mama. I've got to pack my stuff and get back to Wisconsin. That murder I'm investigating is starting to heat up."

"Can't you stay for lunch?"

"I'd love to, but first I need to stop in Gillespie. The sheriff's department is making copies of computer files that I need. I'm getting some arrest warrants."

"Don't do it all yourself, little girl. Take some big ol' cop with ya. Maybe that cop in Gillespie, your sweetie, Stoner, can help."

"Everyone calls him Stoney, Mama, not Stoner."

"Can't he help ya?"

"I'll bring some Wisconsin cops with me for the arrest. That won't happen right away. When it does, maybe the sheriff in Gillespie will assign local deputies for backup."

"Maybe your boyfriend?"

"He's not my boyfriend. He's a boy and a friend. But he'd be perfect for backup. Used to be a star linebacker for the Salukis. Grew up on a farm south of Murphysboro."

"A local boy? From SIU? Maybe I like him already."

"If you ever meet him, you'll like him."

Ida left her mother munching on toast and jam as she showered, dressed, and stuffed her clothes into the bag she'd brought from Howard. She fixed her makeup quickly, fluffed her hair, and then returned to the kitchen.

"I'll call you when I get back to Wisconsin, Mama."

"What time?"

"Might be as late as ten tonight. But don't worry. I'll drive carefully."

They hugged at the kitchen door, and Ida trotted to her Mustang. She dropped her bag into the trunk, then grabbed a pebble from the driveway and lobbed it near the feet of Old Henry, the current rooster. It was something she'd always done as a girl, regardless of the rooster du jour.

As Old Henry fled in a frenzy, Lula Belle spoke her lines from their long-ago barnyard drama.

"Leave Old Henry alone, Ida," she mockingly scolded. "He needs his energy for the chickens."

"That old lecher should keep his feathers hitched up," Ida laughed. Then she flicked the ignition, gunned the motor, and spun a handful of gravel out of the driveway.

It was still early in the morning for city people, but Ida knew country girls rose early. She was betting that Thad Elliott's mother was awake, alert, and working in the kitchen. Ida drove from Cobden to the scenic overlook at Alto Pass, pulled her Mustang to the side of the road, and looked across the deep valley and up to the giant cross at the peak of Bald Knob Mountain. She found Wanda Elliott's number in her cell and placed the call.

"Elliott residence, Wanda speaking," said a friendly voice.

"Mrs. Elliott? This is Ida Mae Rollins, the detective from Wisconsin."

"Oh God. Please don't let this be bad news about my Thad."

"There's no easy way to tell you this, ma'am. We used your son's dental records to identify a body. Your Thad was murdered. I'm very sorry."

Ida heard a faint gasp, then heard the phone being jostled, perhaps from being muffled by an apron. A long silence followed. Finally there were the sounds of rapid breathing and of a woman clearing her throat.

"Are you sure?"

"Positive, Mrs. Elliott. I had to be sure before I called."

There was another long pause. Ida expected to be disconnected. But the call was not yet over.

"How could this happen? He was a hardworking boy. He worked up north because of the money. Yankees pay better."

"We think he met some bad people online. It looks as if he was pursuing a romantic interest," Ida said. The full truth could wait; nothing would be served by telling a murder victim's mother of her son's sexual interest in both men and women.

"Online? With his computer?"

"That's the way it looks. I'm very sorry."

"I guess I need to call some people, then the funeral home. I hope you don't mind if we cut this short. I'm upset."

Ida provided the phone numbers for the Howard County medical examiner and coroner. The remains wouldn't be released for burial until all forensic needs were addressed. But that news could be accurately provided only by pathology professionals.

"May I call you again?" Ida asked. "I'd like to know more about your son—biographical information. It might help us get a murder conviction."

"I'll do anything I can. Wisconsin has the death penalty, doesn't it?"

"I'm afraid we don't, ma'am. Not for more than a hundred and fifty years. Most states don't execute people anymore."

"They should. Kentucky does. So does Indiana, Tennessee, and Missouri. Illinois used to execute, but they went soft on crime when the liberals took over."

"Yes, ma'am. I'll call you tomorrow."

"Goodbye, Detective."

•⸴∙ ∙

Ida drove into Gillespie and stopped at the sheriff's department. Freddie Sherman had agreed to make digital copies of all communications between John Michael Thomas and Maddy Connelly, along with all their communications to and from the late Thad Elliott and the late Ronald Bernard Foster III.

Ida knew the importance of the copies made by Sherman. Taken as a whole, the digital communications entangled two men who'd been murdered and dismembered with the two Missouri drug-dealing suspects—who had sought intimate relations and exchanged spicy chatter with bisexual men in Wisconsin and Iowa.

Because the computer evidence was essential, Ida expected some type of hiccup or lengthy delay. She got a bad feeling when Stoney and the sheriff met her at the door.

"Good morning, men," she said. "You look like you've been waiting for me."

"We have, Detective," Bing Thompson replied. "We've got something for you. Don't we, Stoney?"

"This is from Freddie," Stoney said as he handed Ida a padded mailing envelope. "He said everything you need is in here."

"Feels light, Stoney. I expected a pound of paper."

"Freddie hates paper," Bing said. "He's even got me relying on the computer."

"Maybe I should look inside the envelope before I start driving north."

"I doubt you'll need to," Stoney said. "I looked at what he compiled. It looks comprehensive and complete. I'm glad you told me about the crimes. I sort of knew what I was looking for."

"Where's Freddie?" Ida asked.

"He's on assignment with the Saint Louis PD," Bing said. "Freddie told us what we needed to tell you before he hit the road. And his contact numbers are in the envelope, if you have questions."

"I hope this is stuff that doesn't require an advanced degree in computer technology."

"It's stuff I could use, and I'm way more low tech than Freddie," Stoney said. "He told me that everything can be accessed from the cloud with the links he emailed to you at the Howard County Sheriff's Department. He also put all the stuff on a couple CDs and memory sticks, which are in the envelope, along with a few printed copies of key communications."

"Mind if I check my email before I hit the road?" Ida asked. "It'll ease my mind. I'm prone to worrying about things."

"Suit yourself, Detective," Bing said with a smile. "I'm gonna have coffee at the Jury Box."

Stoney led Ida to his desk, tucked inside a neat, well-organized cubicle. There were no personal items on display, other than a well-worn football and a Saluki team picture from his college days. The desktop contained only a blotter-style calendar that was devoid of any scheduled activities.

"Don't you keep a calendar?" Ida asked.

"It's all on the computer and my phone. Sometimes I doodle on the blotter."

Ida checked her email and found the messages sent by Freddie Sherman. She clicked on several links and found what she needed.

"That Freddie's really something, isn't he?" Stoney said.

"Bing was right. He's the best."

Stoney offered to walk Ida to the Mustang, but she declined.

"We should keep things quiet about us," she said. "At least for now."

"I guess I can live with that. Can I ask you for a date the next time you're here?"

"Shucks, I'll agree right now. I just don't wanna be teased about having a boyfriend. Not yet anyway."

"OK, Ida. Drive careful. Maybe you can call me sometime, huh?"

"You should be calling me, Lieutenant Stonewall. I'm a proper southern girl, remember?"

"I'll call. Just let me know if I start calling too much. Sometimes I get carried away."

Ida thought about Stoney as she drove north. It was lucky to meet a man who'd pursue her. Make that a handsome, well-built man. But it was bad luck that he worked in a distant state. And it was worse luck that he had to be another cop. The last thing she wanted was romance with anyone like Bill Rollins.

After battling rush-hour traffic that turned Chicago expressways into parking lots, Ida still planned to roll into Wisconsin before sunset. She'd talked to Sheriff Clark several times during the drive and knew he was anxious to seek arrest warrants for Maddy Connelly and John Michael Thomas.

"Those two will fight extradition with everything they've got," Clark had said. "They'll be facing murder charges here. We've got to get the ball rolling."

"Yes, sir. I understand, sir." She knew Clark wanted to host a press conference and take a bow for the homicide charges. It would help his reelection campaign overcome accusations of bungling a murder probe.

"That asshole Calvin Krebs has it in for me. We've got to move quickly, Ida."

"I can be in your office around seven. Maybe a little later."

"Can't you make it earlier?"

"Not without lights and siren, sir. I'll push it as much as I can, but the traffic is brutal. I'll make better time once I'm north of O'Hare Field, but that's still ten miles away."

"Call me when you cross the Wisconsin state line. I'll drive back to the office. It'll mean leaving my fundraiser early, but murder arrests will shake more money loose than handshakes and smiles."

Ida walked into the Howard County Sheriff's Department headquarters just after seven. A beaming Clark held the door open for her, then poked at the padded mailer she cradled against her chest.

"Is that the stuff?" he asked. "Let's take it into the conference room and spread it out on the big table."

"I just need my computer. You can pull up a chair, and I'll share what I've got."

It took Ida two hours to lead the sheriff through the evidence compiled in Missouri. He wasn't especially computer literate, but he saw the strong underpinnings of a murder case. There were digital links between the suspects and Thad Elliott that tied everyone to the time, place, and date of the murder.

"This ought to be enough to get a search warrant for George and Caroline Connelly's barn," he said. "We can show the judge that the suspects planned a tryst in Maddy's apartment. That's in the loft of the Connelly barn, isn't it?"

"That's right, sir."

"But what about physical evidence? You don't have enough to make arrests."

"Not yet, sir. I'll want the inside of the barn's floor drain tested for blood and tissue. We'll need to dig up some of the sewer line, too, and seize any screens or filters we find."

"You say the medical examiner believes the victim was hoisted off the floor, then cut apart?"

"That's right, sir. We'll want to get the chain off the pulley hanging from one of the beams. It's not possible to eliminate all traces of tissue and blood, especially not with the amount of blood shed by Thad Elliott."

"What about DNA? Any sources aside from what we get in the barn?"

"We'll get some of Thad's DNA from his mother's home. It'll match up."

Ida was ready for sleep when she returned to her apartment, but she made two phone calls before getting into bed. Her mother was pleased that Ida was safe. Stoney sounded surprised, maybe a little hurt, too, by what she said.

"You're a great guy, Stoney," she said as he caught his breath. "But I don't think we should start thinking of ourselves as maybe someday being a couple."

"Is it the distance between us?"

"That isn't my main concern. I visit my mother a lot."

"What, then? We've sure got a lot in common. My ex was a cop too."

"Too much in common. My ex expected a subordinate little wife. He made fun of my job with a small-town police force. He spent most of his free time drinking with other cops."

"Drunks are mean. I hope he didn't abuse you."

"He finally did. Once. I moved out while he was at work."

"That's how Darlene left me. All of a sudden. We never quarreled; she just got really quiet and withdrawn. Then she was gone."

"I'm sorry, Stoney."

"I was working when she split. She left a note on the kitchen table saying she was starting over in Saint Louis. The note was folded around her engagement ring and wedding band."

CHAPTER 28
WHAT'S GOING ON?

It had been a good day for the diner. There was a waiting line for breakfast. And the lunch crowd filled every stool at the counter, as well as a few tables jammed into the modest confines. It was almost as good as it had been in the early days of the murder investigation, when I was identified as both the owner of Eddie's and a person of interest in a dismemberment killing.

Back then, it had felt like I had a starring part in a local freak show, which was a lousy way to make money. I resented the gawking from strangers, even as they paid for meals and left generous tips. Sometimes I saw a customer pointing at me as he talked to another. Mothers noticeably kept their children away from me, sometimes crouching low and whispering in a tiny ear. It was galling to overhear their chatter, especially the time a young woman glibly told her friends, "The cops think he might have killed a man."

There wasn't a single day when I didn't feel like shouting out my innocence. But I kept my mouth shut, as my lawyer urged. It took time, a lot of it, but eventually the public curiosity had waned. Some folks relish being in the spotlight. I prefer the solitude and privacy that surround yesterday's news makers.

In fact, I seldom thought of the unsolved homicide after the one-year anniversary had passed. Detective Ida no longer seemed interested in me, nor did the bumbling fool wearing the sheriff's seven-pointed star. I certainly hadn't thought of the gruesome death on this busy day.

My cell phone changed things. It was Becky calling just as we'd nearly finished the daily cleanup and prep work for the next breakfast.

"Something's happened," Becky said, her voice cracking with fear. "There's a bunch of cop cars at Caroline's house. She doesn't answer the phone. George is working out of town, so I didn't try calling him."

"He'd probably worry if you did. He'd think Caroline was attacked or—"

"Don't even say it, Eddie. I hate being scared. But a killer is still out there somewhere."

"Whoever killed that poor guy isn't likely to return."

"I thought killers always returned to the scene of the crime."

"Only on TV or in the movies."

"I'm still worried. Can you come home now? Anita knows how to close up and make the bank deposit, doesn't she?"

"I'm on my way."

During the drive, I wondered whether Becky was exaggerating the amount of police activity. She wasn't. Multiple sheriff's department squad cars were parked near the Connellys' barn. There were also cruisers and SUVs from the state patrol and two unmarked cars that looked like what detectives drove. There also was a late-model red Mustang parked near the barn.

"See what I mean?" Becky said as I walked into the kitchen.

We both leaned over the sink and peered through the bay window, trying to make sense of the scene.

"Hear that noise?" Becky asked. "Right after I called you, a helicopter started circling. It's a news crew from Milwaukee, I guess."

I saw the network's logo on the chopper and nodded.

"I wish Caroline would answer the phone. Something must have happened to her."

"The cops probably won't let her use the phone. They don't want her to do anything that might interfere with their investigation."

"I wish we knew for sure. Not knowing is driving me crazy."

"I'm gonna walk over there," I finally said. "Caroline and George are good friends. Staying away probably seems suspicious. Remember—I used to be a person of interest."

"Like I could forget."

I heard the noise of police activity before spotting any officers. Police radios crackled, popped, and blared the ten-code messages of several departments.

"10-50 PI, eastbound Ryan Road at the I-94 overpass."

"Subject is 10-96. Please advise."

"Citizen report of possible 10-55 southbound lanes of I-94."

The calls concerned a crash, a mentally ill subject, and a drunken driver, but it was electronic gibberish to me and likely unrelated to activity on the Connelly property.

I walked among the vehicles, confused and growing more worried by the minute. Had the killer somehow decided Caroline could identify him? I wasn't a cop, but I knew that someone who'd killed once wouldn't hesitate to kill again—especially if that person endangered their continued freedom.

Just as I reached for my phone to call Becky, Detective Ida walked away from the barn and toward me. She looked less scary than I remembered, probably because I wasn't worried about being arrested on the spot. I smiled and waved hello.

"That you, Mr. Norwood?" she asked. "What're you doing here?"

"My wife is worried that something happened to Caroline. So am I."

"You can stop worrying. She's fine. She's watching what we're doing in the barn right now. I've ordered her to stay off the phone."

"What are you doing?"

"Executing a search warrant."

"What for?"

"I can't say anything else, Mr. Norwood."

"How does it connect with the murder?"

"I really can't say."

"Can you at least let me know if I'm still a person of interest?"

"I personally think you're very interesting, Mr. Norwood. But you probably don't need to worry so much about getting arrested."

"I'm in the clear? No connection at all?"

"What I told you is unofficial and off the record. I'll deny saying it if you tell anyone else. But I hate to see you worrying so much. Becky tells me you're a pretty good guy."

• ∴ •

Becky and I watched the TV news, the station with the helicopter. They reported that the search was for evidence in the unsolved homicide, then showed footage shot from the chopper—a useless video clip of uniformed officers walking between the barn and squad cars.

The highlight of their "special report" was an "exclusive" live interview with Calvin Krebs. I thought it probably was exclusive because nobody else would talk to a creep like Krebs, someone I'd be willing to hit with a mallet—without regrets. But despite my aversion to Krebs, what he said was interesting. He'd obviously asked good questions and visited the search site.

"I'm being told by Sheriff Peter Clark that his department has identified the man whose remains were found scattered along county roads," Krebs said. "He's scheduled a news conference for tomorrow afternoon to identify the man and to answer questions about today's search at the rural home of George and Catherine Connelly."

I spit a mouthful of beer at the TV over Krebs's cocksure misidentification of our female neighbor. Becky looked as if she'd just been poked with an electric cattle prod.

"How did he get Caroline's name wrong?" she said. "It's even written on their mailbox."

"Krebs is a doofus. He'd screw up a one-car funeral."

• ∴ •

We learned the next day that Krebs wasn't nearly the fool I suspected. The newspaper story contained a correction—an "Editor's Note"—clarifying the name of Caroline Connelly, along with the rarely used phrase "The *Howard Register-Press* regrets the error in earlier broadcast and online reports." The note also said Krebs was repeating an erroneous identification provided hastily by Sheriff Clark.

I had a quick chuckle over the carelessness of our buffoon sheriff. But the bulk of the newspaper story was no laughing matter. It turned out that the chopped-up body I'd mistaken for trash two years earlier was Thad Elliott, the construction worker who owed me money.

It was no wonder Ida had been so careful in the way she spoke to me. I worried that the search of the Connellys' barn would prove to be a red herring. The dangerous and cunning Angelo Calacia would be able to have a man murdered and make it look like the work of another. If Ida for some reason started asking Angelo about Thad's gambling, my life span might be considerably shortened. And my days would be spent locking doors, scrutinizing new customers at the diner, and constantly looking over my shoulder.

I'd never been a praying man, but I began begging God for another chance. I'd made mistakes as a gambler, I admitted, but nothing worth my life.

That's what *I* thought. God wasn't sharing *His* thoughts—or Angelo's.

CHAPTER 29
WATCHING AND LISTENING

The realities of police work were often frustrating. TV murders were solved in a few hours, but seldom were arrests made quickly in unsolved killings. Ida could prove Thad Elliott had been planning kinky sex with Maddy and John Michael in the barn's loft apartment, thanks to the seized laptop. But it would take time to determine whether the tissue scraped from the barn's drain, sewer pipe, and filters was human, more time still to learn whether the DNA matched Thad Elliott's.

Ida needed help from Wanda Elliott, and soon. But it wouldn't be done without first establishing trust with the dead man's mother. A personal visit would be best, especially for a woman raised in the South, but Ida didn't have enough time for a round-trip drive into Kentucky.

She used a landline from the sheriff's department and a private office to make the call. There was an answer after the second ring.

"Elliott residence. This is Wanda speaking."

"This is Ida Mae Rollins. How're you getting along, Mrs. Elliott?"

"I'm breathing, eatin' a little bit, and reading the Bible. Preacher says God never gives you more'n you can handle. I'm not convinced."

"I won't insult you by saying I know how you feel. No one in the world knows how you feel about losing a son."

"I'm as low as a woman can get."

"Can you tell me a little about your boy? I'm trying to find a motive for whoever killed him." Ida actually was pretty sure sexual desires had led to his death, but it wouldn't be right to share all the details. Not now. Not with his mother.

"Thad was a well-behaved boy. He got pretty good marks in school. He could have gone to college. But me and Edgar—that's my late husband—didn't have the money. Edgar did field work his whole life. He died of a heart attack in his fifties."

"I'm sorry, Mrs. Elliott."

"Thad played baseball, but not good enough to make the high school team. Other kids picked on him. I guess he didn't quite fit in around here. And he didn't want to end up like his dad."

"My daddy worked himself to death too. He often talked about how he might make more money in Chicago, but never got around to moving. Mama and my sisters wouldn't stand for it either."

"What about you, Ida? Why did you move to Wisconsin?"

"I married another cop straight out of school. That was a mistake. We both were too young. He changed after taking a job with a big police department. We split up, and I moved to Wisconsin. I'm paid well and treated all right, I guess."

"My Thad liked it around Milwaukee. He liked to see baseball games and hang out with friends. He said the people were friendly, especially the girls."

"Did he have a girlfriend? Did he ever mention betting on games?"

"If he had a girlfriend, it never came up. If he was gambling, he'd never mention it. We're Southern Baptist. We don't drink, dance, or gamble."

"Sounds like he was a good son. You'll always miss him."

"Thank you, Ida. Are you really a detective? You sound too considerate."

"The work's tough, but I don't have to be. I need help from people. That's easier to come by when you treat them decently."

"Have you learned anything more about Thad? Is there a way I can help you out?"

"Actually, there is, Mrs. Elliott."

"Please call me Wanda."

"OK, Wanda. I'll tell you what would help."

"I'll do whatever I can."

"I need you to box up as many personal items as you can used only by Thad—stuff like a hairbrush, toothbrush, underwear, bed linens. Do you still have any gym gear he used in high school? What would really help us is an old gym bag with sweats and stuff that needs washing."

"I'll wash the stuff for you, Ida."

"Please, Wanda, don't do anything to clean his items. We need a DNA sample in case we come across a suspect or a murder scene."

"Will you?"

"I believe we're close."

"I hope so. What should I do with his things after I fill a box?"

"I'm going to find someone who'll bring the stuff to me. A police officer. I'll call you back when I know for sure."

As Ida placed her call to Kentucky, Caroline Connelly phoned her daughter.

"Hi, Maddy. This is Mom."

"I'm still at work, Mom. I've got to keep this short."

"The police searched the barn, everything from your apartment to the floor drain."

Maddy's pulse surged at the mention of the floor drain. She caught her breath, then acted confused.

"You're kind of breaking up on me. Are you still using that cheap cell phone? What did you say about the barn?"

"The cops were digging around in the floor drain and then pulled out some of the sewer pipe and filtering screens. I couldn't see all of what they took from your apartment, but it was hard to miss holes in the barn floor."

"Weird! What the heck are they doing?" Maddy asked as a cold sweat trickled down her back. Only one other living person knew of the possibility of murder evidence being in the floor's drainage system: John Michael Thomas, the guy who'd gotten her busted for drug dealing.

"I thought maybe you'd know what they were looking for."

"That's silly. How should I know? They're like a bunch of Keystone Cops, anyhow. They're probably just trying to get Sheriff Clark reelected. They've gotta act like they're trying."

"It looked really serious, Maddy."

"I can't talk now, Mom. My client's getting color work done, and it's time for me to finish the job. I'll call you tomorrow. You're getting too worried over nothing. G'bye!"

Maddy stared at the phone, then tucked it into her purse. She needed time to think, even if it cut into the normal happy chatter between stylist and client. It must have been noticed, because the tip was smaller than normal. But when Head Quarters closed for the night, Maddy knew what had to be done.

CHAPTER 30
OUT OF JAIL

John Michael Thomas was trying to make the best of his release on bond. He owed his freedom to his mother and was determined to reward her faith in him. It required behaving like a Boy Scout and blaming the drug dealing on Maddy, but lying wasn't difficult for John Michael. He'd done a lot of it. And it was easier to lie while sober. Details mattered. Even little ones.

Martha had worked with Pastor Driscoll to find a furnished two-bedroom apartment for herself and John Michael. He'd met with Gillespie's Lutheran minister, Jason Stein, who helped members of his flock find deserving tenants for their rental units. Reverend Stein first expressed concern about having a suspected drug dealer living in a parishioner's rental, but he was impressed by his fellow pastor and especially by Martha Thomas.

"All he's facing are *accusations*," Driscoll said.

"My son's wrongly accused," Martha added. "He's going to fight the charges."

"That's right, Pastor," John Michael said. "I'm also looking for work. Maybe you know of something?"

"Probably some farmwork, if you don't mind manual labor. Might be some dishwashing work downtown too."

"I'll take anything. I can't let my mother support me."

"We're family, son," Martha said. "I'll take care of you as long as it's needed."

"I know you will, Mom. But I want to do what's right."

They moved into a second-floor apartment in a neighborhood of older homes, a mix of large single-family dwellings and multiunit homes created by subdividing other once-grand homes. There was a bay window overlooking a park with a formal garden, a bench-lined walkway, and seldom-used tennis courts.

It was one of the few available apartments meeting Martha's main requirement: it could not be located downtown. She wanted plenty of space between John Michael and Maddy because of the no-contact condition of his release on bond. She suspected he was being watched by the police. And the judge who'd approved his release didn't seem like he'd be forgiving if John Michael somehow bumped into Maddy at a coffee shop.

While Maddy was still in jail, Martha and her son had cleared his belongings from the apartment they'd shared. John Michael left his key on a kitchen counter before pulling the locked door shut behind them.

"Maybe we should've left a note," John Michael said.

"What if the judge saw that note? You can't have *any* contact with that woman. A note is contact, isn't it?"

"I guess you're right."

"I don't think you should be going downtown either. If she gets out of jail and goes back to work, you'll cross paths."

"I'd rather work outdoors, anyway. Pastor Stein gave me some names and phone numbers. Some farmer will hire me."

Martha planned to stay in Gillespie until her son was cleared. Any income he generated would help, but most of the financial pressure had been eased through Pastor Driscoll's efforts back in Milwaukee. His church paid Martha to rent her home to a family of refugees from Guatemala. The market-price rent she received for a Milwaukee single-family home was more than enough to cover food and housing costs in Gillespie.

John Michael took a job on Ernie Nadolski's dairy farm in rural Gillespie County. Things were looking up.

"I'm happy to be working, but there's nothing easy about farming," John Michael said as he ate supper with his mother. It was after sunset. He was so tired he was dizzy.

"Hard work drives people away from farming," Martha said. "Some city folks used to live on farms."

"I can see why they left. After they drop the drug charges against me, I want to go back home. I'll finish school and get a job in Milwaukee."

"That sounds like a good plan, son. I hope your lawyer can help you. He's got a good reputation."

"I just wish I'd never met Maddy."

"I wish you hadn't either. Why didn't you just leave her?"

"It was fun traveling, and she was making good money. I didn't really know her very well."

"Maybe you should have asked more questions. Didn't it all seem too good to be true?"

"Not really. Maddy can be very persuasive."

"Didn't you wonder why she didn't want you calling me or knowing where you were?"

"She told me it was for our protection."

"What? Protection from what?"

"She said she was afraid of a guy she used to live with," John Michael said. "He'd beaten her up, even put her in the hospital. Maddy said he'd sworn to kill her if she ever left him."

"But I'm your *mother*."

"Maddy thought he'd be able to find us if *anyone* knew our whereabouts. She said he'd kill me too."

"I just don't understand how he would find you."

"I was scared, Mom."

John Michael cut the talk short by rinsing the dishes and saying he needed to get to bed. It was true that he needed plenty of rest for farmwork. But he'd spun enough tales for one night. Too many specifics were the downfall of a liar. Even the best tripped up over details.

Dairy farming wasn't John Michael's idea of a career-level job, but the steady toil of milking, feeding, and cleaning up after Ernie Nadolski's dairy herd kept his mind occupied. Physical labor helped John Michael suppress his sexual fantasies, aided by total abstinence. There were cravings at first for the heroin he'd chipped while dealing. But he wasn't really a junkie. He'd avoided the hellish withdrawal from quitting cold turkey.

Alcohol was the easiest to avoid. He had never been a big drinker and had heeded his dad's warnings against imbibing at home.

"You don't find booze bottles in a rich man's trash," Arnie had said. "There's a reason for it."

The only alcohol ever consumed in the Thomas home came from a single bottle of wine that was purchased for and entirely consumed on Thanksgiving, Christmas, and Easter. One bottle per holiday. That was a way of life for Arnie and Martha Thomas.

Early in the morning, John Michael was shoveling manure out of the Nadolski barn when a sheriff's department car crunched noisily into the gravel entryway.

"That's for me, Ernie," John Michael said. "While I'm free on bond, I've gotta pee in a cup whenever I'm asked."

"You'll be happy when your name is cleared, I'll bet."

"You better believe it."

John Michael stepped into a stall and, under the steady watch of both a deputy and a probation officer, relieved himself in a specimen jar. "That's all I've got, boys. Hope ya don't need more!"

They'd heard similar remarks before. Neither man smiled nor said a word as they quickly departed.

"They probably avoid being friendly with anyone," Ernie said. "Prob'ly makes it easier if they gotta come back with handcuffs for you."

"Only if the urine is dirty. I've got nothing to worry about."

"That's good. Now finish scooping that cow poop. We need to buy some feed and haul it back here."

John Michael worked twelve-hour days, breaking only for coffee in the morning and afternoon and for lunchtime sandwiches and an apple packed by his mother. At night, he ate dinner with his mother, watched TV, and often fell asleep on the couch.

The routine would have him bored out of his mind if he hadn't been so exhausted.

Although Martha missed her Milwaukee home and neighborhood, she found Gillespie comfortable. Her only daily obligation was driving to the dairy farm to pick up her son after work. John Michael left for work at six in the morning, catching a ride with Nadolski's wife, Janeen, who worked nights as a nursing assistant at Gillespie Memorial Hospital.

Martha passed her mornings by watching TV news and reading the *Gillespie Gazette*, a weekly paper. One of the biggest stories during her first week in the apartment concerned the release on bond of two drug-dealing suspects.

It was reported that her son's codefendant, now identified as Madeline, a.k.a. Lynne, a.k.a. Maddy, Connelly, had returned to her downtown apartment and was again styling hair at Head Quarters. The story included a quote from the drug suspect: "I never broke the law. I'll be acquitted, unless the charges are dropped first."

The only mention of John Michael Thomas— "address unknown"— was that he was "thought to be working on a farm in rural Gillespie."

Martha's daily routine made her time in Gillespie more pleasant. Midmornings found her walking to a strip mall at the edge of town. It housed a grocery store, a Laundromat, a drugstore, and a coffee shop called the Daily Grind. The twenty-minute stroll boosted her pulse and tightened her waistline.

Martha enjoyed her stops at the coffee shop, which also served herbal tea and breakfast pastries. Martha sometimes requested a decadent cheese danish but usually ordered an english muffin with cream cheese. She spent some of her time reading the big daily newspapers from Cape Girardeau and Saint Louis, though she couldn't help people watching as an eclectic mix of patrons came and went.

Another regular customer was a woman who reeked of cigarette smoke and drank her coffee black. She usually bought two more coffees in to-go cups and paid her bill with a credit card. Although Martha abhorred smoking, and generally steered clear of smokers, the woman's pleasant smile and friendly manner were compelling—a demeanor that balanced out her well-coiffed auburn hair and the almost-garish turquoise jewelry she wore from her ears and neck and on several fingers.

Since the woman sat at a nearby table, Martha nodded and said, "Good morning."

"You're new here, aren't ya?" the woman replied with a warm smile. "You sound like someone from up north."

"I just moved here from Wisconsin. My son and I live by the park."

"The little one downtown?"

"No, the big park not too far from here. It has a nice garden and some tennis courts."

"What brings you to Gillespie? I've always wanted to leave but never got the chance."

"My son is taking care of some business," Martha said after a thoughtful pause. "We'll be going back to Wisconsin before too long."

"Are ya lookin' for work?"

"Honey, I'm too old for a job. My son works on a dairy farm north of town."

"Nadolski's?"

"Yes. How did you know?"

"This is a small town. Only dairy farm north of town is Ernie Nadolski's. I know his wife, Janeen."

"John Michael—that's my son—says they're real nice folks, the Nadolskis."

"Janeen's a real sweet girl. We went to high school together."

"About ten years ago?"

"More'n twice that, but thanks for the flattery. Hey, what's your name? Mine is Lorraine Gallagher, but everyone calls me Lottie."

"Nice meeting you, Lottie. I'm just plain old Martha."

"The pleasure was all mine, Martha. I'd visit some more, but I've gotta get this coffee back to the girls at work. I can't handle more'n a cup a day. Makes me ornery."

Martha watched as Lottie carried a cup holder laden with coffee, opened the door with an elbow, and dug into her shoulder bag with her free hand. She stuck a long skinny cigarette between her painted lips—a frosty coral hue that complemented the turquoise—and then flicked a lighter as she walked across the parking lot, puffing a trail of smoke. Lottie finally set the coffees on the roof of her minivan, opened the door, and grabbed her keys before retrieving the coffees and settling into the driver's seat—in one fluid motion.

"She must have been a dancer," Martha said to the ponytailed and tattooed male barista who wiped Lottie's table clean.

"I think she was, before the kids and all," he said. "She's got about five kids from three different husbands, I guess."

•⋮⋅•

Maddy was scheduled to work the Head Quarters late shift, a schedule avoided by newlyweds and working mothers. It suited Maddy perfectly. She didn't get up until she felt like it, then drank a quick cup of coffee before donning her fitness gear—top-of-the-line running shoes, skintight performance top, and satin shorts—and pounding out a brisk five or six miles. Afterward, she'd work her arms and upper body with a pair of rubber-coated ten-pound dumbbells, followed by floor exercises that maintained her core.

The routine gave her plenty of thinking time. That also was a routine. As she began her mileage, Maddy battled pent-up frustration about being sexually abused as a child. Then she struggled through resentment of her mother for refusing to believe she was being molested by her own grandfather. Finally, in the third mile, she felt good about having evened the score with her mother. Why couldn't an only child claim her inheritance when she needed it?

The bitch is lucky that's all I've done, she thought as she ran. *I earned that money keeping my mouth shut about her boy toy.*

By the end of her run, Maddy was thinking about what she'd do after the drug charges were dropped. The cops might be able to prove John Michael was a drug dealer, but she'd never had anything to do with it. Once she gave a video statement to the police—a statement her lawyer was arranging—they'd have an ironclad prosecution for John Michael.

Why mess with me when they've got everything against him? I'll tell the cops about his supplier in New Orleans, too, once they agree to cut me loose, Maddy thought as she climbed the stairs to her apartment. *I never even used drugs. My clean urine at the jailhouse proved that.*

Maddy was nothing but positive energy and high expectations when she reported for work at one o'clock. She nodded a friendly hello to Jasmine, who was deep in conversation with a young blond aiming to go even blonder. Then she ducked into the tiny office that doubled as a breakroom, where the manager had left her favorite coffee—a large blond cappuccino that stayed amazingly warm in a covered carryout cup.

"How's the coffee, girl?" Lottie asked after returning from the alley that served as a smoking lounge.

"Best in town. I sure do appreciate it, Lottie."

"I'd like to pay you more, but I can afford coffee. And you girls keep all your tips. Franchise hair places take all the tips and dole them out equally."

"That ain't equal for the best girls," Maddy said. "And it's more than the worst ones deserve."

Lottie nodded enthusiastically as she sprayed perfume to smother the smoke smell. Maddy knew it didn't work worth a damn, both from her nose and given the fact that all of Lottie's clients were smokers too.

Maddy slipped into her smock, then grabbed her coffee and walked into the shop. Lottie followed, then nodded back toward the doorway, apparently to share a confidence.

"Hey, what was the name of that druggie who got you busted? Some Wisconsin guy, wasn't it?"

"Yep, we met in Wisconsin. I wish I'd never seen him."

"His name? What is it?"

"John Michael Thomas."

"You'll never guess who I ran into this morning."

"Him? Where?"

"Not him, his mother. She's a nice older gal. Said her name was Martha."

"That's his mom, all right. She have anything else to say?"

"Said he's working on Ernie Nadolski's dairy farm. It's on the highway north of town."

"He can stay there for all I'm concerned. Until he goes to prison."

CHAPTER 31

ON THE ROAD

There was time. Not a surplus, but enough. Maddy knew the police in Wisconsin wouldn't be able to make a speedy arrest on murder charges unless they'd seized immediately damning and certain physical evidence—something like the ear of a murder victim snagged on a sewer screen, or perhaps a boozy selfie video boasting of having committed a perfect crime.

There was nothing of the sort. Maddy avoided selfies. And if there was any type of physical evidence to be found, it could only be exceedingly minute traces of blood or tissue. Maddy wasn't certain any could be recovered. She'd flooded the barn's drainage system with water on three separate occasions; how could anything human still remain?

It would take several days at the very least for even the ultrasophisticated state crime laboratory to examine and analyze whatever lingered in the drain. More likely it would take weeks to determine whether any potential DNA matched with that of the sex-obsessed young construction worker she'd dispatched last year. She'd suffered at the hands of abusive men most of her life, beginning with her grandfather, and had no use for men aside from whatever complicity she could elicit from a generally violent and lecherous gender. She'd learned the hillbilly's real name was Thad Elliott only after emptying the cash from his wallet and then dumping the billfold and other personal effects into the unmonitored trash barrel of a car wash near downtown Howard.

Maddy's greatest fear was John Michael Thomas and his conscience.

There was no telling what he'd say while under the spell of his mother. She also knew what would happen once John Michael faced a certain drug conviction. He'd do what other inmates had done when Maddy was jailed in the past. Their stories hadn't been used against *her*, but this time would be different. John Michael would spill his guts about the murder and agree to testify against Maddy in exchange for reduced charges. He'd say the murder was entirely a surprise and all Maddy's doing. Under his mother's goody-goody influence, he'd avoid a death penalty, perhaps a life sentence too. Maddy knew he was a good-enough liar to make his hollow claims ring true.

It was too big a risk to allow, Maddy decided as she finished a cup of coffee and rinsed the cup in her kitchen sink. She descended the stairs and walked into Head Quarters early on a Friday morning, a big smile on her face and a plan firmly in mind.

"Morning, girls," she said to Lottie and Jasmine. "Isn't it a beautiful day?"

"You been drinkin'?" Lottie said. "I can't ever remember you being so chipper in the morning."

"I just feel good about myself. The drug charges are gonna be dropped next week, my lawyer says. I'm hoping to take a long weekend, starting this afternoon. I've only got two appointments. Both are early."

"I s'pect y'all want me to cover for you if we get busy this afternoon?" Jasmine asked.

"I'll make it up to you next week. I just need to get away for a few days."

"I thought you were supposed to stay in Missouri," Lottie said. "What's up?"

"Missouri's a big state. I'm just gonna spend a couple days in Saint Louis. Maybe see a play, hit a nightclub, go shopping."

"Maybe find a rich boyfriend?" Jasmine said.

"You never can tell. But I need some help from you, Jasmine. Can you give me a whole new look this afternoon? I noticed you're free after two."

"How are you paying for it?" Lottie asked.

"You can take it out of my next check, can't you? I'll give Jasmine a cash tip."

"How much?"

"I was thinking twenty bucks," Maddy said.

"Make it thirty," Jasmine said, "and you've gotta deal. OK with you, Lottie?"

Lottie frowned, then opened a window. She lit a smoke—a rarity in the shop and only for times of high stress. She took a long drag and then blew the smoke out the window. She let a few more seconds pass as she gazed outside. She hated to limit any walk-in customers, who paid a premium. Friday's late shift was often lucrative.

"I guess it'll be OK," Lottie said. "Just as long as I get thirty bucks too."

Maddy paid both women and then got ready for her first appointment, a simple cut and style for a new mother. It had to be short, the woman said. She was sick of getting her hair pulled by a surprisingly strong baby boy.

The cut was a big success. It looked flirty and feminine, Jasmine said.

"That's kind of how I want my hair cut," Maddy said. "Give me some layers and a wedge in the back. Leave enough on top so I can spike it up sometimes."

"It's an awful big change. You sure about this?"

"Let's do it after my next appointment. Before I change my mind. OK?"

"Can do, girl."

An hour later, Maddy settled into Jasmine's chair.

"Let's do this thing," she said.

"You want it to look boyish for normal, slutty for night?"

"That's it. Also, I want to change the color to jet black."

"Get rid of your blond hair?" Lottie said. "Are you nuts?"

"Just give me a complete makeover. I want to look like a city girl in Saint Louis."

Later in the afternoon, as Maddy stepped out of the salon and into the bright sunshine, she looked at her reflection in the front window. It was a startling change, one that so radically altered her appearance her mother wouldn't recognize Maddy without a long and studied look. Absent the mousse-spiked top, dangling hoop earrings, and flashy gold-plated necklace she contemplated for a night in Saint Louis, the look was boyish.

Maddy correctly guessed there wouldn't be many questions when she rented a car. All she needed was the credit card her dad had recently supplied and one of the bogus IDs the cops hadn't grabbed in their drug bust.

"Here's the keys," the rental agent said. "You've got the red one in front. Will that be all?"

"Thank you, Sam," Maddy said. "Please call me Lynnette. I'm sure to rent from you again."

By four thirty, Maddy had stashed the few belongings she would need in the rental car, then locked the apartment door. She thought about dropping the keys through the mail slot in the door, hating to inconvenience the landlord, Lottie's husband, Carl. But if she left the keys behind, even an idiot like Carl would realize she wasn't coming back. Maddy was counting on a little bit of mystery aiding her disappearing act.

⁘

John Michael no longer needed to look at his cell phone to tell the time. He'd spent enough time working outdoors at the farm to learn more than brush-cutting techniques from the seat of Nadolski's big red tractor. He knew that when the sunbeams dipped toward the distant tree line west of the farm fields, it was late in the afternoon, close to five o'clock. Sometimes he'd check his guesstimate against the time posted on his phone, a cheap burner that offered little more than the correct time, a scanty weather report, and telephone service. It was the only type of phone he could be trusted with, his mother had decided when she bought him the prepaid device at the discount store.

It was four thirty when John Michael checked the phone. He was working only until five today, so he drove the tractor into the field, killed the engine, and began to secure the giant machine for the night. He heard a vehicle approaching on the county road and thought it might be Nadolski, who'd agreed to drive John Michael home if he hadn't decided to walk or hitch a ride. He was looking forward to the weekend for two reasons: his mother was returning to Milwaukee to check on her home and retrieve some personal possessions and he'd been given the weekend off by Nadolski.

It wasn't Nadolski approaching, just a late-model red car that was traveling slowly, unlike the farmland drivers who knew the roads and were always racing against the clock. John Michael wasn't an agricultural expert by any means, but he'd learned farming would be a great way to work himself to death. Any puffiness he'd developed as an idler, drug dealer, and partner in crime had vanished. He now had the tan and rawboned look of Nadolski.

John Michael tracked the car. He wondered why it was moving so slow. He wondered whether the driver was lost. Then he watched as the car pulled to the side of the road near the fence line at the northern border of the field.

His curiosity grew as the driver stepped out of the car. It was either a young man or a woman who didn't play the girlie-girl fashion game— someone wearing a ball cap, an unbuttoned denim shirt over a black T-shirt, jeans, and boots. The driver looked up and down the rural road, then slowly circled the car while peering at the ground, finally kicking at the loose gravel on the shoulder, perhaps out of frustration. Then the driver opened the hood of the car and peered into the engine compartment.

John Michael believed only a man would act as if the clue to a breakdown might be quickly spotted under the hood. A woman would have returned to the car's shaded interior and used her cell phone to summon help. He started walking to the car after the driver looked up from the engine and waved at him.

"Need some help?" John Michael called. "You can probably get back to town with me. My ride should be here around five thirty."

"Thanks," said a female voice. "That sounds good."

"Maybe you're just out of gas? I can get you a couple gallons back at the barn."

"Don't bother," the driver snarled as she backed away from the engine and pointed a silver-plated handgun at John Michael. It took him a moment to recognize Maddy. He might have recognized her quicker if his attention hadn't been entirely consumed by the gun barrel of a snub-nosed .38 revolver and the bullet tips visible in the cylinder.

"Maddy! We aren't supposed to see each other. You better get out of here."

"We're gonna take a little ride first. We gotta talk. Get in the fucking car."

"How did you get a gun?"

"My dad bought me this when I started traveling for work. It was hidden in the apartment, but those hick cops missed a lot of stuff."

"What do you want? I don't want to get shot."

It might have been possible to run away, but John Michael's thoughts were clouded. He didn't know a basic fact of police work. Fleeing suspects are almost impossible to hit squarely with a handgun, especially those with a short barrel. If he ran as fast as possible while ducking and weaving, Maddy would need incredible luck to hit him. Or a scope-equipped rifle mounted on a tripod.

Terror freezes most people accosted with a gun. And John Michael didn't have either the time or the training to explore his options. He hoped Maddy would listen to him. She held the gun on him as he climbed into the car, a low-slung two-door that wasn't easily entered or exited. She kept the gun in her left hand as she started the car, shoved it into drive, and drove away from the Nadolski farm.

CHAPTER 32
FAST-TRACK HELP

Ida expected little help from her sheriff, but he surprised her at times. Sheriff Clark had political connections statewide, not just within the rectangular borders of Howard County. One of those connections was with the state crime laboratory, which was usually at the beck and call of the big police agencies in Milwaukee and Dane Counties.

"Ida, what kind of timeline are you expecting on this Elliott murder?"

"It might take weeks to get what we need from the crime lab, sir."

"I've been told we can get some fast-track service on this. How would you feel about knowing something solid in seventy-two hours?"

"Like I was in a dream. Whenever I call, the first thing I hear is how busy they are with rape-kit tests from Milwaukee and Madison. Maybe you remember the news stories about their backlog, sir?"

"I do. But you were superfast submitting evidence from the Connelly farm. I'm owed a favor. I asked for a little help."

"From who, sir?"

"If I told you, I'd have to kill you," Clark said, a full smile doubling his ample chin and crinkling the corners of his steel-blue eyes. "They'll have preliminary results Monday afternoon."

"How preliminary?"

"Not enough for a trial, but we should be able to get arrest warrants and extradition requests."

"I'll get the DA prepped, sir. He'll find a judge to sign the orders."

"How do you plan to make the arrests, Ida? Missouri is a long way off."

"I know where John Michael Thomas and Madeline Connelly live. And the Gillespie County sheriff and his guys will give us any support we need. You'd like their sheriff, sir."

"I expect I would. Old Bing Thompson and I went to FBI training together. Place called Quantico."

"You've already called him, haven't you, sir?"

"Yup. Bing says he and your boyfriend Stoney will be glad to help."

"He's not my boyfriend," Ida said, her face blushing.

Martha didn't worry when John Michael didn't answer the phone Friday night. She left a message that she'd arrived safely in Milwaukee and would be staying with her good friend Helen Voorhees. She didn't ask John Michael to return her call quickly. It could wait until Saturday, she decided, allowing her boy some freedom for the night. He might see a movie, maybe stop for coffee and a snack, perhaps even meet a girl.

Anything not involving drugs or Madeline Connelly would be OK, she'd decided. Helen agreed, and so did Pastor Driscoll, who paid a visit to Helen's home Friday night.

"John Michael's a good kid," Driscoll said. "He got mixed up with the wrong people, that's all."

"He's under a court order to avoid that woman," Martha said. "He can't drink or use drugs either. They randomly check his urine all the time."

"You need some time of your own too," Helen added. "I'm glad you'll be meeting with your renters tomorrow. I'd worry about leaving my house with strangers."

"I don't think of the Rodriguez family as strangers," Pastor Driscoll said. "I think you'll be impressed with your tenants. Fernando, the father, has a full-time job as a meat packer. Then he works until midnight five nights a week cleaning the church and our school."

"Goodness! When does he sleep?"

"He's in his twenties, Martha. He doesn't need much sleep."

"What about the mother and kids?" Martha asked.

"Her name is Isabella. She's got three boys under the age of five. She's a full-time mom, but she takes in laundry to help make ends meet."

"Sounds like a hard life."

"They never complain," Driscoll said. "Life is better in Milwaukee than Guatemala. A lot better. Here, there's hope."

After the pastor went home and Helen retired to her bedroom, Martha broke a promise to herself and called John Michael a second time. He wouldn't be troubled by a late call or too tired to talk. But the phone rang seven times, then dropped into voice mail.

"Hi. This is John Michael Thomas. Sorry I missed your call. Please leave a message."

"It's just Mom, John Michael. I hope you're OK. Call me tomorrow, OK?" Martha said, trying to stifle the fear in her voice. "I guess that's all for now. I love you, son."

Ida spent Saturday morning cleaning her apartment and trying to coax life back into the parched houseplants she'd neglected while on the road. Encouraging chatter and a lot of water might help, she decided. There were no other options.

Just past noon, she made a second pot of coffee and started watching a TV news channel when her cell phone vibrated powerfully on the counter. It made such a clatter Ida often wondered why cell phones also needed ringtones. The supposedly silenced phone still rattled her out of a deep sleep whenever police emergencies arose.

Ida grabbed the phone, frowning when she spotted the caller's name: Martha Thomas.

"This is Detective Ida Mae Rollins," she answered, wondering how freely she would be able to speak to the mother of a suspected killer.

"I'm sorry for calling you, Ida. But I don't know what to do. I can't get hold of my son. I'm in Milwaukee, and he's back in Missouri."

"Why? What's happening in Milwaukee?"

"It's a long story, but I needed to check my house here. I also wanted to get some things we can use in Gillespie."

"You left your son alone?"

"That sounds awful, doesn't it? But he's an adult. And he's not allowed to leave Missouri. I wanted to make sure my house is being rented by good people."

"Is it?"

"They remind me of the way Arnie and I worked endlessly when we were young. And the house is cleaner than when I left it. I don't know how Isabella does it! She's mothering three lively boys, taking in laundry, and keeping house at the same time."

"Is she married? Or just living with the guy?"

"Married. His name is Fernando, and he works eighteen hours a day."

"Where are they from?"

"Guatemala. They're refugees."

"So, what's happening with John Michael? I can't be much help, though. He's facing drug charges, and I'm a cop."

"I didn't know who else to call. His attorney is out of the country, fishing in Canada. Something called the Boundary Waters. No cell phone service. He's not accessible before Monday."

"When were you expecting to talk with your son?"

"He promised to call me today before noon. He keeps his promises. I've called and left messages, and now his voice mail is full. What should I do?"

"I can call one of the sheriff's deputies in Gillespie. They'll know where he is. He's probably got to give them a urine sample today or tomorrow."

"Will you tell me what they learn?"

"I've got to stay out of this, Martha. But I can give the deputy your phone number."

Ida thought about the propriety of making such a call. She decided it wouldn't be a problem if the call was cast as police business.

"Hi, Stoney. This is Ida."

"I recognize your voice. Is this a personal call or police business?"

"Police."

"Damn it. I'm feeling kinda lonely today."

"I got a call from the mother of one of your druggies—the male one. She can't get hold of her son. I can't help her out, obviously, but maybe he's skipped town? Isn't he scheduled for a weekend urine check?"

"We always check on Saturday *and* Sunday. If someone wants to drink or use drugs, they usually mess up over the weekend."

"If he turns up missing, I'm thinking his mother might eventually know where to look in Gillespie. You might check with the female druggie too."

"I would have thought of that, Ida. This ain't my first rodeo."

"I'm sorry, Stoney. Of course you would. The mother's name is Martha Thomas. I can give you her number, but I've got to stay out of this. You've got a legitimate police reason to look for him."

"You do too. When are you going to pick him up? Sooner or later?"

"Sooner looks promising," Ida said. "But it won't be today. I'm just trying to help Martha out by calling you. She's already half out of her mind."

"She's an OK lady?"

"Very OK. Bighearted churchgoing type, widowed and lonely. Rented her house in Milwaukee to refugees from Guatemala."

"She'll need an exterminator when they move out."

"That's not fair, and you know it. I didn't know you were a racist."

"Guess I meant it as a joke," Stoney said.

"I sure hope so. My ex is a huge racist as well as a sexist wife beater."

"I'm not that way. If we see more of each other, I'll have a chance to prove it."

"I'll think about it. Right now I'll give you Martha's number and step away. If I don't, it could mess things up for your prosecutor. Why give a defense attorney something that can be twisted and turned?"

"OK, Ida. I've got a pen and paper. What's the number?"

"Wireless Caller" flashed on Martha's cell phone when it rang at four in the afternoon. She answered, hoping it wasn't a scam, a sales pitch for hearing aids, or an inane political survey.

"Mrs. Thomas?" a deep male voice asked.

"Yes, it is. Who's calling, please?"

"This is Lieutenant Bedford Stonewall calling from the Gillespie County Sheriff's Department. I'm looking for your son. We need to check his urine today, and he's not at home or work."

"Oh God! Are you going to arrest him?"

"Too soon to tell, Mrs. Thomas. Thought maybe you'd know where we might look."

"He goes to the coffee shop in the strip mall. You might check with that woman you arrested too."

"We can't find her either. Her boss at the hair salon said she was going to spend the weekend in Saint Louis. If we can't find her or test her urine, she'll eventually be arrested and charged with bail jumping."

"What about John Michael?"

"Same for him."

"I just have a feeling something terrible has happened to my son. I was hoping he'd give me a call today. He's really a good boy, just got mixed up with a bad crowd."

"Don't worry. He'll turn up. We get a lot of drug suspects who skip town. They start using again, get arrested elsewhere, and we get them back on warrants."

"That sounds awful."

"They sure don't like it either. But at least they're alive and can get straight while they're locked up."

"Can you call me when you know more, or have him call me?"

"I'll try, Mrs. Thomas. Try not to worry so much."

CHAPTER 33
LOOKING FOR ANSWERS

I couldn't figure out what was going on. For some reason, George Connelly hadn't been home for more than a month. I expected to see him last weekend, today at the latest. He never showed up.

That was highly unusual. Normally I'd spot his truck parked outside the barn when I got home from the diner on a Friday afternoon. It was usually part of a four-day weekend he was allowed from the jobsite in Tennessee. George said it was a privilege he enjoyed as a longtime union carpenter.

"I got seniority, Ed," he'd explained as we drank beers in the barnyard. "I can afford to do it too."

"How's that?"

"I work all the overtime I can get. I rack up enough OT to more than make up for losing two days of work."

George also liked to be with his dogs, check on the well-being of Maddy's neglected horse, and allow poor Lucky a few days of pasture time. "Horsing around," George called it. Caroline made sure Lucky was fed and had hired a farmer's fourteen-year-old son to shovel manure and pitch hay in the barn. You could say the horse was neglected, but not that he was ignored or mistreated.

I couldn't remember exactly when I'd last seen George. I wondered whether he'd gone to visit Maddy. She hadn't been home for more than a year, not since before I'd spotted bagged body parts along the roadway. I

210

knew from Becky that there was some recent bad blood between Caroline and Maddy, but I hadn't listened closely to the details. It's not unusual for me to take flight from female squabbling. My mother and her younger sister hated each other. Their verbal sword fights often sent my father and me to the solitude and mechanical tinkering of our garage.

On a lazy Saturday afternoon, I was fighting to stay awake in my recliner, petting Muffin. She'd slipped into a deep slumber on my lap. I again thought of George's absence. What would keep him away from home? Trouble between a distant daughter and his wife seemed an unlikely reason, at least to me.

I remembered hearing about the mother-daughter trouble around the same time Maddy got arrested in Missouri. That might have been the last time George was home, but I couldn't be sure. It made me nervous for some reason, and I began to look for reasons to call George. On a big spread like his, there was always some unfinished business on the property. I decided to give him a call once I found something needing attention.

Then something else happened. Becky was going through our mail on the kitchen table when a utility bill slipped from between slick flyers advertising mattresses, fast food, and new cars. It was addressed to George and Caroline Connelly.

"I better get this over to Caroline," Becky said as she darted out the kitchen door. I thought about following, but a nap with Muffin was more inviting. I'd barely fallen asleep when the door banged open against the jamb.

"Eddie!" Becky said. "Where are you?"

"Trying to sleep."

"Something's going on next door."

"With Caroline?"

"Of course. Who else could I mean? We don't have other neighbors."

"What's going on?"

"Caroline said she was too busy to talk."

"That's odd."

"Usually she'll complain about Maddy or George. You know how she is. All she said was 'There's nothing new with either of them.'"

"Where's George? When's he coming home?"

"He's still working in Tennessee. That's all she said."

"Caroline got red in the face when I asked about George. Then she started talking about feeding Lucky. She changed the subject."

"Why would she do that?"

"I don't know," Becky said. "Then she grabbed her keys and phone off the counter. Said she was going out to the barn, she'd call me later."

"So?"

"Caroline didn't go into the barn. I saw her drive away before I opened our back door. And I think there was someone riding in the passenger seat, slumped way down."

It was a weird story. Too weird for Caroline. George and I had sometimes teased her about her conventional, straight-laced ways. "Norma Normal" is what George called her.

I didn't give the matter much thought. Minutes later, I was deep into the splendor of a nap, pinned securely by a purring cat.

After dinner, I tried calling George. Becky had inspired the call, which was useless. My call immediately went into voice mail and a recording saying the mailbox was full. I tried the number several times over the weekend and got the same nonanswer each time.

Becky also saw something Monday while I was at the diner. The kid helping care for Lucky drove into the barnyard in a heavy-duty pickup truck with a horse trailer. A few minutes later, he walked Lucky into the trailer, bolted the gate, and drove away.

Becky phoned Caroline but didn't get an answer. She waited a few minutes, then walked next door. Caroline came out of the house as Becky approached. My wife said it looked as if Caroline expected her visit and didn't want her in the house. She was carrying her car keys and acted as if she were in a hurry to get to the gym.

"She's always in a hurry, Ed. Caroline used to have time to talk. Now she doesn't."

"So what? I'm sure you've been too busy with school a few times. Caroline will come around."

"There's something else. I'm almost certain I saw someone looking at us from an upstairs window, peeking between the blinds."

CHAPTER 34
NOW WHAT?

Ida felt lost. Since her return to Wisconsin, the crime lab had developed enough physical evidence to charge John Michael Thomas and Madeline "Maddy" Connelly with the dismemberment murder of Thad Elliott. A judge signed their arrest warrants and the extradition paperwork. They'd be brought to Wisconsin before their drug charges were resolved in Missouri.

That was Ida's plan. But the two murder suspects had disappeared while the charges were pending. Ida's biggest professional triumph suddenly turned sour.

It was like losing a championship football game from a last-second desperation throw into the end zone. No, it was much worse. And Ida still had to deliver the bad news to Thad's mother. In their last talk, she'd predicted arrests would soon be made. Ida had spoken too soon, though it seemed safe at the time. This new information might be taken as a betrayal.

Ida knew it was best to pay a personal visit with bad news, but a quick trip to Kentucky wasn't possible. She closed the office door and used her cell phone. Five rings later, it was answered.

"I'm calling for Wanda Elliott," Ida said in what she hoped was a heartfelt voice.

"Speaking. Is that you, Ida? You sound kinda formal. What's happened?"

Ida explained that her boy's two killers had been positively identified and that a judge had authorized their arrests and extradition to Wisconsin.

"That's good. They need to be executed."

"Remember? Wisconsin doesn't have a death penalty. They might get life in prison, though. But first we've got to find them."

"Find them? You let them get away? What kind of police are you? Cops here in Kentucky woulda killed them both. They'd shoot first, ask questions later."

"It's not as simple as that, Mrs. Elliott. They were free on bond and facing drug charges in Missouri, a little town called Gillespie."

"Don't they have a jail?"

"They made bail. Now they're being sought on bail-jumping charges. They'll be locked up when the Missouri cops find them. They're being sought statewide."

"What if they don't find them?"

"They'll get caught somewhere."

Ida explained that photos of the suspects and news releases about their disappearance were distributed to the news media by the Howard County and Gillespie County sheriff's departments. The news would spread quickly across Wisconsin, Missouri, and the Midwest.

"My sheriff already gave our local paper an interview about the murder charges and the suspects. The story will get sent nationwide by the Associated Press. Your son's murder was big news."

"Think the Kentucky papers will print it?"

"I can't say. But you can read it online right now."

"I don't have a computer."

"Find someone who does. You must know somebody. They can print it out for you."

Ida had checked the local story for accuracy, expecting to find something screwed up by her sheriff or Calvin Krebs. She couldn't find anything to complain about. It was a solid, factual report, and the mug shots were top quality. Sheriff Clark had given Ida full credit for building the case. There was also a comment from Gillespie County sheriff Bing Thompson on the "ongoing" and "intensive" search for Thomas and Connelly.

Ida knew from her most recent talk with Stoney that he personally was searching for the two, mostly on his own time. His updates were appreciated, though not encouraging.

"They haven't been seen since Friday. She rented a car using her father's credit card. He left the Nadolski farm in the late afternoon, which wasn't unusual."

"Did you check with the phone company? Cell phones track our movements."

"Jeez, wish I'd thought of that," Stoney sighed sarcastically. "You say phones know where we are?"

"Sorry. Of course you'd check phones."

"They were both using prepaid burners. They've been dumped and replaced, I'm sure."

"What about Saint Louis? Didn't she talk about going there for the weekend?"

"No trace of her. She was probably going anywhere *other* than Saint Louis."

"In other words, we're screwed."

"That's about it. Until someone makes a mistake. They always do."

CHAPTER 35
NORTH OR SOUTH?

Maddy had headed north on the highway from Gillespie. After belligerently confronting John Michael at gunpoint and ordering him into her rental car, she softened her tactics during the drive and urged her former roommate to cooperate.

"Listen, John Michael. I'm sorry about the gun, but I needed to get your full attention," Maddy said, her once-harsh expression melting into a warm smile. "We need to talk. Let's get our stories straight about Wisconsin and Iowa."

"Maybe you're right. Can you put the gun away? Please?"

"Sure. I'm not much of a shot, anyway. I'm just looking for this place Jasmine told me about. It's a quarry where high school kids skinny-dip. Supposed to be off a gravel road to the east, just after a billboard for the Gateway Arch."

"That big arch along the Mississippi River in Saint Louis? My mom and dad took me there when I was in junior high."

"What the hell for?"

"They said Saint Louis was the gateway to the West. They liked looking at historical sites."

"Sounds about as interesting as watching paint dry," Maddy said while stifling a yawn. "That looks like our billboard ahead."

"Yeah, that's the arch. Great views from the top, I thought."

Maddy scanned the road ahead and checked her mirrors before turning onto the gravel road. There was no traffic anywhere in sight. Nobody saw a red car slipping onto quarry property.

Jasmine had said the land was fenced and posted with numerous No Trespassing signs but the ancient wooden gate wasn't latched. Today it was. Maddy stopped the car, unhooked the simple latch, and then drove toward the quarry. She soon pulled beyond a thick grove of poplars and parked near an overview of the quarry.

"Let's get out and stretch," she said. "We can walk and talk. It won't take long."

"Leave the gun in the car, OK?"

"No problem," Maddy said, as she pulled the handgun out of her purse and shoved it in the glove box.

"Thanks. I feel better now."

"You should. Hey, let's get a better look at the quarry. Jasmine said kids dive from the rocks into the water. It's really deep and cold too, she said."

"Sounds fun."

"I think so too. Hey, give me a second. I think there's a rock in my boot."

As Maddy loosened her boot, John Michael walked to the rim of the quarry, then turned toward Maddy. He hadn't paid attention to her hands since she'd left the gun behind. The lock-blade knife she'd pulled from the top of her boot took him by surprise.

"What the—" John Michael said as Maddy plunged the knife into his throat. The stab severed an artery, and a billowing fountain of blood stained the ground.

John Michael grabbed at his throat, trying to stop the blood, as Maddy plunged the blade into his stomach. He doubled over and staggered clumsily. Maddy pushed him toward the quarry's edge and shoved him off the precipice. The only sound he made was a splash into the water sixty feet below. In less than a minute, he sank out of view.

Maddy threw her knife into the water, wiped her hands on the grass, and stepped carefully around a pool of blood. She grabbed the gun from the glove box, then threw it far into the quarry. Finally she kicked gravel and grit onto the bloodstain, which soon became barely noticeable— certainly not recognizable as blood.

She was unaware of any blood on her clothes or body. But she checked her reflection carefully in the windows of the car, then did the same with her face in the rental car's lit mirror. She was clean and hadn't even worked up a sweat. It had all happened so fast it almost didn't seem real.

A few minutes later, Maddy pulled onto the still-deserted highway and headed north. She was positive she hadn't been seen.

George Connelly drank beer and watched the TV news after leaving the jobsite in Memphis. There wasn't much else to do on the Arkansas side of the Mississippi River, where rent was cheaper and questions seldom asked. It was either watch TV in the mobile home or chug beer and snarf burgers in one of the nearby roadhouses—all featuring lit signs advertising GIRLS, GIRLS, GIRLS or TOPLESS WAITRESSES or TOTALLY NUDE DANCERS.

It was a trashy trailer in an even dumpier mobile home "park," a treeless rock lot that buzzed with the noise of truck traffic from the interstate. George wasn't looking for anything more than a cheap place to sleep when he rented it on a month-to-month agreement.

Most of his money paid the bills for the family home in Wisconsin. What a joke! George's family had disintegrated after Maddy's drug arrest. But he was still paying the bills for a home where his estranged wife, Caroline, was playing house with a Latino boy toy she'd met at the gym.

It was something he'd learned about in the hours after bailing Maddy out of jail. She had a furious argument with her mother after they'd driven her home to her apartment above the hair salon.

Caroline started the verbal brawl by refusing to give Maddy any money.

"You want five hundred bucks until payday? I wouldn't give you fifty cents until dawn."

"Be reasonable, *Mother*," Maddy wailed. "It's not like I've got a sugar daddy. I'm not as lucky as you."

"Watch your mouth, young lady. You're lucky we got you out of jail."

"You're lucky I haven't told Daddy about your live-in boyfriend. You'd have to pay your own bills."

"You little bitch!" Caroline said as she tore into Maddy's hair.

Maddy flailed wildly, then pulled Caroline to the floor by grabbing her necklace and twisting it tight around her throat.

George pulled the women apart, then grabbed his wallet. He gave Maddy all his cash—$743—and begged them to keep their voices down.

"The cops will be here! We'll all be in jail with no one to call for bail. Shut up! For God's sake, shut up!"

"Gimme that money, bitch!" Caroline snarled as she grabbed for the bills. "That's *my* money. I earned it."

"Is that how it works? You sometimes fuck him and he pays you? We call that something else wherever I've been."

Caroline turned red with rage and shoved Maddy aside as she raced into the kitchen. She pulled open a drawer and fumbled for a knife before George grabbed her from behind, bear-hugged her arms, and told his wife and daughter the fight was over.

"Your mom and I are leaving. You've got money and your freedom, Maddy."

"Get that bitch outta here," Maddy snarled.

"You're dead to me, you little tramp. I never want to see you again."

"You both need to cool off. We're still a family. Call us when the charges are dropped."

George still held Caroline's hand as they left Maddy's apartment, but it wasn't a gentle squeeze. Her fingers were painfully mashed together and bruised from her rings. He'd never touched Caroline in anger, but George believed he was all that stood between the women and bloodshed.

"You're breaking my hand," Caroline said through tears as George opened the truck door and lifted her inside.

He slammed the door shut and then raced behind the wheel, warning Caroline to stay seated. She sobbed and massaged her hand as they drove toward the highway.

"I'll see a doctor when we get home," she said. "I'm sure my hand's broken."

"That hand ain't broke. You'd never use it again if I really wanted to hurt you. I can still swing a hammer all day long."

"Yeah, you're quite the big man. Beating up a woman. Think that makes you tough?"

"I didn't beat you up. I stopped you from killing my daughter."

"She's not *your* daughter, George. You couldn't satisfy me even when we were newlyweds."

George rarely thought about that fateful night. He'd been beaten as a boy by both his father and his stepmother. He'd learned to stay silent as he was whipped with a belt, punched in the face, burned with cigarettes, and jabbed in the hands with a kitchen fork. If he wept, the beatings grew more severe and painful, especially the attacks on his hands. And when the attacks ended, he'd locked the violence deep into his mind—where it couldn't hurt him.

That's what became of the night his family life ended. He'd been silent throughout the long drive back to Wisconsin, never responding as Caroline raged endlessly. He recalled the details, but from years of practice, he knew how to lock it away. What's learned as a child never leaves.

She'd said they were through, of course. She'd taunted him to take a blood test to prove he hadn't fathered Maddy. And she'd bragged about the way Jerry Maldonado made her scream with pleasure.

"He's twice the man you are, Georgie boy," she laughed.

She'd said plenty more too, but George's hearing had partly disconnected from his brain.

At home, he'd packed his things quickly. He calmly told Caroline to look after the dogs and Maddy's horse and then drove away from Howard County and his country spread—a place he'd always considered a dream home for his family.

George left the Memphis jobsite at noon. Work ended early on Saturdays, and his thoughts wandered as he drove across the Mississippi River into Arkansas.

He thought of the last time he'd seen Caroline and Maddy. Not so much the details, which hurt too much. Broad brushstrokes of thought were possible without mental agony, and George needed to think about what to do next. He believed the eventual divorce and homestead sale wouldn't ruin him financially. It also seemed likely that he might get ahead without the financial millstones of a jailbird daughter and a cheating wife.

In the trailer, he kicked his boots off at the door, then stretched out on the couch and stared at the TV. He clicked through the channels until he found an old black-and-white western, which put him to sleep for several hours.

Around suppertime, George walked to the nearest roadhouse, a tin-roofed shack known as the Red Rooster. The topless dancers weren't especially pretty, but they weren't pushy gold diggers. Mostly they danced and hustled drinks, though a few would agree to bedtime fun for the right price.

George wasn't looking for action. He was hungry, and the place served a passable burger and fries. Plus he hated drinking alone.

The company wasn't ideal, but George had worked with feed-cap rednecks long enough to tolerate their inane chatter. He even grew to enjoy bantering with Red, a burly field hand who occupied the same barstool every night.

"Hey, George," he drawled while exhaling the last drag off an unfiltered cigarette. "We ain't seen ya here at the titty bar for a few days. Ya been in jail?"

"They'll never take me alive, Red. Who's winning the ball game?"

"Cardinals. Just like last night. They're gettin' hot at the right time."

"Yeah, yeah, yeah," said George, a Cubs fan who despised the Saint Louis team.

Red chattered as George pretended to be absorbed in the game. He'd made up his mind about Caroline; they were through. It didn't bother him a bit. But his heart ached when he thought of losing Maddy. Even if Caroline was telling the truth about their daughter's paternity—no certainty—he'd been nothing short of a loving and supportive father. He was having second thoughts about trashing his cell phone, a rash act meant to keep Caroline and her hurtful words out of his life. Only after he'd dropped the phone into the Mississippi River from a railroad bridge had he considered it was the only number Maddy had for contacting him, though she still had his address.

"Nice ass on that dancer, ain'a?" Red suddenly said.

"Yeah, sure, sure," George replied. "Maybe a little top heavy, though."

Red lit up another smoke, then studied the dancer's upper body as if he'd never seen it before. "Yer nuts, George. She's a babe."

George seldom watched the poorly paid dancers, who relied on tips and 50 percent kickbacks received on every ten-dollar split of cheap "champagne" sold to the gullible and horny. It was low-dollar sparkling wine. Whenever a new dancer sat next to him and said, "Want to buy me a drink, handsome?" George knew what to say.

"You're wasting time, honey. I'm so broke my paydays don't hardly matter. It's all gone as soon as I get it."

It wasn't exactly the truth, but it was close enough. He was under no obligation to confide in topless female strangers. His legal obligations were to a cheating wife and the property they owned together—though he'd paid for all of it.

CHAPTER 36
SURPRISE VISITOR

George had a belly full of beer and the deadened reaction time of an overserved sloth but still was jolted awake by the heavy pounding at his door. It was either the cops or someone seeking the kind of attention triggered by a cop knock.

He grabbed the fully loaded .9 mm handgun from his nightstand, cinched up his sweatpants, and walked quietly to the trailer's door. Then he stood silently, peering through the security peephole on the high-security metal door. On the other side was an attractive young woman, perhaps a dancer from the Red Rooster who'd watched his alcohol-fueled stumble home.

As an armed marksman, George wasn't worried about robbery. But he wanted to avoid dealing with a lying con woman only after his money. If he'd wanted that kind of life, he might have stayed with Caroline.

"What do you want?" George finally bellowed.

"Daddy, it's me. Please let me in."

George took a closer look—beyond the jet-black hair, flashy jewelry, and severe makeup. It was Maddy! He unlocked the door, and she stepped inside, slinging her duffel onto the couch and hugging her father tightly.

"What are you doing here?" he asked while returning the hug. "You're not supposed to leave Missouri."

"They dropped the charges against me," Maddy lied. "I gave a statement and agreed to testify against John Michael."

"That's great, I guess. How come you look so different?"

"I changed my hairstyle and makeup because people in Gillespie kept looking at me funny. Being arrested was bad, but the newspaper really messed me up."

"Huh?"

"Their so-called news story made me out to be a big-time drug dealer. And the mug shot must have been seen by everyone in town. People at the coffee shop whispered when I was around. Some of them pointed at me when they thought I wasn't looking."

"You kind of look like some rock star."

"People don't recognize me now. That's a big deal in a small town like Gillespie."

"How did you get here?"

"I keep your address and phone number in my purse. How come you don't answer the phone?"

"I got rid of it. The only calls I got were from Caroline, asking for money."

"I ditched my phone too. It was more hassle than it was worth."

"Did you drive here? Where's the car?"

"I got a friend to drive me to Saint Louis," Maddy fibbed. "I took a bus to a small town in Illinois, a place called Carbondale. They've got an Amtrak station."

"I drove through it a few times. Carbondale is on US 51, right?"

"I guess so. I bought a train ticket to Memphis and took a cab to your place."

"What are you going to do now? Need some money?"

"I can't go back to Gillespie. When the charges were dropped, the newspaper printed a tiny news story. Nobody even saw it. I'm still one half of Bonnie and Clyde, to the local yokels."

"You can stay with me if you want. Your mom and I are through, in case you ain't heard."

"Is she still seeing Jerry Maldonado?"

"I guess so. There were other problems too."

"She's gonna try to take everything you own. She was bragging about it the last time we talked."

Again and again, Maddy instinctively lied without missing a beat. It was the path she chose whenever opportunity knocked, or when times got tough.

"You knew about it? That she was cheating on me?"

"Last time I was home, I had suspicions about all the time she spent at the gym. She always dressed like she was going on a date."

"You should have told me."

"I didn't know for sure, Daddy. I wanted to be fair."

"I'm still paying for everything back home. Think your mother will get a job? That'd help."

"That's not what she's planning. Jerry's already living in your house. You can figure the rest out, I'm sure."

"I just wish there was something I could do. How did everything get so messed up?"

"I've got some ideas. We can talk more later. I need some sleep."

Ida spent most of her weekend at home. She talked at length with her mother both Saturday and Sunday morning, bought groceries, and tidied her apartment. Most of Sunday afternoon she spent looking through the big paper printed in Milwaukee, watching sports on TV, and thinking about the two fugitives from justice in Missouri.

Just as she started running the hot water in the shower, her cell phone chirped and buzzed noisily on the kitchen table. It might have been OK to let the call go to voice mail; her showers lasted no more than ten minutes. But it was neither the way she'd been raised nor what was expected of the best cops.

Stoney was calling. Again. For some reason, he couldn't believe there was little chance for a shared future. She'd already tried marriage to another cop, but the comforts of having had a spouse on the job, too, were far outweighed by professional rivalries and jealousies.

"This is Detective Ida Mae Rollins."

"Hey, it's me."

"Hello, me. Any chance you're calling to say you arrested our druggie murderers?"

"Not yet. But I've got a lead. Want to hear more?"

"Spill it, Stoney. Don't make me wait. I've been beating myself up since talking to Thad Elliott's mama."

"Why? You didn't do anything wrong."

"Try explaining that to a woman with a murdered and dismembered son. One you've told the suspected killers are on the loose."

"Why not blame the cops in Gillespie? We were supposed to keep track of them."

"If anyone can be blamed, it's the parents who posted property bonds and the judge who approved the deal."

"All they were facing were drug charges. It was just one of those things. You know the job as well as me."

Ida paused at his final words. It was the kind of remark Bill had never made. Not once. He'd always acted as if her police work was second rate.

"I guess you're right," she said. "But I can't expect Wanda Elliott to be understanding. She asked me why we let them get away."

"We can't win them all, Ida. But we win most."

"Thanks. Maybe I needed to hear some encouraging words."

"You're a smart cop. If you work hard, good things will happen. The harder you work, the luckier you get."

CHAPTER 37
LATE-NIGHT CALLER

I had just fallen into bed and pulled the cat onto my lap and was drifting toward sleep when the phone rang. If it had been my cell phone, I'd have let the call go to voice mail. Calls on the landline tended to be more serious. Was someone in Becky's family ill or injured? In mine?

"Norwood residence, Ed speaking."

"Mr. Norwood, this is Detective Ida Mae Rollins. We need to talk. It can't wait until morning."

I shivered involuntarily as my thoughts ran wild.

"Am I in trouble?" I finally stammered.

"I'd already be in your house showing you a warrant if you were getting arrested. But something might have happened with the murder. Can we talk?"

"Sure. Want me to come downtown?"

"I'm pulling into your driveway now. Got any coffee?"

"I'll get Becky to make us a pot. Once the phone rang, she was wide awake."

I let Ida in the front door. She was wearing her uniform and badge, which was unusual. There was a gun, handcuffs, and a police radio on her duty belt. Maybe she wasn't going to arrest me, but it looked as if she might arrest someone. Normally she wore khakis, a knit shirt, and a jacket that covered her shoulder holster—an everyday look intended to put others at ease.

"What's up?" I asked.

"I can't tell you too much. I'm hoping you're still friendly with the Connellys?"

"We haven't seen George for weeks, and I can't reach him by phone. Caroline's been sort of funny too."

"Funny? How do you mean?"

"She's never got time to talk anymore," Becky said. "All she's said about George is that he's busy on a jobsite in Memphis. She said she doesn't know when he'll be home."

"That's not normal," I said. "He usually came home once a month for a long weekend."

"And you remember the horse Maddy left in the barn?" Becky said.

"You mean Lucky?" Ida asked.

"You've got a good memory, Detective."

"We never know what might be important. We observe and record a lot. I'm partial to animals, especially horses. How is poor ol' Lucky? His name sure ain't accurate, unless you think it's lucky to be neglected."

"That's the thing, Detective."

"It's Ida. What happened?"

"I saw the kid who helped care for the horse take him away in a horse trailer. And Caroline is hardly ever home. And she's not good about answering the phone."

"Is that different from the way it used to be? I figured you two were close friends."

"We never got *really* close, but yeah, we were friends. We'd usually chat outside and sometimes have coffee and cookies in her kitchen or mine. That stopped a few weeks ago."

"Anything else?"

"I'm almost certain there's someone else staying in the house. A man. I've seen him looking from an upstairs window, peeking around the curtains."

"Interesting. Who is he?"

"We don't know," Becky said. "Eddie's suspicious, but I don't know if we should say this to you."

"This is a murder case. You're both material witnesses. Anything you've seen or heard could be helpful."

I took a deep swig of coffee, wiped my lips with a sleeve, and spoke slowly.

"I hate gossip, Ida. As much as I hate gossip, I hate gossips even more."

"Yeah? So what?"

"I've never told this to Becky, but one of the guys who eats breakfast at the diner brags to his buddies about this married woman he's been, well, intimate with."

"Who is this guy?"

"Everyone calls him Jerry. The woman he describes sounds just like Caroline, and the place where she lives has got to be George and Caroline's. He's described the place and says he's going to be taking it over."

"That might mean George isn't coming back."

I nodded as Becky shook her head sadly.

"You got an address for George?" Ida asked.

"I'm sure you can get it from Caroline," Becky said.

"It's best that she doesn't know anything about this visit or what we've talked about. I can't say why, but you've got to keep this a secret."

"We will," Becky said as she stared at me.

I finally stood up and pushed away from the table. It took me only a few seconds to reach the stairs leading to our bedroom and the home office.

"Where are you going, Mr. Norwood?" Ida asked.

"I've got a mailing address for George," I said. "It's some jerkwater little town in Arkansas. He gave it to me when he went to work in Memphis, in case of an emergency."

Once I gave her the address, she thanked us and disappeared into the night.

CHAPTER 38
PLAYING A HUNCH

Ida sometimes doubted the police work of Bill Rollins. Her ex-husband too often acted on impulse, while she dotted all the i's, crossed all the t's. But as much as Bill's confidence and quick trigger bugged her, Ida admitted there were times when it was better to listen to the heart than the head. Bill's gut instincts sometimes led to headline-making arrests and celebrated acts of courage.

He had once saved three small children from a raging house fire and was hailed as a hero on TV news. But it also earned him a three-day suspension for violating departmental rules against entering a burning structure.

"They should have looked the other way," Ida had said at the time. "How could you remember a policy on burning buildings while kids were being killed?"

"I knew the policy," he'd said. "I just didn't care. Those kids were screaming from the attic. They'd have died if I hadn't dragged 'em out."

Ida thought about that rescue as she gathered her thoughts about Stoney's phone call and the interview she'd just wrapped up with the Norwoods. If she went by the book, her next move was writing full reports on the search in Missouri and the information supplied by Ed and Becky. In the morning, she would review her findings with Sheriff Clark, then spend more time on a conference call with Missouri authorities. By the afternoon, maybe evening, she'd have a well-considered plan for what to do next.

Ida wasn't waiting that long. She headed toward Interstate 94 after leaving the Norwoods' home. By midnight, she was cutting past the Chicago Loop and aiming at the Interstate 57 interchange.

Before dawn, she'd make a choice between heading west to Gillespie or continuing south.

•⠀•⠀•

Maddy slept well on the couch, which wasn't exposed to the blazing Sunday-morning sunshine. Then she loafed around the trailer the rest of the day, talking with George, watching TV, and raiding the trailer's well-stocked refrigerator. She slept a full night into Monday morning.

It was her father's heavy footsteps and the smell of fresh coffee in the kitchen that finally roused her from slumber.

"You going to work today, Daddy?" she mumbled as she shuffled through a pile of dirty dishes for a coffee cup.

"I took today off. Boss man thinks I needed Monday off for a trip back home. What he doesn't know won't hurt him."

Maddy rinsed her cup under scalding water, then squirted a dab of dish soap in the bottom and swished it around with a sponge. Finally, she rinsed the cup again and dried it with a paper towel.

"When did you get so neat?" George asked. "How come you never kept Lucky and his stall so clean?"

"Lucky is a horse. I'm a woman. Is that so hard to understand?"

"Whatever. I think we need to head up to Gillespie today. I need to make sure that property bond is quashed. Didn't they say something about that in court?"

"Maybe they did," Maddy said. "I was so excited I didn't ask."

"I guess I understand. But just so you know, that property is all that I've got left. I can't afford to lose it."

"You worry too much, Daddy."

"Just the same, we're going to take care of that business today."

"No problem," Maddy said, though she had no intention of ever again seeing Gillespie or the rest of Missouri. This visit with her father was getting too complicated. Maddy had hoped to catch the train to New

Orleans at the Memphis station. She'd been counting on her father to give her the fat roll of bills he carried, wish her well, and watch her wave goodbye from the southbound train.

But when they talked about her plans late Sunday afternoon, Maddy learned her dad didn't have his customary roll of cash. He was living paycheck to paycheck and just barely getting by.

Now she needed a new plan—one that would keep her father from poking around in Gillespie. As George showered, noisily singing an off-key rock hit from his boyhood, Maddy searched the kitchen drawers and found a boning knife. She hid the blade in her purse, then chased her father out of the bathroom so she could "freshen up."

Maddy told her father the best route to Gillespie was via I-55 northbound. It would very soon involve traveling through the bootheel region of Missouri, but Maddy wasn't planning to visit the Show-Me State.

She'd beg him to take a bathroom break while still in Arkansas, explaining, "It's that time of the month, Daddy." She'd ask her dad to pull into a rest stop or an isolated spot in a busy truck stop. She'd plead for "a little privacy" so it would be possible to change into fresh panties.

Then she'd ask him to crawl into the back of the pickup truck, under the low-slung camper top, to retrieve the duffel she'd thrown near the cab. She couldn't do it because of her cramps, she'd explain, and tearfully ask for her tampons and underwear. Maddy would have the knife ready as he handed over the duffel with one hand, balancing himself with the other. She knew his arms would be too occupied for self-defense. It wouldn't take long for a plunging knife to render a man helpless.

Once Maddy had decided emotional attachment with a father was illogical for a grown woman, her decision was made. Taking the life of a parent who'd already had a full life was less of an offense than murdering younger men in Wisconsin and Iowa—one barely an adult, the other a married breadwinner. She felt even less remorse about killing John Michael Thomas. He simply had to disappear. There would be no retribution from a make-believe God in the sky. Maddy was out of options. George had to go.

"I'm all set for Gillespie, Daddy," Maddy said as she left the bathroom, her hair teased into a rooster-like comb and her makeup carefully applied.

With dangling earrings and a heavy gold necklace, a pullover top, tight jeans, and half boots, Maddy looked both attractive and feminine.

"You look real pretty, Madeline," her father said, using the name he'd reserved for their happiest and closest times.

"Oh, Daddy," she said. "I'm still your best girl, aren't I?"

"There's nobody like you," George said. "You've always been my baby girl."

⁂

As Ida rolled south, Stoney met with Sheriff Thompson. He'd need extra horsepower to confirm what he suspected about the missing drug suspects—a theory he'd explained to Ida in their phone call. Stoney would need Bing's blessings to step away from his regular duties.

"Got a minute, boss?" he asked as the clock inched toward seven.

"What the hell are you doing here so early?"

"It's about Connelly and Thomas, the two druggies who made bail."

"You found them?"

"Not exactly, but I found a place to start looking."

"I'll drive. Let's go," Bing said as he jumped to his feet.

It was the kind of reaction Stoney had wanted. Bing was a cop long before he was elected sheriff, and he liked action on the street more than desk work. A lot more.

"It's not quite that simple," Stoney said. "We're going to need a boat, divers, and a search warrant."

"We can do that. First you gotta tell me why."

"You remember that lady detective from Wisconsin?"

"Your girlfriend?"

"I wish."

"What, then?"

"We happened to talk about our druggies right after she got murder warrants for them. That dismemberment killing in Wisconsin she'd talked about."

"I remember."

"She was plenty shook up when Connelly and Thomas disappeared. I felt bad for her. I got to thinking about where they might have gone. I did some driving around, thinking maybe I'd spot the car Connelly rented."

"Any luck?"

"All I knew was that she'd talked to her coworkers about going to Saint Louis. I looked south of town first, figuring the Saint Louis story was a lie to send us in the wrong direction. Didn't find anything."

"You might as well have been looking for a needle in a haystack."

"I was depressed about it. So I drove to that quarry north of town, the place where the high school kids skinny-dip."

"I used to do that, too, back in the day."

The sudden mental image of a nude tubby lawman frolicking froze Stoney. It was an alarming thought, one that caused him to lose his train of thought.

"You skinny-dipped?"

"All of us did. I'll bet you did too. Hey! Is that what you did in the quarry over the weekend?"

"Of course not. I go there to think sometimes. It's quiet and deserted most of the time."

"Get any great thoughts?"

"There were fresh tire tracks in the gravel, and not from a truck. It looked like a passenger car had been there."

"So what?"

"They must have been in a hurry. The wooden gate was standing open. Someone unhooked the latch, drove near the quarry, and parked. When they left, the gate was left open."

"Coulda been anybody."

"Maybe. But it made me call Randy Carlsen. He's a foreman for the contractor who owns the quarry. We played football together in college and stayed in touch."

"He know anything?"

"That gate is linked to a couple security cameras hidden in the poplars. One shows who opens the gate. Another tracks motion in the parking area near the quarry. The cameras sit dormant unless something moves in the field of focus."

"We need a warrant for that?"

"Maybe. That's for the prosecutor to decide. But Randy let me look at what the camera recorded for the last few days. The first thing it recorded was a passenger car matching the description of one rented by Connelly.

The driver opened the gate, but it didn't look like Connelly. This was someone with short black hair."

"Stoney, she's a hairstylist. She could change her appearance fast."

"I figured that too. There was a passenger too. He looked just like Thomas. They walked away from the car together, then went out of view. Less than ten minutes later, the driver hurried back to the car. Alone. The camera got a good facial view. It was a woman. Then she drove away from the gate and disappeared."

"Where's the guy?"

"I think he's in the water. I looked everywhere near the parking area after seeing the security video. There were two sets of footprints going near the rim of the quarry, but just one set heading back to the car."

"Get the boat and dive team ready. I'm going to the courthouse for a search warrant. Let's meet here in an hour."

Ida drove her Mustang into Arkansas before the rush-hour traffic began surging east to Memphis. She'd talked with Stoney before dawn, getting coffee and using the washroom in an I-57 truck stop in southern Illinois. He told Ida about using the dive team in Gillespie to search the quarry where Connelly and Thomas had last been seen. It was something she'd wanted to witness before learning Connelly was almost certainly on the loose.

Ida remembered the way George and Maddy had looked at each other in court during her bond hearing. She also vividly recalled the way the two hugged when Maddy was released from jail. It was in stark contrast to her brief, cold-looking embrace with Caroline. It wasn't so likely that Maddy would seek help from her mother, Ida thought, especially with her father living much closer—just one state away from Gillespie.

Ida hoped to catch Maddy by surprise. She'd brought the Wisconsin murder warrants and Missouri bail-jumping warrants in her laptop bag, which doubled as a desktop in her car. She'd also brought copies of all Wisconsin DMV information on George Connelly, including the make, model, and color of his pickup truck. It would be helpful to spot that truck parked outside the address she'd punched into her GPS. Ida believed Maddy had ditched the rental car, maybe at an airport or train station.

She still had doubts about what she was doing. She was merely playing a hunch that Maddy would run to Daddy for help, based solely on brief observations from court and outside the jail. This wasn't by-the-book detective work. That type of training would put her at the scene of a possible body recovery. Searching for Connelly was something she felt in her heart.

She'd grown close to John Michael Thomas's mother, Martha, before the young man was identified as a murder suspect. If his body was found in the quarry water, someone would have to tell Martha Thomas. Ida wanted that responsibility. She knew how to do the job properly, sparing none of the facts but presenting them in accordance with the milk of human kindness.

That sad duty might still be possible, Ida realized, once she'd paid a visit to George's trailer home in Arkansas. If she struck out in the search for Maddy, she'd still be needed in Gillespie. It could take hours, sometimes days, to find a submerged body. And there was no certainty of finding a body, just a probability. It was better than a hunch, though. There were images of two people walking toward the quarry rim, but only one returning to the car driven onto the property.

Once Ida was in Arkansas, her GPS led her to a run-down-looking cul-de-sac across the highway from a crummier-looking topless bar, the Red Rooster. A single trailer of three looked habitable. Parked in the gravel near the front door was a pickup truck licensed in Wisconsin to George Connelly. It was easily visible from the highway, where Ida slowed but did not stop.

Instead, she pulled next to the Red Rooster, giving herself a clear view of the trailer. The bright morning sun would prevent anyone from seeing inside the Mustang, but Ida could see into the trailer with binoculars.

Now it was a waiting game. She hoped the game would end before anyone got nosy about an out-of-state car parked near the obviously closed Red Rooster. Or before she was forced to seek a toilet.

CHAPTER 39
WAITING AND WATCHING

Ida struggled to stay alert as she watched George's pickup truck. She'd been awake for more than twenty-four hours, fueled by investigative adrenaline and coffee. But tedium combined with a comfortable bucket seat and warm sunshine invited slumber. She wished she could exit the car and trot around the Red Rooster's parking lot. A jog would have pepped her up, but Ida couldn't risk being spotted from the trailer, especially not while clad in a police uniform.

She finally nodded off but jolted awake at the sound of a truck door being slammed. One door only. She was sure of it. But she couldn't be sure that there hadn't been earlier sounds of another door closing and a tailgate banging into place.

Cursing herself, Ida started the Mustang and watched the truck drive out of the cul-de-sac. She couldn't see into the truck without binoculars, which had fallen from her lap to the floor. But even if they'd been used, there were just seconds available for a glimpse through the windshield or the driver's side window. Ida believed a man was driving—maybe because that's what she expected—but had no idea whether anyone else was in the cab, or, less likely, the truck bed. Even if someone other than the driver was in the truck, there was no guarantee it was Maddy.

Another possibility. Someone else might still be in the trailer, not the pickup truck.

It was decision time. Follow the truck? Watch the trailer?

If Maddy was in the trailer and Ida followed the truck, she'd lose her murder suspect. A by-the-book strategy would keep the trailer under surveillance, with Ida using her radio to alert other squads to follow and stop the truck. But Ida was alone. And she was in Arkansas, not Wisconsin. She didn't have a backup standing by.

Ida went with her gut and hit the gas. Gravel spun off her tires as she aimed for the highway. She easily kept the truck in view but didn't get close enough to arouse suspicion. The job of tailing became easier once she'd followed the truck onto Interstate 55, a straight shot into Missouri. It caused Ida to consider whether she'd made a mistake leaving the trailer.

Why would Maddy go into a state where she was wanted for jumping bail and dealing drugs? It was an unnecessary risk. But if Ida ended the pursuit and returned to the trailer, she'd lose both the truck and the time frame that would have been most likely for the departure of anyone else from the trailer.

Ida kept rolling north, always keeping other vehicles between the Mustang and the pickup. As she noticed the first sign advertising a Missouri attraction, her cell phone chirped and buzzed. She saw the call was coming from Stoney.

"This is Detective Ida Mae Rollins."

"Hey, Ida. It's me, Stoney. I'm towing the boat. The dive team is following in a van. We'll be in the quarry soon."

"Let me know how it's going, OK? Did Sheriff Bing slow you down?"

"Bing's in the van. He practically ran to the courthouse for a search warrant."

"My sheriff would stay in the office."

"Hey, did you ever let him know what you're doing today?"

"Oh shit. I knew I was forgetting something."

"Call him. I'll get back to you."

As Ida punched in the speed dial for Sheriff Clark, the truck signaled for a turn on the approaching exit.

"Hey, Ida, where the heck are you? I thought we'd have a conference call with Missouri and Iowa today."

"I'm on the trail of our female murder suspect," Ida said, hoping her hunch was right. It had grown more foolish, she thought, as the miles and minutes disappeared in interstate travel.

"Where are you?"

"Near Memphis. I've gotta go, sir."

Ida merged right and followed the truck onto the exit for Paragould, a name and Arkansas location that meant nothing to Ida. She anticipated the truck heading east, avoiding Missouri, but it instead turned west toward Paragould and a truck stop.

Ida followed the pickup into the truck stop. She parked near the building as the truck pulled into a space near the edge of the parking area, the kind of spot favored by dog owners. But there were no dogs or other vehicles.

She watched both doors of the pickup truck open, then saw a man and a younger woman walk toward the rear of the vehicle. The woman lowered the tailgate and stepped back. Then she stretched her back and gestured to something in the truck bed.

Ida jogged toward the truck as the man, watched closely by the woman, started crawling inside. Their backs were turned, and Ida took care to stay on a path shielded by vehicles at the fuel pumps. She ran softly, the sound of her breath more noticeable than footsteps.

Maddy finally whirled away from the truck bed and faced Ida.

"Police! Freeze!" Ida shouted as she took a shooter's stance and aimed her service pistol for a center-mass hit—by-the-book training Ida had committed to muscle memory.

"Hands up! Drop your weapon! Hands on top of the camper."

Maddy dropped her knife and held her hands aloft. "Don't shoot! I haven't done anything."

She then raised her hands as directed, her back to Ida.

Ida holstered the pistol and snatched her handcuffs. It took just a moment to cuff Maddy from behind. Ida then looked at the knife and the man in the truck.

The blade was bloody. The man inside the truck was holding the side of his lower abdomen.

"I'm hurt," George Connelly said. "You better call an ambulance."

"Can someone call 911?" Ida barked at a small crowd of onlookers. "I'm a little busy right now."

"What's goin' on?" a heavyset truck driver demanded.

"Police business, sir. This woman's under arrest," Ida loudly replied.

"It appears this man has been stabbed. I saw her drop that knife on the ground."

"That's a lie!" Maddy said. "My dad got cut on the tailgate latch. I was trying to help him."

Ida said nothing. The murmuring crowd encouraged Maddy.

"This is a false arrest. I didn't do anything. She threw that knife on the ground herself. Police brutality! Someone help me!"

Ida pushed Maddy inside the cab of the truck, slammed the door, and leaned against it. Then she turned to the crowd. "You can see that I'm a police officer. This ain't a disguise. I've got warrants for the woman's arrest from Missouri and Wisconsin."

Her remarks registered with the trucker. He blocked the other truck door before Maddy could crawl out, and then he spoke slowly and carefully to everyone.

"Our cops and an ambulance will be comin' soon. They'll sort this out. If this lady in uniform ain't a cop, they'll know what to do."

"Much obliged, sir," Ida said as Maddy futilely screamed, thrashed, and kicked in the truck cab.

"I used to be on the job too," he said. "Finally got sick of the heartache and started driving trucks. I was Memphis PD."

"Tough town," Ida said. "Hey! Is there anyone here with medical training? The man in the back of the truck is hurt."

"I'm a CNA," a young woman said. "I can put pressure on the wound, maybe stop the bleeding."

"Please. That would help," Ida said, taking a good look at the samaritan. She was no more than nineteen, obviously pregnant, and perhaps malnourished. Her pink tank top revealed little of the baby bump, but her bony arms and crude tattoos were easily seen.

Despite her worn-out and mud-spattered flip-flops, the CNA moved nimbly to George Connelly's side. She used George's shirttails to stanch the bleeding, her wispy brown ponytail swaying rhythmically as she covered the bloody wound.

"How bad is he?" Ida asked.

"I've seen worse. He'll live," she said as an ambulance and two squad cars pulled into the truck stop, sirens screaming and emergency lights flashing.

Ida breathed a sigh of relief, then identified herself to a state trooper. She was a stranger to Arkansas, but she was still confident she'd acted properly. Another cop would be able to see the truth about a raving, confined woman, an older man with a puncture wound, and a bloody knife on the pavement.

Or would he?

Stoney and Bing remained in the boat as two divers began a search of the quarry waters. The sun was directly overhead and hot, reflecting off the water in shimmering heat waves. There was good visibility below the surface because of the sunlight, but the quarry bottom was much darker and covered with debris—car parts, automotive wheels, even a metal bed frame. Anything plunging into the depths might snag on the junk and stay put for weeks, months, maybe years.

Stoney anchored the boat below the rim of the quarry, just a short walk from the parking area where a man and woman had walked toward the water a few days earlier. He'd seen the security video enough times to make an educated guess of where a falling body might have landed.

"I'm sure this is where we ought to look," he finally said to Bing.

"Water's a funny thing," the sheriff replied. "I've been on a lot of these. This might be the best place to *start* looking, but a body could drift."

Just then, a diver surfaced. "We need the lights down at the bottom. Can't hardly see a thing with these flashlights."

Stoney lowered the lights into the water on a marine rope cinched to a net holding the lights. The diver took the lights off the rope and plunged out of view.

"This could take a while," Stoney said.

"And we might not find anything. I've got a grid started on a map of the quarry. We'll move the boat whenever the divers come up for air. We'll mark the areas where they've looked."

The broiling boredom in the boat was occasionally interrupted by their police radios. Finally, Stoney's cell jangled noisily. Bing saw the call was coming from "Ida," a contact that didn't include her last name or position.

"I think your girlfriend wants you," Bing laughed.

"I bet it's police business," Stoney said and grabbed his phone. "This is Lieutenant Bedford Stonewall. May I help you?"

"I need some help, Stoney. Can someone from your department talk with the cops down here? They want to verify what I've said. I guess they're being extra careful, but doggone it, I showed 'em the warrants and paperwork."

"Would a call from the sheriff suffice?"

"That would be perfect. Put him on your phone. I'll give mine to the friendly trooper who's watching me like a hawk."

Bing took the phone from Stoney and identified himself. He then was quiet for a long time, occasionally muttering, "I see," or "Is that right?" and "You ain't serious, are you?"

As Ida listened to the trooper, she felt as if her head might explode, unless her bladder burst first. She'd downed half a dozen cups of coffee to stay alert, but her equally caffeinated all-male counterparts apparently had basketball-sized kidneys.

Stoney was baffled by the half of the conversation he heard. He tried to have a quizzical look on his face as Bing ended the call.

"OK, then. You call my office to verify who I am," Bing said. "Then call me back on the cell phone number they give you."

"Ida's in a jam, huh?" Stoney asked.

"Them Arkansas cops must think they're in some reality show. They're actually checking out the claims our suspect made."

"What'd she say?"

"Stay calm, now. She says the guy back in Wisconsin was killed and hacked up by a guy who runs a diner and cuts meat. It's a big cover-up, and she's been framed by Ida."

"What?"

"There's more too. We've charged her with a drug crime only committed by Thomas, she says."

"That's bullshit."

"Wait—there's still more. The guy who was driving Connelly north on

I-55 apparently was stabbed by her at a truck stop. But she says Ida planted the knife at the scene."

"That's crazy. What's the stabbed guy say?"

"He's been stitched up. No organs or arteries damaged. And—get this—he says his daughter didn't stab him. He stuck himself with a screwdriver. That's his story, even though said screwdriver isn't bloody."

"This is all going crazy."

"He also refuses to sign a complaint against his daughter. Anyhow, we just gotta be patient. I'll be getting called back, and I'll give them the straight scoop. They'll be calling Sheriff Clark in Wisconsin too, and he'll do the same. The truth will win out."

"I hope you're right."

"All we gotta do is float here and wait on the divers. When my phone rings, I'll set the record straight. Until then, I suggest we enjoy the sunshine."

CHAPTER 40
GETTING BACK TO WORK

It was dark when the Arkansas cops finally believed Ida was telling them the truth. They'd verified her claims, determined the official paperwork was legitimate, and, thankfully, allowed her to freely use the bathroom. When the ordeal was near an end, long past supper hour, she was treated to a surprisingly good pork tenderloin sandwich and a piece of blueberry pie à la mode.

"This is really great," she said to the friendliest of her law enforcement colleagues.

"Yew surprised by that? Y'all think we's just a bunch of redneck crackers?"

"My mama cooks like this. We're from southern Illinois. It's more like Dixie than Chicago," Ida said and scooped the last of the ice cream into her mouth. She couldn't remember eating a better meal. At least not recently.

"No offense meant, Detective. About anything," the trooper said with a grin. "We don't get many Yankee cops down this way. Y'all got us confused."

"I'm free to go, then?"

"No reason to hold ya. Not now. We sure do 'ppreciate you stickin' around to answer our questions," Trooper Burton Bloodworth said. "Y'all been real professional, Detective."

"It's Ida, please."

"Everyone calls me Bloody. You might as well too."

After she supplied her cell number and other contacts, Ida retrieved her gun from the locker where police weapons were kept in the office. She snugged the piece into her holster, stretched her legs, and walked to the exit—pleased that she'd been allowed to drive her own car to the office.

"I guess this is goodbye, Bloody," Ida said with a smile and a handshake.

"Or until we meet again," he replied with a light-pressure grasp.

Ida appreciated the gentle touch since his large hand felt like chiseled stone. Also, she had minor aches and pains from taking Maddy into custody.

Ida left town as fast as legally permitted, then headed north on Interstate 55. She had no desire to linger in Arkansas. She'd drive into Missouri to Cape Girardeau and then veer northwest to Gillespie. She'd be either in the town or near it by midnight.

That was the plan. Reality took hold minutes after Ida rolled into the bootheel of Missouri, near the center point of the 1811–12 New Madrid earthquakes. Perhaps it was the influence of the seismic zone or, more likely, relief at being out of Arkansas, but Ida struggled to grip the steering wheel and keep her eyes open. She left the interstate and looked along a county highway for a place to stay. She skipped two small motels—mom-and-pop operations—that looked as if Hitchcock might have considered either as a location for *Psycho*. She opted for a bright, obviously busy inn that was part of a national group.

"We've only got one room left, but I hate to let ya take it," the clerk said between messy bites of an egg-salad sandwich. "It ain't got a TV, and the AC don't work too good."

"I'll take it," Ida said. "I just need a bed. Here's my credit card."

The room was accurately but incompletely described by pimply-faced "Noah," a high schooler further identified on his badge as "Asst. Mgr." He failed to say the room was stiflingly hot, filthy, and alive with flies.

Ida opened the sliding glass door of her second-floor room, a security taboo for nonpolice travelers—those without handguns. Then she kicked off her boots, tucked her gun under the pillow, fell into bed, and passed out. Morning sunshine and troubling thoughts woke her just after six o'clock.

What had Sheriff Clark been doing because of the phone calls from Arkansas? Ida hoped he'd quickly alerted Deputy Brooks to Maddy's insane claims, then stepped out of the way. Iowa needed notification that one of the homicide suspects was in custody, the other being sought and possibly deceased. Brooks could handle it.

Another possibility was Sheriff Clark deciding to have another look at Ed Norwood, who had come to the attention of police only because he'd reported roadside trash that turned out to be body parts. She'd learned Norwood was a gambler who sometimes fibbed about his whereabouts to his wife. But she'd also learned he wasn't involved in the death of Thad Elliott. That was entirely the work of Maddy Connelly and John Michael Thomas.

Her blood ran cold as she remembered the sheriff's initial suggestion to take Norwood into custody and stand on his toes to induce a confession. It was nutty, but he'd never entirely let it go. She brewed a watery cup of motel-room coffee, gulped the java when it cooled, and then called her boss.

"This is Howard County sheriff Peter Clark," he said in a deep, polished voice. "How may I serve you?"

Ida suspected he was heading to a breakfast fundraiser. The voice was pitch perfect.

"It's Ida. How did everything work out with Arkansas?"

"What do you mean? They playing football against the Badgers or something?"

Ida thought she might scream, but she kept her voice calm and professional. "About my arrest of Maddy Connelly. Yesterday in Arkansas? You took a call from the state cops down there."

"I was just having fun with you, Ida. Things went fine. Me and Scotty gave them what they wanted. Then we took another look at Ed Norwood."

Ida almost dropped the phone. She was silent for seconds.

"Ida? Are you still there, girl?"

"Yes, sir, I am. Just hoping to hear more of what happened in Howard County. And, sir, please don't take this the wrong way, but if you can't call me Ida or Detective, please don't call me 'girl.' It's demeaning."

"Sorry, Ida! Don't get all feminazi on me. I meant no harm. It was a term of friendship when I grew up. Still is, to some. I call Scotty 'boy,' and he doesn't mind."

"That's different, sir. You're both men. There's no imbalance of power."

"Imbalance of what? What are you talking about?"

"We can discuss it later. What's happening with Ed?"

"Maybe you got a little too close to Mr. Norwood. Can't see the forest because of the trees."

"That's nonsense, sir. I never looked at anyone harder. He's clean."

"Maybe. I'll have a better idea later today."

Ida was tumbling down the rabbit hole. She needed to disengage—and quick.

"Can I give you a call late this morning?" she said. "I'm heading into Gillespie. I'll update you when I get there."

"They ever find that body? Maybe he's not in the water. Maybe he's on the loose?"

"It's not likely, but it's possible. I'll know more later. The Gillespie cops said they'd call me if they found him. They haven't called."

"Not even your boyfriend?"

"He's not a boyfriend," Ida snapped. "Can I call you sometime before noon?"

"That'll be fine, *Detective*. Call me at eleven if it fits your schedule, *Ida*."

"Yes, sir, I will. Have a good day, sir."

The sheriff hung up without another word.

Ida couldn't remember the last time she'd been as angry. She felt hot beads of sweat forming on her scalp, soon to be forehead bound. She quickly stripped, ducked into a coolish shower, and then checked out and hit the road.

$\bullet \cdot \cdot \bullet$

Stoney spotted Ida's Mustang as he hitched the boat trailer to the SWAT team's SUV—one of few department vehicles with enough power to pull the heavy rig. The dive team's van would work, too, but not as well when it was fully loaded with four divers and all needed equipment—as it was today.

"We need to talk with the detective," Stoney said to Sheriff Bing. "She needs to know where we're at."

"Let's bring her with us. We've got room in the boat. We can talk while keeping track of the divers and updating the grid."

"Good idea, sir. Also it's a good idea to use two teams of divers today. Less downtime. Maybe we'll find something."

"There's a lot of water in that quarry. Don't get your hopes up. But if we don't find a body soon, it might have to wait until it floats up on its own. We can't tie up our staff indefinitely."

"Let's keep that to ourselves, OK, Sheriff? At least for now," Stoney said as Ida stepped near.

"Fine with me. Hey! Good morning, Detective. How's my favorite Yankee cop on this fine day?"

"Like I was rode hard and put away wet. Getting anywhere on the body search?"

"Didn't find anything yesterday," Bing said. "All we know is where the body *ain't*. We've got *two* diving teams today. Maybe we get lucky."

As the sun rose higher in the sky, Ida described her dealings with the Arkansas police and the troubling call with Sheriff Clark.

"That doesn't sound like the Peter Clark I knew in Quantico. Ain't he still trying to catch the bad guys?"

"He's an elected sheriff and faces the voters every two years. He spends at least half his time raising campaign funds and kissing butt. The rest of his time, he second-guesses me and his men."

"I'm an appointed sheriff," Bing finally said. "I focus on the work and trust the county to keep me employed. It's working so far. But if I spend too much time and money on any single task, the bean counters come after me."

"How much time can we spend out here, Sheriff?" Ida asked.

"One more day. Max."

For nearly twenty minutes, not another word was spoken. A hawk screeched from high in the treetops, and bugs bobbed and weaved in the shimmering heat waves coming off the water. One team of divers probed the water as the other rested. A blue heron streaked from a rocky ledge to just above the water—a feathered heat-seeking missile with a taste for fish.

"Any chance of taking me to shore real quick?" Ida asked as eleven o'clock approached. "Gotta talk with my sheriff. I'd like a little privacy, please."

"Once all the divers are on top and safe, we'll do it quick. But I mean quick," Bing said.

Minutes later, the four frogmen gave thumbs-up signals as Bing gestured between the boat and shore. In just a few minutes, Ida was on dry land and the boat was back helping the divers—two who rested and two who descended.

∴

The call to Sheriff Clark wasn't as bad as Ida had feared. Both kept calm and on topic. Ida soon learned that Ed Norwood had been reinterviewed at length the night before in his home. Deputy Brooks taped the interview while he and the sheriff asked questions and took notes.

"All we're going to do is see if he tells essentially the same story. People mostly remember the truth, but if they lied earlier, they mess up their stories. The details of a lie disappear."

"You're right, sir. I'm sorry about being peevish before."

"It's OK, Ida. You sounded kinda knocked out."

"I didn't get any real sleep till last night. I was awake for two days straight—mostly driving, but there was a little arrest I made too."

"You did good work, Ida. I hope you didn't get hurt struggling with Ms. Connelly."

"Coupla bumps and scratches. Nothing major. What's next for Mr. Norwood?"

"Once we compare what he said last night with his earlier statements, we'll know where we're at. How's it going in Missouri?"

"The divers are still searching the water. I'll call you if something happens. Even if nothing happens, I'll call you after sundown, and we can talk about what's next."

"Sounds good. I can spare you another day, but we need a detective here. Poor Scotty's getting run ragged."

"He's young. Got a lot of energy. Just like me."

∴

Sunset ended the day's body search, with no guarantee of more than another day devoted to the tedious and grim task. It would be a scaled-down two-diver search. Ida had come to realize she had better odds of winning a lottery jackpot than seeing the team quickly find anyone in such a large and deep body of water.

"Water is a living thing," Bing had said. "Even when there isn't a current, surface winds and seepage to groundwater keep things movin'."

"Won't the weight of a body hold it still?" Ida had asked.

"Only when it's held down by rocks, concrete, or heavy metal chains. If that was true, we'd have found young Mr. Thomas pretty quick."

Ida watched Stoney and the sheriff put the boat away, then decided to spend the night with her mother in Cobden. It was nearly an hour-long drive, but she'd have time at the wheel to make a phone call to her sheriff and then think about what she'd say to Martha Thomas and Wanda Elliott when she called in the morning.

The call to Sheriff Clark was the least time-consuming, so she got it out of the way. The sheriff was an old-school buffoon at times, but he knew how to quickly tell Ida what she needed to know. It took less than ten minutes. Ed Norwood's story had checked out; he was in the clear. Scotty Brooks had updated Iowa on the arrest of Maddy Connelly and the continuing search for John Michael Thomas. Iowa was told the search included a dive team, though it wasn't a 100 percent certainty that he wasn't alive and fleeing justice.

"Iowa says they're gonna hold their prosecution until we're finished," Clark said. "I bet Missouri does the same. You coming home in the morning?"

"I'll stay one more day. I've got a feeling about tomorrow," Ida said.

Actually, the only feeling she had was that they'd strike out. But it would give her plenty of time to telephone the mother of a murder victim, then the mother of a suspect who also might be dead.

It was the second phone call that especially troubled Ida. She wouldn't mislead Martha Thomas, but she couldn't just blurt out, "We think your dead son is at the bottom of a flooded quarry."

A night of watching TV and eating popcorn with her mother, a good night's rest in her childhood bed, and an early-morning breakfast would put her in the right frame of mind.

CHAPTER 41
BREAKING THE NEWS

Ida woke to the breakfast sounds of pans rattling, a wooden chair scraping the floor, and a window banging open. It was barely dawn on the farm, but she soon felt warm sunshine slip past the curtains and onto her pillow.

A cloudless day began easing across the valley and into the barnyard. Ida caught a whiff of fresh-brewed coffee as she grabbed a robe from her closet, then shuffled barefoot into the kitchen.

"Morning, Mama," she said. "You aren't making pancakes, are you? I don't need the weight."

"Shucks, honey. You'd blow over in heavy wind. You ain't eatin' right. Your mother can tell."

"Well, maybe it'll be OK."

"I'm throwing blueberries in the batter. Just picked 'em. And there's maple syrup too. The real stuff, not store-bought."

Ida loved her mother's breakfasts, though it was hard to pick a favorite. Was it today's fruit-laden hotcakes with real maple syrup? Or was it scrambled eggs with hash browns, onions, peppers, cubed ham, and jalapeños?

She was on the road before eight o'clock. Her call to Wanda Elliott was answered on the second ring.

"I was just headin' to the store, Detective. I just grabbed my list off the counter, and the phone rang."

"You can call me Ida. I'd be pleased if you did. I'm calling because there's been a development with your son."

"What happened?"

"We've got the female suspect in custody. She's being held without bond in Missouri, pending extradition to Wisconsin."

"Extra what?"

"Extradition. It's a legal term. We'll go to court to have her ordered back to the county where your son was killed."

"What about the other killer?"

"We think Maddy Connelly killed John Michael Thomas. Divers are looking for his body."

"I wish they were both dead. God's justice is better than what we get in court."

"I'd feel the same with my kin."

"Thank you, Ida. Sometimes I just feel like a mean, angry old woman. Like I've lost my faith. Maybe it's not so unusual."

"It's not unusual. Not at all."

"It must be awful doin' police work. How can ya stand it?"

"Some days are pretty bad. But it feels good bringing someone to justice."

"I'm not sure there really is any justice. Not in this world."

"I sure don't fault you for feeling that way."

After a long pause, Wanda Elliott said she needed to get groceries.

"Life goes on, I guess," she added.

"Yes, it does. Even with heartache."

"So long, Ida. Please call me again before this goes to trial. I plan to be there."

"You can count on me. I won't let you down."

The call went about as well as it could, all things considered. But Ida logged a few more miles before calling the second worried mother. Two-lane driving settled her nerves. It was a welcome distraction.

Ida was rolling near the bridge into Missouri as she searched her phone's contacts and clicked on the cell number for Martha Thomas.

"Good morning, Mrs. Thomas. This is Ida."

"Oh God! What's happened? Have you found John Michael?"

"We've got Maddy Connelly in custody on a murder charge. She got caught in Arkansas."

"Arkansas? How did the cops get her?"

"I helped a little. Followed a hunch and watched her father's trailer. Pretty much she just fell into my lap."

"What about my son?"

"He's still missing. I hate to tell you this, but it's better to hear it from me than by word of mouth or the news. Divers are searching a quarry for a body. In Missouri."

There was a moment of silence. Ida finally heard a brief gasp, then steady breathing. She let the silence linger before she spoke again.

"It is also possible that John Michael is still alive. We don't think it's likely, but we can't rule it out. I'm very sorry."

Ida could hear the sound of a phone being jostled, then the rattle of a cardboard box and gentle sniffling into a tissue.

"Where are you at, Mrs. Thomas? Are you going to be all right?"

"I'm staying with Helen. Maybe you remember her?"

"Can't you get back into your own home?"

"My house is rented to the nicest young family you ever met. They're refugees. From Guatemala. I can't just put them out on the street."

"I guess not."

"Reverend Driscoll is talking to them. He says he's got a plan. I don't know the details, but he's a good man."

"I remember him too."

"Ida, can you do me a favor?"

"If I can, I will."

"Promise to call me as soon as you know what happened to John Michael?"

Ida promised, then completed her drive into Gillespie and called Sheriff Clark. She left a voice mail, saying she'd call again when the quarry search ended for the day.

It ended long before sundown. Angry low-hanging clouds crept into the southwest sky early in the afternoon. Even before the police radio warned of an approaching severe thunderstorm and possible tornado, Sheriff Bing called the divers to the surface. He spoke quickly and effectively with a few easily understood words.

"Some of the clouds we see have a yellowish-greenish tint near the bottoms. I've seen it before. Might be a twister. We're done here."

"Kind of a short day," Ida said. "We coming back tomorrow?"

"Can't spare the time or men. That storm's gonna do some damage. We've got to get back to the barn, pronto."

Once they were back in the storage structure—a secure metal building laughably known by the sheriff and his deputies as "the barn"—the full weight of the day's brief and disappointing search hit Ida. She hadn't expected success, but it was troubling to leave the body of Martha's son underwater.

"Isn't there some way to keep looking for the body?" she asked.

"Pretty much we're waiting on help from nature," Stoney said.

Lightning and thunder shook the barn's walls as heavy hail battered the metal roof. It sounded like machine-gun fire during an artillery attack. Once Ida could be heard, she again spoke.

"I'm not sure I understand what you said about nature."

"We'll send a deputy to look in the quarry daily," Bing said. "But there won't be much to see for weeks. Water bloats and misshapes a body. Then it comes to the surface."

"Are you sure?"

"If there's a body down below, it'll eventually come up. But it'll look bad and smell worse."

Once the storm passed, somehow sparing Gillespie from a tornado, there was still heavy damage throughout the community due to straight-line winds: downed trees, torn-off roofs, a few flattened barns, and severed power lines. It would be a busy night followed by hectic days of recovery.

Ida knew what the damages would mean for the sheriff's department. Endless toil. Overtime expenses that burst the budget. Families overburdened and miserable.

"I feel guilty leaving you after a major storm," Ida said as she thanked Bing and Stoney for their help.

"You've got your own troubles, Detective," Bing said. "Better get back to work in Wisconsin. Y'all won't forget about us, will ya?"

Ida smiled, shook her head, and started walking slowly to her Mustang. Stoney followed.

"I hope you won't mind if I stay in touch," he said. "I'll let you know what's going on with Connelly, or if we find something in the quarry."

"I guess you'll have to," Ida said. "I just wish I knew what to tell John Michael Thomas's mother."

"Tell her we didn't find anything in the water. But we're still searching. It might be the kindest way to tell her the truth."

CHAPTER 42
COLD OCTOBER WIND

After she'd cleaned out the Gillespie apartment and moved back to Milwaukee, Martha Thomas fell into a routine. It was a new one but growing more comfortable with time. At the suggestion of Pastor Driscoll, she'd decided to share her home with her tenants and then cut their rent in half.

"Feels like it could snow, Isabella," Martha said as they washed the breakfast dishes. "Did you ever get snow in Guatemala?"

"Fernando remembers seeing snow in the mountains. My family lived near the Pacific Ocean. It was warm. We didn't have snow. What's it like?"

"Real pretty when it first falls. Your boys will like playing in it. My son loved the snow when he was little. We used to get more snow."

Wisconsin winters weren't always as frigid and snowy as Martha remembered from childhood. But light snow was still possible in October, heavier snow probable in November. It certainly never surprised anyone who'd lived in the Badger State for a few years. There was a resolute, Germanic acceptance of lousy conditions that sharply contrasted with hysterical TV weather forecasts hinting at atmospheric Armageddon.

Martha looked into the living room as she hung a dish towel to dry. Isabella's three young boys were playing with some of John Michael's childhood toys that she'd fished from the attic. They appeared fascinated with a red plastic barn and realistic-looking tiny farm animals, also with sturdy metal trucks and a bulldozer with a movable scoop and rolling wheels. Occasionally the oldest, Pedro, would tell his brothers about the animals. But mostly the boys were quiet and contemplative.

"Your boys are so well behaved. I remember John Michael making more noise all by himself."

She thought about her son continually, hoping that he somehow was still alive—despite the passing weeks. It was the slimmest of hopes, as fragile and ultimately useless as a slice of wedding cake kept in a freezer for years. But even the tiniest of hopes were better than lifelong losses, Martha knew.

●ↆ·•

The day looked more wintry in the afternoon. The shadows grew long, and a wind from the north rattled the pine branches against the siding.

"I need to have the trees pruned," Martha said. "If Arnie was here, it'd be done already. Or John Michael."

Isabella looked as if she were thinking about something else as Martha spoke. It wasn't like her to be inattentive. Isabella's English continually improved because she listened carefully and mimicked the phrasing of Martha and her visitors.

It was as if she'd heard something outside. Finally, Isabella looked toward the door.

"Martha, are you expecting someone?" she asked.

As she spoke, Martha heard a car door slamming in front of her house. Then there were footsteps on the stairs and a knock at the front door. Through the eye-level panes of glass, Martha recognized Detective Ida Mae Rollins.

"I'm sorry to drop in like this, Mrs. Thomas, but we need to talk. It's important."

"What's happened? Did you find my son?"

"We need to be alone. Can we have some privacy?"

"I guess we can use my bedroom. I've got a couple rocking chairs we can use. Let me just talk to Isabella a little. I don't want her to think this has anything to do with her family and immigration."

"That'll be OK. I'd like to get a better look at the boys' little farm. They might like to hear about how I grew up on a farm with a red barn."

"Really? Where?" Pedro asked.

"A place called Cobden. It's in Illinois."

"Is it near here? Can we go there?"

"It's a long way to drive. Too far for us."

Martha returned a few minutes later and led Ida into the bedroom.

"I'm sorry the bed isn't made. I usually make the bed after the breakfast dishes are done. I was talking with Isabella and her boys. They love John Michael's old toys."

"Don't worry about an unmade bed. It's not important," Ida said as she softly closed the bedroom door. "Please sit down, Mrs. Thomas."

"Oh God. This is bad, isn't it?"

"I'm afraid it's the worst. Your boy's body was recovered yesterday from the quarry. His remains matched the fingerprints taken during his Missouri drug arrest."

Martha dropped her head into her hands, her shoulders rising and falling with sobs. "My poor, poor boy. Why does God allow such heartache? First I lost Arnie, and now John Michael."

"I'm sure you know I'm sorry for your loss. That's why I came here in person," Ida said, slowly rising from a bentwood rocker and placing a comforting hand on Martha's shoulder. "I called your friend Helen and the pastor just before I drove up and asked them to meet me here."

"You told them before me?"

"No, Martha. I'd never do such a thing. I just said you were going to need some support today."

As she spoke, Isabella tapped on the door.

"Senora, your friend and the pastor are here."

"Let them in, Isabella. You can stay too. I'm going to need all the friends I can get."

"I'll be letting myself out, then," Ida said. "Unless you have some questions."

There were many questions. Ida calmly and as kindly as possible explained that the police in Missouri suspected Maddy Connelly of killing John Michael and dumping his body in a quarry. She said high school kids swam in the quarry during summer but parked on the gravel road throughout the year, either for beer parties or for romance—sometimes both.

"How was his body found? Police divers?"

"A high school kid spotted him," Ida said. "He saw something unusual in the water, then climbed down the rocks to get a closer look. He called the sheriff. The sheriff called me after John Michael's body was recovered."

"How did he die?"

"The coroner said it looked like he was stabbed to death."

"Ohhh God. I need to call the funeral home. The one I used for Arnie."

"Just have them contact the Gillespie County Sheriff's Department. They'll know what to do."

"Excuse me, Detective," Pastor Driscoll said. "May I ask a question? What's going to happen to the woman accused of killing him?"

"We're trying to figure out what happens first. Maddy Connelly is facing a murder charge here. But she'll also be going on trial for murder in Missouri for John Michael's death. Missouri still has the death penalty and regularly executes convicted killers. She's also charged with a murder in Iowa."

"I don't believe in the death penalty, Ida," Martha said. "Even now."

"I'm not sure that I do either. But the mother of our Wisconsin murder victim wants Missouri to go first. She lives in Kentucky."

"But her son was killed in Wisconsin."

"Wanda Elliott wants Maddy Connelly put to death. That won't happen in Wisconsin. She's reached out to the Kentucky governor's office, and they're trying to work with Missouri."

"I don't know what's best," Pastor Driscoll finally said. "I pray that by the grace of God we learn to accept and live by his final judgment."

Ida bowed her head and clasped hands with Martha and Helen as they and Isabella repeated the Lord's Prayer with the minister. Then she stood up straight, nodded to everyone, and hugged Martha.

"You gonna be OK?" she asked.

"I'm never alone with God," Martha said. "Helen and Pastor Driscoll will support me. Isabella and her boys will take care of me too. I don't need to worry about taking care of the house. Fernando can fix anything. I'll get him to trim those trees too."

"Would you like to know what's going to happen in court? Before it happens?"

"I guess so. It would be better than suddenly hearing about it on TV or in the paper."

CHAPTER 43
BACK IN THE GAME?

Business fell off at my diner once the holiday season ended. It always dipped after New Year's, but this downturn was steeper than ever. I tried to concentrate on other things, including the approaching pro football playoffs, but I was thinking more about paying the bills than anything else. Worrying, I should say.

My fretting in the diner's basement office was interrupted by the cell phone stuffed into my back pocket. I answered finally, hoping it wasn't a creditor.

"Hey, man. It's me," a gravelly voice rasped.

There was no mistaking the less-than-sonorous tones of Angelo Calacia.

"I know your voice. What's up?"

"Lotta football comin' up. Mebbe you wanna get back in the game?"

"Ain't I still too hot?"

"Been more than a year. They ain't lookin' our way anymore. I got a guy in the courthouse who told me."

"Sounds risky—too risky."

"You got a business, right?" Angelo said. "No risk, no reward. It would be doin' me a favor too."

"How?"

"Things are slow in Kenosha. A Chicago guy started workin' way north, near the state line. Some of my local guys had to take jobs in northern Illinois. The new guy's more convenient for 'em. He hangs in their bars."

"He must do a lot of driving."

"He's based near Skokie. Drives the Edens to Highway 41. Ain't too far to drive if the money's right."

"I can't do anything about Illinois," I said.

"Not what I mean. You were one of my best earners. Mebbe you could get some Milwaukee business?"

I didn't say yes, but I didn't say no either. I didn't say anything. I quietly listened to Angelo's heavy breathing—too many cigars and single-malt scotches. He sounded just this side of death, but at least he was rich.

I finally said I'd think about it. Angelo said he'd call Monday and hung up.

After we spoke, I seriously thought about running a sports book again. I was in the clear with our sheriff's department. And if I kept a smaller book, one for nobody other than Milwaukee County residents, I'd probably be OK. The money would come in handy, especially after Becky's Christmas spending came due.

By Sunday morning, as I walked to get the newspaper from a cheap plastic tube hung below our rural mailbox, it seemed like a risk worth taking. I'd have to keep it a secret from Becky, of course, but as long as my getting-home-from-work time didn't change, she'd be none the wiser. She wasn't the snoopy type, anyhow. Other guys tell me about wives looking through their text messages, phone records, and email, but Becky never was that type of woman. Come to think of it, I'd never looked through her stuff either.

I was thinking about earning hundreds of dollars more every week and working my way to owning our home and the diner free and clear. If I put half my new income to paying extra principal on each monthly mortgage payment, I'd cut the length of the loans in half. Half!

The sunshine felt good on my face, and there was a hint of eventual spring in the breeze. Then I opened the paper—the big Sunday paper from Milwaukee—and got a double whammy. Make that a triple whammy.

The front page was dominated by a jailhouse booking shot of Maddy Connelly from her arrest in Missouri. She looked exactly as I remembered. And there was a second booking shot, too, taken more recently by the

Howard County Sheriff's Department. Maddy now looked like a punk rocker or maybe someone transitioning to manhood. She looked awful. Tough too.

The other whammies came from the massive black headline "Serial Killer?" and the byline of Calvin Krebs.

It took me an hour of determined reading to get the full gist of an eighty-inch "exclusive." Krebs's rants and ramblings in the *Howard Register-Press* evidently had been admired by the editors in Milwaukee. They'd hired him. And now the newspaper idiot would be interviewed by TV reporters too lazy to do their own research about a murder spree. As if Krebs alone knew something.

I still remembered the last time I'd spoken with him, threatening legal action and questioning his intelligence.

"So sue me!" he'd said. "All I do is report what people tell me."

The phone went dead right after I shouted, "You only report what you *think* people told you!"

Krebs's big jump into the journalistic heavens bothered me tremendously, especially since I wondered whether any of his sensational claims were accurate. I gave Becky a snapshot version of the story as she poured a cup of coffee and sorted through the advertising inserts. The kitchen table looked like a landfill, but that was normal for any Sunday.

"Some of this we knew in bits and pieces," I said, "but it looks like Maddy Connelly is charged with killing men in Wisconsin, Iowa, and Missouri. Supposedly she was assisted in the local killing of Thad Elliott by a Milwaukee guy named John Michael Thomas. He's also suspected in the Iowa death, some rich guy named Ronald Bernard Foster III."

"You mean that guy who was cut into pieces? Thrown along our roads?" Becky asked. "I thought John Michael Thomas was the victim."

"He was missing, remember? His mother was worried, a nice lady from Milwaukee. We talked on the phone. She wanted to sue Krebs too."

"They found out it wasn't him, right?"

"Yeah. DNA testing ruled him out as the victim."

"Who got killed near us?"

"Guy's name was Thad Elliott, a construction worker from Kentucky who found a job in Milwaukee," I said, intentionally omitting a reminder that the poor guy had owed me money for bad sports bets.

"Did we know him?"

"No," I lied. "He came to a bad end, according to Krebs's story. It says Maddy killed him in the Connellys' barn. That John Michael guy supposedly helped. Some kinda kinky sexual motivation involved, Krebs suggests."

"What happened to John Michael? Is he still alive?"

"This story says he was involved in the Iowa murder, also a dismemberment. He and Maddy both got arrested on drug charges in Missouri, then posted bond and disappeared."

"How come this story focuses only on Maddy? That doesn't seem fair."

"John Michael is dead. Maddy is accused of killing him and ditching his body in a quarry near Gillespie, Missouri. It's a place high school kids use for swimming, beer parties, and making out."

"Did they catch her at the quarry?"

"Nowhere near it. She was hiding out with her dad down south. She supposedly was attacking him with a knife when she was arrested in Arkansas, across the river from Memphis."

"Is George OK?"

"I guess so. He gave police a statement saying the puncture wound near his belly came from accidentally laying on a screwdriver! Hard to believe, isn't it? George is careful with tools."

"How did he get hurt? Really, that is."

"The cops say Maddy dropped a bloody knife during the arrest."

"How'd they find her?"

"You remember Ida? She somehow tracked Maddy down and made the arrest. There's a little photo and story about Ida inside the front section, along with more photos and maps of crime scene locations."

"Ida was decent to me and Caroline," Becky said. "Sure seems like a long time ago, especially since Caroline and George split up and their place went on the market after Missouri declined to seize their property. What's going to happen next?"

"The paper says Wisconsin, Iowa, and Missouri are working together on Maddy's court dates. It's not a done deal, I guess, but it looks like Missouri will put her on trial first."

"Why?"

"The story doesn't say. I bet it's because Missouri has the death penalty.

I remember a story last week about them giving someone the needle for killing two store clerks in a holdup."

Becky settled back into her advertising research as I scanned the sports section and read the betting line on the playoff games next weekend. Milwaukee gamblers would be betting on Green Bay. A lot of money would be involved.

I took the news story as a good sign that the local murder investigation was closed. Nobody would be looking at Eddie Norwood.

Second thoughts were looming, but of course, I had no idea.

Those thoughts came after a Howard County Sheriff's Department squad car slowly crunched gravel in our driveway and came to a halt—engine idling and police radio squawking. The driver was the now somewhat famous Detective Ida Mae Rollins. I opened the door to her as she padded up the front steps, not an easy task in heavy police footwear.

"Afternoon, Mr. Norwood," she said as we shook hands.

Her grip was even stronger than I remembered.

"Hello, Detective. It's Ed or Eddie, remember? Hey, what brings you out here?"

"Please call me Ida. I'm touching base with some folks I met during the murder investigation. The whole thing started with you reporting roadside trash."

"Like I could ever forget."

"Did you see the big story about it today in the Milwaukee paper?"

"I glanced at it. Krebs probably made the whole thing up, right?"

"No, sir, he did not. It's remarkably accurate. He even used my full name and spelled it right. Most Yankees think someone named Ida Mae spells their middle name m-a-y."

"Damn. I was hoping to read the corrections tomorrow."

"I stopped here on my way back from Milwaukee. Maybe you remember Martha Thomas? The mother of the guy we *thought* might have been murdered?"

"Talked to her a couple times. Seemed like a real nice lady."

"There was a little memorial service today for her son," Ida said. "Just some close friends in her church. I felt kinda out of place, but she invited me. Hugged me like a friend too."

"Too bad what happened to her boy."

"He got hooked up with the wrong woman. He made terrible mistakes. That wasn't the boy Martha knew. She mainly remembers the good son she raised. She'll never get over his death, maybe learn to live with it. In time, that is. With the grace of God."

Becky came into the front room and invited Ida into the kitchen.

"I wondered who Eddie was jabbering with. You're so soft spoken, Ida, sometimes I forget you're a cop."

"That works in my favor at times," Ida said.

"I'm having a hard time believing a neighbor's daughter murdered someone in their barn. It gives me the creeps."

"Once we identified human blood and tissue traces in the floor drain, the rest just took time. DNA science can be trusted, but it takes patience to get results."

"But still, Maddy a killer? She wasn't a good daughter, but I never thought she'd murder someone."

"We still don't know everything she did," Ida said. "She moved around a lot, especially in the West. Other states are looking at her for their unsolved killings."

"How many others?"

"We don't know and maybe never will. I shouldn't speak ill of other cops, but some departments rush to conclusions on likely suspects—even if they're never convicted."

I looked out the kitchen window as Ida spoke. A small group of deer—two yearlings and three does—wandered from our yard into the Connellys' field. The last of the day's bird feeder visitors, mostly woodpeckers, nuthatches, jays, and pesky blackbirds, swooped into the sunflower seeds, peanut splits, and thistle. It gave me a peaceful feeling, even if our conversation was unsettling.

I'd heard enough about murder. Becky's fidgeting told me she'd had more than her fill too. I changed the subject.

"I can see why you reached out to Mrs. Thomas. It was an act of kindness. But why touch base with us?"

"Guess I want to make amends for spooking you. My sheriff wanted to put you in jail and squeeze you. See what you *really* knew. I leaned on you a little bit, even though I knew it wasn't right."

"You've got a tough job, Ida," I said, resisting the urge to describe my sleepless nights, constant worry, and anger with the news media. I don't have a charitable nature, but sometimes it kicks in. Parochial school and catechism dug deep roots, I guess.

"I want to make amends with you and Becky. I'm thinking about making some changes. Maybe I'm trying to get rid of some emotional baggage."

"I can understand that," Becky said as I stared dumbly at the two women. The only baggage I ever got rid of was some cheap fiberboard that I'd carted to college.

"I want to think clearly," Ida said, "without pangs of conscience."

"What are you thinking about changing? Looking for a new place to live?"

"No offense to you Wisconsin folks, but I can't figure out why y'all wanna live in this deep freeze."

"It's not so bad today," Becky said. "Didn't you ever get used to it?"

"No," Ida replied. "I must have thinner blood. Back home, daffodils bloom in February and we open our windows in March. It's a different world."

"How about some cookies, Ida?" Becky asked, obviously warming to the topic. "Maybe you just need a new place to live. A warm and homey place. You could get George and Caroline's spread for a song."

"Cookies sound good, but only if you baked them. I don't like store-bought."

"Baked this morning. Chocolate chip."

We all munched cookies as Becky poured coffee for me and milk for Ida. Without a bit of hesitation, she dunked a cookie and gobbled it down.

"Reminds me of the snack I'd get after school," she said, "when I was a little girl."

I finally thought of something to say, though I dreaded the idea of a cop moving in next door. Especially since I was thinking about working with Angelo again.

"I bet they'd be willing to sell for less than they paid," I mumbled between gulps of cookie. "George always talked about being property rich and cash poor."

"That's too much land for me," Ida finally said. "And it's too cold to live here for any length of time."

As we polished off the cookies, Ida spoke more freely. Her working relationship with Sheriff Clark was never great, downright troublesome whenever an election approached. He'd dip into ongoing investigations and push her toward hasty conclusions, which she'd strongly resisted.

"Peter's basically a good man, but he's facing reelection every two years. It takes a lot of money to keep the job. He's always campaigning and raising funds. Some of his contributors expect something in return. It'll be especially nasty now."

"I don't see why," Becky said.

"He's gonna be out of his mind because of that big newspaper story. It doesn't give him enough credit, though he won't admit it. He'll be jealous and sulky all week."

"Hard to live with, huh?"

"I guess I'd like another woman's opinion on what I'm considering."

Ida then explained how she'd worked in partnership with the Gillespie County Sheriff's Department. It was a professional department from top to bottom, she said.

"The sheriff, Bing Thompson, is appointed and retained at the discretion of the county board. He doesn't waste time and energy campaigning for office. He's the boss, no doubt, but he still does the work too."

"Did he offer you a job?"

"You got it. He made me an offer that doesn't require me to immediately reside in Missouri. I'd be living with Mama for up to a year, if I wanted to. That'll give me time to decide where I might put down roots."

"You probably can find a cute apartment near their courthouse," Becky said. "Someplace that's easy to clean, easy to leave on weekends."

"Well, there's another thing too," Ida said. "One of the deputies is interested in me. I've tried to discourage him, but lately I'm thinking maybe he's not such a bad prospect."

"Another cop?" I asked. "Wouldn't that be trouble?"

"Hold on, Ed. You're getting way ahead of me. This guy isn't like Bill, my ex. He's kinda quiet, but he really listens. When he *does speak*, it means something."

Becky was smiling happily, straining to ask a question—maybe ten.

"What's his name?" she asked. "Would he be your boss?"

"His name is Bedford J. Stonewall. He's a lieutenant, but I'd be reporting directly to the sheriff. The sheriff is the head of the detective bureau."

"Bedford?" Becky said. "That sure sounds like a southern name. Is he a southern gentleman?"

"He treated me like any other cop when we were working. But when we went to dinner, he treated me like a lady. It reminded me of the way Daddy treated Mama."

"Bedford sounds nice."

"Everyone calls him Stoney. Me too. He was raised in southern Illinois. Stoney grew up less than an hour away from our farm in Cobden."

"This sounds like it could get serious."

"If I accept the job, we're going to be moving slow and easy. Dinner dates, maybe some movies too. I don't want to be taken in a heated rush. That's the way it was with Bill. Never again."

"Eddie and I took our time too. Didn't we, sweetie?"

I nodded, fearing they might hear crystallized chunks of my brain clattering inside an empty male skull. Their talk of dating and romance seemed a part of a parallel yet invisible reality. I heard their words but comprehended little.

I let the women talk privately and wandered into the front room. A fiery-orange sun was starting to dip toward the horizon, and the wind was kicking fallen leaves across the lawn. I slipped into a hoodie kept on a hook near the door, stepped into my rubber ankle boots, and walked toward the roadside.

I busied myself picking up discarded fast-food wrappers and three empty beer cans.

I jumped when the front door banged shut and Ida walked into the yard.

"Still worrying about litterbugs, huh?"

"Always. The stuff's usually not gruesome. You know, like when we met."

"Ed, if you wouldn't mind, I'm going to call Becky later tonight. Just some more girl talk. She's such a warm person. You're really lucky."

"You're right about that," I said. "She'll give you good advice."

Ida got into the car and lowered the driver's side window. She first tested the squad's emergency lights and blipped the siren. I watched as she checked her mirrors and looked over her shoulder before backing away. It felt like I was watching a driver's ed video.

As the police car neared the road, she braked to a stop. I walked near her window after she gestured for me to come closer. Ida spoke softly, for my ears only, but there was a trace of steel in her voice. Her eyes locked on mine as she spoke.

"Just one last thing, Ed. You need to be careful about the company you keep."

Printed in the United States
by Baker & Taylor Publisher Services